HELEN

THE FIRST TROJAN HORSE

HELEN

THE FIRST TROJAN HORSE

Michael Lally

Helen, The First Trojan Horse
Copyright © 2018 by Michael Lally. All rights reserved.

Published in the United States of America

ISBN: 978-1-949362-31-2 (*sc*)
      978-1-949362-30-5 (*e*)

Library of Congress Control Number: 2018955115

Published by Stonewall Press
4800 Hampden Lane, Suite 200, Bethesda, MD 20814 USA
1.888.334.0980 | www.stonewallpress.com
1. Romance
2. Historical
18.11.20

CONTENTS

Chapter One　　　Helen's Youth 7

Chapter Two　　　Helen's Courtship 36

Chapter Three　　Agamemnon's Plan 59

Chapter Four　　　Call To War 82

Chapter Five　　　The War Begins.. 105

Chapter Six　　　　Hector And Achilles 128

Chapter Seven　　Death Of Achilles..................................... 149

Chapter Eight　　Paris And The Palladium........................... 172

Chapter Nine　　　The Wooden Horse 197

Chapter Ten　　　The Fall Of Troy 216

Chapter Eleven　Helen Goes Home.................................... 238

CHAPTER ONE

HELEN'S YOUTH

"I want to go home!" the thought screamed in her head, it had dominated Helen's thinking for the last seven days. "Has it only been seven days? It seems as though I have been here much longer." She longed for home; oh, how she longed! She was constantly under guard, no matter how many ways she thought of to escape her imprisonment, the impracticality of each plan immediately disqualified it. It is as if everyone here is her captor, even when walking through the courtyard, too many eyes focused on her for her own comfort level. Helen looked out the tower window, at the townspeople bustling about below. She let out a heavy sigh and watched the children rolling hoops with sticks. She loved rolling the hoop with a stick, and she became so good at it, she used it in her dances. Her mind drifted back home, to just seven days ago, when she had been looking forward to Theseus's arrival. She missed home, she missed her siblings, and she missed her dear friend Menelaus.

Helen smiled lightly when she thought about one of her favorite games, Day and Night. The children would pick teams, and then flip a shell with one side painted black to determine which team would be "it." That team chased the opposing team, and when a player would catch someone, the person who was caught had to carry the captor on his back and chase the other players. Helen smiled. Menelaus always let her catch him, and they would chase the others while she rode on his back. When Menelaus did catch her, she struggled to carry him. His long legs dangled almost to the ground, and the two of them would topple over, laughing and giggling. Her two brothers Castor and Pollux, and her sister Clytemnestra, also loved playing this game.

Helen's consciousness returned to the dank tower room she sat in. She looked around at the gray walls and let herself crumble to the ground. She bowed her head, and wept. Now, she didn't believe she would ever see her family or friends again. Besides, she sighed to herself, no one would want to be around her now that she has been damaged so. Her weeping turned into heavy sobbing. How could things have gone so wrong? Her she was looking out a window in her captor's tower, daydreaming about a freedom she may never have again.

Just seven days ago, Helen was anxious to meet Theseus and Perithious and had been gazing out her own bedroom window as she prepared to meet the heroes. That day, the townspeople down the hill from the palace had been rushing about, preparing for the heroes' arrival. She thought again of the tales she had heard of Theseus. Her father had told stories of how Theseus disguised himself as a young boy and killed the Minotaur at Crete. He also had cleared the road from Troezen to Athens of bandits and murderers. Now, as an adult, he had taken the throne as the King of Athens, and his traveling companion, Perithious, was the King of Larissa.

Helen spat from the nasty taste thinking about the two men left in her mouth. "Some hero," she muttered aloud, then glanced around the room to see whether anyone heard her, then she returned to her thoughts. She had gone over the events of the day of her kidnapping endlessly—trying to figure out what she should have done differently to prevent this fate. Helen wondered whether anyone would bother to come after her. Perhaps she shouldn't have danced for the men, but she had been so excited to play her own part in welcoming the kings on their goodwill tour of the many kingdoms of Greece.

As soon as the sun finished rising, Helen rushed to find her sister Clytemnestra, and the two of them ran to the back of the palace, where the servants roasted a wild boar and prepared for the evening's large banquet. They slowly turned the spit and spread savory smelling sauces over the boar. Other servants shuffled quickly, taking baskets of fruits and vegetables into the great hall. Clytemnestra turned to her sister, "I can't believe that the preparations are almost finished."

"All of the local merchants and dignitaries are coming tonight. We'll be dancing for everyone!" Helen tried to control the excitement in her voice. It would be their first performance. Although they were only twelve years old, their parents had given them special permission to dance for the guests of honor.

The girls had to hurry, or they would be late for their studies. First, they attended arts and sciences class, then weaving, and finally, the rehearsal for that night's festivities. The day seemed to drag on.

During lunch, Helen continued to shift about in her seat. More than 500 people would be coming for the evening's celebration. Helen rushed through her meal so that she and Clytemnestra could begin their dance rehearsal.

Meanwhile, a few miles away, Theseus and Perithious were on the road to Sparta. Theseus was getting on in years. He had traces of gray in his hair, and his once muscular, well-defined body was showing signs of softening from the leisurely lifestyle of a king.

Perithious looked over to Theseus, "Do you think Helen will be as beautiful as they say?"

"We will soon see." Theseus smiled, "They say she is so beautiful, she glows."

"I find that hard to believe. No one can be that beautiful." Perithious shook his head.

"Well, if what they say is true it's possible. People say she can't be the child of mortal parents. They say that she is so beautiful; she must be one of Zeus's daughters. That's why we're going, remember?"

"We'll see; we'll see."

"Yes, we will. I hope they're right," Theseus said, smiling again.

"Are you sure traveling without an entourage was a good idea?" Perithious looked around. They were approaching the outskirts of town, and people were recognizing them. "We could run into trouble."

"Now that wouldn't help our plan, would it? No, we need to travel light and fast so—"

A man ran about shouting, "They are here! Theseus and Perithious are here!"

People emerged from the shops, lined the streets, and cheered as the kings walked their horses through town. "Thank you, Theseus!" a shopkeeper shouted out. "I was once robbed on that road!"

"Did the Minotaur really have a bulls head? How did you kill it?" Another man called out. Theseus exchanged glances with Perithious and smiled. Nothing beat a hero's welcome.

"You're welcome." Theseus shook hands and waved at people as they pushed through the gathering crowds. "Yes, thank you."

As they approached Sparta's center, scarlet and gold banners waved, and signs greeted them with "Welcome, Theseus the Great," and "Thank you, King Theseus!"

Theseus and Perithious finally forced their way through the throngs of people up the small, manicured hill to the palace. Two attendants took their horses to the stables, and a third attendant led them through the massive, gilded front doors to the palace reception room, where Tyndareus and his gorgeous wife Leda, awaited them.

Tyndareus was a tall, slender man in his late forties with gray hair and a full beard. He had aged a bit since the two had last met, and his embrace was that of a king who had been long out of battle. His wife was tall and statuesque, dressed in a long golden gown, and draped in jewels. She appeared to be also in her late forties, gray streaks running through her hair, yet she had retained the classic beauty of her youth. "Welcome, old friend. It has been many years."

"Too many years," he replied. "I would like to introduce you to my friend, Perithious, King of Larissa."

"It is a pleasure," Tyndareus said and nodded toward Perithious. Perithious returned the nod and turned toward the tall woman standing next to the king. "Ah, yes! This is my beautiful wife, Leda."

Theseus looked at his traveling companion and smiled. Acknowledging the beauty of the fabled Leda most certainly insured that Helen must be at least as beautiful as she was. Both he and Perithious bowed and nodded toward the queen. "My lady," they said in unison.

"You must be tired from your journey," said the Spartan King.

"Not at all; we are energized by the greeting we received from the people of Sparta! There will be time to sleep later, but first, I would like to take a tour of your beautiful palace," Theseus said. As he followed Tyndareus and Leda through the tour, he could tell they were quite proud of their home and enjoyed receiving visitors. Every room had a story. Theseus noted the family's sleeping quarters, but he was also taken through the great hall where they would feast that evening, more than fifty other rooms in the palace, and then his guest quarters. After a quick lunch and a tour of the palace's grounds and stables, Theseus and Perithious retreated to the guest quarters to rest before the evening's festivities.

Helen and Clytemnestra stood with their parents at the corral, where their brother, Pollux, readied himself to demonstrate his talent for riding and jumping horses. More than 500 people had gathered, and Helen decided to have a little fun with the crowd. Many of the men gawked and pointed at her, and she felt compelled to use her talent, mimicking others' voices, to draw attention away from herself and back to the riding demonstration.

"Please pay attention to the great Pollux! He is a champion horse jumper and rider!" She mimicked her mother's voice in an uncanny impersonation.

"Echo, this is not the time!" Clytemnestra whispered harshly at her sister while grabbing her by the arm."

"Those men are staring at me. I want them to look at Pollux." Helen pointed toward a group of leering men, and then started to speak in her mother's voice again. This time, her mother put a hand on her shoulder and shook her head in disapproval when Helen met her glance. Helen stopped and smiled slightly at her mother, but she could still feel the men's gaze as she stood by her parents and watched the demonstration.

After Pollux finished, the crowd moved into the great hall to ready themselves for Castor's boxing display. Helen wove between guests, again mimicking her mother's voice to distract the crowd and open up a way through.

"Hey, Echo! Over here!" Helen looked up to see Menelaus waving at her. She waved back and ducked through a few more people to reach him. "Your brother did a great job out there. I can't wait to see how Castor does with his boxing display. When we sparred earlier, he was in top form."

Helen smiled back at her sixteen-year old friend. He and his brother, Agamemnon, who was a few years older than Menelaus, had come to live in Sparta as exiles from their own home in Mycenae when their half-brother Aegisthus murdered their father, King Atreus. Agamemnon was far more brash and vengeful, and while Clytemnestra appeared to have a fondness for him, Helen herself was not at all impressed by his outspoken nature.

"You can't fool me with that trickery. I know you are good at fooling everyone else with your impersonations when we play our games, but I know you, Helen." Menelaus put his arm around her, and she finally felt herself relax for the first time that day. The two then walked to the great hall to watch Castor.

"We will be performing soon." Helen whispered, "Clytemnestra and I."

"Are you nervous?"

"Not anymore." Helen ceded. Inside the great hall, scarlet and gold banners hung, just as they had in the town. All the tables were decorated with flowers. At the far end of the room, people gathered to watch Castor. The next hours flew by in a blur for Helen. Dinner was savory and delicious, just as she had expected it to be when she smelled the boar roasting. Jugglers and acrobats preformed, and then, finally, it was Helen's turn.

Helen and Clytemnestra stood in front of the crowd, the two men who had been staring at her during Pollux's demonstration now sat to the side of Helen's father at the table of honor. She shuddered once again at their stares—it was almost as though they were devouring her with their eyes. Clytemnestra noticed Helen's gaze and leaned in, "Those men are King Theseus and King Perithious. We need to make sure we end our dance in front of them.

The kithara player began his melody. The sisters portrayed girls about to be sacrificed to the Minotaur. A performer with a bull-headed costume chased them around the hall and between the tables, before an actor portraying Theseus confronted the Minotaur and slayed him in the middle of the hall. Helen and Clytemnestra used their hoops to perform a dance of joy and gratitude, ending their dance in front of Theseus and Perithious.

Theseus had enjoyed all the pomp that had been afforded to him, welcoming him to the palace. He clapped as the girls stood in front of him smiling. Helen was, indeed, shining, though she appeared to be nervous as well. He turned to Tyndareus. "You have very gifted children. You must be proud."

"Thank you. Yes, we are quite proud. Now Helen, Clytemnestra, you two must be exhausted from the long day. It is time for you to head off to sleep. Tomorrow will be no less tiring."

As the king wrestled with sending his daughters to bed, Theseus leaned over to his friend. He whispered, "Well, what do you think?"

"The rumors are true. I have never seen a child like her. Her skin *is* so clear it seems to glow. She is graceful and poised, athletic and supple, and her presence is simply enchanting."

"Yes," Theseus said with a raised eyebrow and contented sigh, "She will do nicely."

The two men enjoyed the celebration and festivities until well after midnight when things finally wound down. "Thank you very much, King Tyndareus. This was a wonderful welcome," said Theseus."

"The honor is all mine, King of Athens. We will show you our town tomorrow. Goodnight, my old friend."

"Goodnight."

Theseus and Perithious wandered down the dark halls to their separate rooms and nodded at one another before parting ways.

Helen awoke to a rough hand placed firmly over her mouth. She could feel the sharp edge of a very cold blade against the skin of her throat. She blinked, struggling to see the man in the dark hooded robe through the moonlight that entered her room. A low, gruff voice growled, "Be very quiet." She could smell stale wine on his breath as his stubble scraped against her own soft skin. She followed the stranger's orders, thinking his voice was familiar. Before she could struggle or scream, the man expertly bound and gagged her with black rags before he draped her over his shoulder. She could feel his power as he carried her from her room and met with his partner. The men moved silently toward the stables, her head bobbing behind the man's back with each large step.

The stable master sat, tied to a post by one of the stalls. Her eyes met his, and she knew he was helpless. She blinked back tears. She couldn't scream, the stable master couldn't help her. She was powerless. Her heart sank. The men tied leather sacks onto the horses' hooves, and walked them briskly off the palace's grounds. The whole world was still, recovering from the earlier celebration. Helen did her best to try to wiggle free, but the action was futile. The arms carrying her were just too strong. Once her kidnappers were safely out of the palace guards' earshot, they mounted their horses, draping Helen carefully in front of one of the riders so she wouldn't fall or wiggle free, and rode into the night.

Her mind raced, as it would many times in the coming days. "What did I do? Who are these men to do this to me? What do they want with me?" A chill came over her as she realized why she recognized the gruff voice. It belonged to Theseus. She began to panic and wriggle around, doing her best to make noise and fight the man who now clamped his hand down hard on her back. She began to cry once again, wondering why a great hero would kidnap her in the middle of the night. After what seemed like forever, the trees began to thin. The riders came to a stop. Without the horses' hooves, she could tell they were near a spring. She let out a sigh. Maybe she would be able to get away here.

Theseus rapidly grew tired of Helen's attempts to struggle against him. He dismounted his horse and walked over to Perithious. "Remove the sacks from the horses hooves and stand guard over there," he said and pointed. "I'm going to try to calm her down. The last thing we need is her attracting the wrong kind of attention our way."

Theseus felt his smile widen as he approached Helen. He took her down from the horse and removed her gags and bindings. He touched the side of her face and played with her hair. She flinched away from his touch. "You must be wondering why we are doing this."

Helen remained silent, and Theseus noticed her eyes darting around. "Don't try to escape. Both Perithious and myself are a lot bigger than you, and, well, it would hurt you a lot more than it would hurt us."

Helen recoiled at the words, but stood still.

"Good." He loved the feeling of power he had over this girl, this daughter of Zeus. "You see, my friend and I made a pact with each other that we would each take a daughter of Zeus as a bride." He declared and moved closer, continuing to play with her hair and brought his face close to her enchanting neck. She was putting him under a spell. "I chose you, and a great choice it was."

Something startled the horses and when Theseus turned to see what happened. Helen broke free from his distracted grip. She began to run from him toward the trees. Perithious called. "Don't let her get away."

Theseus began his pursuit of Helen and quickly caught up with her. Perithious had joined them. "A spirited little thing isn't she?" he breathlessly said.

"Nice try," Theseus growled, now holding her by her throat. "I don't care how beautiful you are, if you try that again, I'll snap your puny neck before you can cry out."

Theseus waved his friend back to his post, then turned back toward Helen. "As I was saying, you are to be my bride. After I saw you dance tonight, and after this little activity, I was filled with desire and can no longer wait to make you mine." Theseus grabbed Helen's hand and pulled it to his crotch. "I cannot wait any longer. I must have you."

Helen pulled her hand back and cringed. Before Helen could move any further, Theseus's lips were against hers. She turned her face. She struggled against him. Theseus laughed. Her heart pounded hard. He grasped at her. He tore at her clothes. She struggled more. She kicked him, and she broke her hand free from his long enough to punch him. He slapped her hard. She fell to the ground. He was on top of her in an instant. He ripped her clothes from her body and placed his hand over her mouth. She realized she was sobbing. He slapped her again, and she stopped struggling. A sharp pain tore through her body, starting between her legs and shooting up. A wolf howled. Unconsciousness set in.

When Helen awoke, she was tied to a tree, and Perithious kneeled in front of her, stroking her hair. Her body ached. She felt an uncomfortable wetness between her legs. She let her head hang down and began to cry. Perithious lightly slapped her face to force her to look at him. He smiled at her; his toothy grin breathed stench in her face. She flinched. "This is such a fine beauty!" He called to Theseus. "When do I get my turn?"

"You don't. This one is mine! We'll get your daughter of Zeus after we drop this one off at Aphidna." Helen wished she could disappear into the tree. Her lip throbbed, and she tasted dried blood when she licked it. Her clothes were tattered and filthy.

The men tried to get her to eat, but she refused the food. Theseus shrugged. "You'll be sorry you didn't eat later. We won't stop again until we have to." Helen didn't care. They tied her up and threw her back onto the horse. Then they rode away.

Menelaus was heading to the palace for his lessons when he heard the commotion. He knew the family would be slowly waking up from the festivities the night before, and he had expected a delay. Clytemnestra, rushed toward the palace, screaming, "They took her! They took her!"

Menelaus ran to meet Clytemnestra. "What is going on?"

Clytemnestra met him with a glare. "Helen. They took Helen!" She began to run again, Menelaus ran at her heels, meeting the King and Queen at their chamber. "Mother, father, they took her!"

"Slow down, child," said Leda as she led Clytemnestra to a chair. "What are you saying?

Who took who?"

"Theseus! He took Helen! I looked all over for her this morning and couldn't find her. I went to the stables, and the stable master was tied up, and he told me Theseus took her last night!" Clytemnestra began to cry. Menelaus felt his fists ball up in his hands. He knew those two were acting suspicious last night, asking too many questions about how the palace was laid out. Leda looked toward her husband and then dashed past Menelaus, followed by Tyndareus. Menelaus followed them and was joined by Pollux and Castor.

"What's going on?" Castor asked.

"Theseus kidnapped Helen." Menelaus responded, the huskiness in his voice surprised him.

When the group reached the stable, they found servants caring for the stable master. He instantly began, "I didn't see them coming. They hit me from behind and tied me up. I saw them carry young Helen away, but I could do nothing to stop them! Please forgive me madam. I am so sorry. I felt so helpless."

Menelaus watched Leda reassure the stable master before she turned to return to the palace. Pollux turned to Tyndareus. "We welcomed Theseus into our home. We honored and celebrated his heroism, yet he has betrayed our family."

Castor chirped in, "What do you intend to do to get Helen back, father?"

Menelaus knew that the king was plagued by indecision, and it was no surprise to him that the king hemmed and hawed before he finally said, "Perhaps it is a good thing that she is with Theseus. After all, he is the King of Athens, and his kingdom is quite powerful."

Leda turned back around and rushed back over. "I can't believe what I am hearing! Your daughter is stolen from us in the night by a couple of so called heroes who are no more than cowardly kidnappers and all you can say is perhaps it is a good thing?"

"I need time to think. Maybe we can form an alliance. Theseus is an old friend of mine."

"Hah!" Leda's voice went up a few octaves.

Castor stepped forward, and although he was also only twelve years old, he was more of a man than a boy. Menelaus found himself often admiring the young man's leadership skills. "I don't care that he is King of Athens. He has kidnapped my sister, my blood! He has no right to do this! He has insulted our family and Sparta. If you won't raise an army, I will, and bring her home, myself!" Castor and Pollux stormed away, tearing down remnants from the previous night's festivities as they went.

Menelaus looked at the king and queen before he walked away. "If they raise an army, I will be in it," he muttered to himself.

For the remaining nights of the three-day journey, the sexual assaults continued. Helen found herself focusing on Menelaus, her brothers, her sister, and even bossy Agamemnon in order to distract herself from the shame she felt as Theseus tore into her body with his own. She didn't have it in her to fight anymore. She struggled less and closed her eyes. Many times she wished she were dead. On what would be the final night, she found herself briefly wishing for a band of bandits to attack their small party, but then realized that her fate with them may be worse.

A few miles before they reached Aphidna, a place she recalled from her studies as a small, fortified town north of Athens, the men covered her with a hooded parka. They warned her not to speak to anyone and Theseus muttered that she'd pay dearly if she tried to escape again, then he cut her free. She didn't have it in her to escape. She was sore, her wrists and ankles ached from being bound, and she'd given up hope that she would get free if she tried. She nodded in agreement when Theseus asked her for a third time if she would behave. It was all a blur.

Once they entered the main house in the town, an older woman greeted Theseus warmly. She met Helen's eyes and then froze. Helen felt the first hope she had in days. Would this woman help her?

"Goodness, child! What happened to you?"

Helen didn't have a chance to speak. Theseus answered for her. "She fell off the horse. Clumsy girl!" Theseus tightened his grip on her arm, a warning that she'd better agree or else. She nodded and let her gaze drop to the ground.

"Dear girl, you must be more careful! Come, let's get you washed up, and into some clean clothes." The woman led Helen through the hallway and into another room. Now that she was alone with the woman, Helen thought, she should say something. But instead, she was silent as the woman handed her fresh robes and directed her to where she could clean herself up.

"That girl did *not* fall off a horse," said Theseus's mother when she returned to the room. "That girl in the back room, she is very bruised. She has blood on her legs. What have you done to her?" Both men ignored her. "I have heard of a young girl from Sparta named Helen. We all have. She is said to be a great beauty. That girl is bruised, but she is still very beautiful. Is she the girl from Sparta?"

The two men looked at each other and remained silent.

"Is that the girl from Sparta?" She repeated.

"Yes! That is Helen of Sparta. I have chosen her for my wife, mother."

"What have you done to her?" Theseus could see the emotion in his mother's face.

"I couldn't very well make her my wife until I found out whether she was worthy," he laughed and Perithious joined in.

"You pig! You animal! What have you become?" She slapped his face hard. It stung, but Theseus refused to flinch or show pain. He instead raised his hand to strike her, but she held her ground. He brought his hand back down. She was his mother, and he did respect her and began to feel a degree of shame for what he had done to the girl. He couldn't help himself, though. She was just that enticing.

Finally, he responded. "Don't give me a hard time over this, woman. Your job is to keep her here until we get back. We are off to the underworld to make Persephone the wife of Perithious."

"Do you really think that is a good idea? It's never good to anger the gods, and Hades is protective of his bride. He is so protective; he keeps her from her mother for half of the year."

Perithious spoke, "I'll be traveling with the great Minotaur-slayer. We can beat Hades and take his bride as my wife."

"Suit yourselves, then." It was what his mother always said when she thought bad things would come of one of his plans.

Theseus turned toward the door, and the two began to walk out. Something made him turn back at the door, and he stared at his mother as though it would be the last time he would see her. He shrugged the feeling off, went outside, and spoke with a few soldiers. He didn't want to delay his quest any more than he had to.

The woman returned to the room. Helen had changed into fresh clothes, and she sat in a chair in the corner of the room, with her knees pulled up to her chin and her eyes cast to the ground. She made herself as small as possible in the empty corner. The woman approached and spoke, "Dear child, you must be hungry and frightened."

Helen just stared blankly back at the woman. Everything was a blur. It almost seemed like a dream, except it was a dream she kept waking up to. She felt dirty, vulnerable, and violated. She blamed herself. "Maybe if I weren't so seductive in my dancing, this wouldn't have happened," she thought to herself.

The woman continued to talk. "My name is Aethra, and Theseus is my son. Your name is Helen?" She asked softly. Helen gave no reply. How did the woman know her name?

"You must try to forgive my son; he has not been the same since his father's death. You see, there was a time when my son was a great hero. He cleared the road from Troezen to Athens of bandits and murderers. By killing the Minotaur, he ended the sacrificing of the children of Athens to the beast. We were so proud of him," she said wistfully. Helen could understand that, at least. She had been proud to dance for him.

"His father, Aegeus, loved him dearly. Before Theseus left on his journey to slay the Minotaur, he told his father he would put up white sails upon his return if he were successful. The crew would raise black sails if he were dead."

Helen heard the woman speaking, but it was hard to process her words when she was deep in her own thoughts. "What is to become of me? Am I to become the wife of this old man? Will my family come for me? Will they find me? What will my friend, Menelaus think of me when he finds out what Theseus has done? Will he care? Will he blame me? What if they never come for me?"

Aethra continued, "Theseus was so elated from his triumph that he forgot his pledge to his father, and upon his return, he flew the black sails. When his father, who had been sitting on a rock cliff overlooking the sea, saw the black sails, he was so overcome with grief he jumped off the cliff into the sea. Theseus has been blaming himself ever since."

Helen felt her body begin to shake. She felt so cold. Where was Menelaus when she needed him for comfort? He always knew how to cheer her up. Theseus's angry face kept popping into her head. It felt like his hands were on her once again, and she tried to shake them off and began to scream. She hadn't realized she'd closed her eyes until she opened them and she wept. Aethra had wrapped herself around Helen and was saying, "There, there, sweetheart. It will be okay. It will be okay. He's not here right now. He can't harm you."

The news of Helen's kidnapping had spread around town, and in the days following, Menelaus, Castor, and Pollux met a large crowd gathered in the center of town. "Is it true?" people asked, "What are we going to do?"

"Pollux stood in the middle of the crowd and shouted, "Yes, it is true! Theseus has kidnapped Helen. We are going to take her back! We will show the world that you cannot come into Sparta and take anything you want. King or no king, we will not stand by and let him have our Helen!" The crowd roared in approval. "We will go to Athens and demand my sister's return, or there will be war!"

Menelaus admired Pollux's ability to command. Tyndareus had finally snapped out of his denial, and he had sent General Loiceteus to lead the quickly forming army. While the king would not be traveling, his sons would travel, as would Menelaus and Agamemnon. After a matter of only a few days, they raised an army of over 10,000 volunteers, but Tyndareus ordered that they take no more than 1,000 men as a show of force.

Menelaus looked at Helen's brothers. They were inspirational leaders, knowing when to stand up and rally the troops, and when to leave military strategy to the military men. They had charioteers with them, and a group in the back carried the makings for a battering ram. The army was prepared to fight as hard as they needed to take Helen back home.

The army followed Castor and Pollux, who rode at the front of the column along with Menelaus and Agamemnon. It didn't take long for them to reach the clearing where the discarded leather sacks were left. Menelaus balled his hands up into fists. Pollux shouted, "They did not take Helen on a drunken whim! This kidnapping was premeditated! They came into our city planning to take her from us."

The army roared so loudly Menelaus wanted to cover his ears, but he didn't. This was his first military action, as it was for both the brothers and Agamemnon. They had all practiced war games and trained in military combat, but the reality of the situation set in. The column started moving again, everyone shouting his eagerness to get to Athens to avenge Helen. Menelaus felt exhilaration and fear. Wearing armor and riding at the head of the company gave him a sense of power, but he knew he was not invincible, though he heard the others bragging about how they would not be brought down in their armor.

Castor turned to Menelaus and said, "If he has harmed her, I will kill him."

"Not if I get to him first," Menelaus found himself saying. Then he muttered again, "Not if I get to him first."

They continued the march in silence; Menelaus was in lost in his own thoughts as, he was sure, were the others. Helen always seemed to understand how he felt when he talked about his exile from his home. She comforted him and made him feel welcome as soon as he arrived in Sparta. He spent time with her as often as he could. Now he was scared for his friend and feared the worst. He'd heard tales of how men would rape girls to take ownership of them. He felt heavy. His armor was heavy. He hoped she hadn't endured that. He began to worry whether they would find Helen at all. The column wasn't moving fast enough for his taste.

In all, it was a three-day march. When the army reached the outskirts of Athens, Castor and Pollux went into the city as envoys. Menelaus and Agamemnon followed. Castor loudly demanded the release of his sister. "We are from Sparta. Your king, Theseus, has kidnapped our sister, Helen. We demand her immediate release!"

A city official replied, "We know nothing of a kidnapping, and Theseus hasn't been here in weeks."

"We don't believe you. Release her now, or there will be war!"

A man, who introduced himself as Academus stepped forward and said, "My friends, Theseus has recently been seen on the road to Aphidna with Perithious and an unknown person. Maybe that is where you can find your sister." The brothers looked at each other and nodded, then back at Menelaus and Agamemnon. When they approached Loceiteus, they said, "We believe him." Let's go." He commanded. So, the Spartans immediately marched on to Aphidna.

Aethra, though her captor, had been kind to Helen. She began to see Aethra as someone she could trust; she represented a glimmer of hope. However, she also knew that the woman couldn't help her escape. Helen sensed that although she was Theseus' mother, she still feared his wrath. She knew that if she helped Helen, he might react violently. Aethra didn't have to communicate that for Helen to know it after her three day ordeal. Nevertheless, she asked, "Why are you keeping me here?"

"It is what my son has asked, dear girl. I know he has harmed you, but in his heart, he is a good man. You will come to see him as I do. He knows what he has done is wrong, but he will treat you well, protect, and care for you when he returns."

"But why me of all the women he could have chosen? Why did he choose me?"

"Dear child, the legend of your beauty has spread throughout the region, and rightfully so. Many believe that your father was none other than Zeus himself. Surely, you know the legend of your birth?"

Helen just stared at Aethra with an agitated expression. As far as she knew, she was Leda and Tyndareus's daughter, and it bothered her that people insinuated otherwise. "Yes, well, I've heard the townspeople speaking, and I have heard some rumors, but I don't want to hear them now!" She turned her back to Aethra and stared out the bedroom window.

Helen looked down at the streets of the town. She saw the shopkeepers and townspeople milling about, and children laughing and giggling as they played in the field behind the shops. She began to feel the familiar anger well up in her. It had been a week. She was tired of weeping, yet the tears came. Aethra moved toward her to comfort her when she heard it.

The alarm sounded, and she heard a loud commotion. A voice cried, "There is an army coming!" Soldiers ran to the tops of their walls.

Helen thought, "Is this real? Am I dreaming yet again? Could they be Spartans? Are they finally coming to rescue me?" She ran past Aethra, past the soldiers, and to the nearest tower to get a better view. She could see the dust kicked up in the distance, and then they came into view. The shopkeepers were closing their doors, and everyone ran behind the walls of the city. She saw the bronze armor and scarlet helmet crests approaching—yes! They were Spartan. She felt lighter than she had in days. Her heart leapt. They had come for her.

Aethra approached with an attendant. "Come, child. This is no place for you. You'll be safer back in your room." As the attendant took her arm and led her away, Helen struggled to look over her shoulder to see what was happening. When she got to her room, she immediately ran to the window.

Outside Aphidna, the Spartans stopped a few hundred yards from the walls. They formed their ranks and waited. A small group of chariots approached the gates. The town became oddly silent, and Helen could hear her brother call to the walls. "I am Pollux of Sparta. I have come for my sister, Helen. Theseus stole her from us in the middle of the night. Return her to us, and we will spare your town."

"Theseus is not here, and there is no one by the name of Helen," the captain of the guards replied. Helen began to feel the sinking sensation she'd become familiar with over the course of the past few days.

Pollux looked back at the others, and Menelaus could tell he was uncertain of what to do next. "If Helen is not here, where could Theseus possibly have taken her?"

Suddenly, her voice called out from behind the gates. "Pollux, I'm here, I'm here! Menelaus, I'm here!" Menelaus and the others looked up and saw Helen just before a woman pulled her back away from a window.

The Spartans looked at each other and then glared sternly at the gate; they knew what they had to do. They turned and rode back to the rest of the army. "She is in there," Pollux reported to General Loiceteus. "They plan on keeping her."

"Is that so?" scoffed the General.

"Stay by my side," Agamemnon said to Menelaus as they returned to their ranks.

Menelaus felt excited and exhilarated. His heart beat strongly in his chest, and he could feel the blood coursing through his veins. He wanted to charge the walls immediately, before they could harm Helen further. He thought of Helen held captive behind the walls. He thought about the site where they had found—he stopped his thoughts there, and changed to focusing on a memory of running, laughing, and rolling in the grass with Helen. If they hurt her at all—a shout in his ear snapped him out of his daydream before he could continue to plot his revenge mentally.

"Stay with me!" Agamemnon ordered once again. "Where I go, you go!" His brother was three years his senior, and had served as his guardian, mentor, and confidant. Menelaus felt more confident because he knew Agamemnon was a great soldier and he would be very protective of him during the battle.

The officers barked their orders, and Menelaus snapped to attention with the rest of the army. Following more commands, the army split into two separate columns ready to attack from the front and the rear. Menelaus was impressed with the sharpness and deliberate actions of the army. He had trained and marched with the army; he knew this was the real thing. His helmet and armor made him feel almost invincible; their weight gave him a sense of security. He glanced around. The army glistened in the sunlight, their bonze armor shimmering, and the sound of the men marching and the horses galloping from side to side added to his excitement. Menelaus joined Agamemnon and the twins to lead the frontal assault. The Spartans had assembled the battering ram, and were going to use it to get through the front gate. The other column planned to advance from the rear with a similar battering ram. The men in front of the city were in place, waiting for the other company to get ready before giving the order to move forward.

Menelaus watched as the defenders scrambled on top of the walls to get into position. They were heavily outnumbered, but he judged that they had the defensive position to their advantage. He took a deep breath as he prepared himself for the battle. "This is real," he whispered to himself. "This is happening."

Helen watched the army prepare for the attack from her window. She was three stories off the ground, and was tempted to jump and try to escape, but she would land in the middle of the courtyard with injuries and nowhere to run. She feared for her brothers' safety. She knew they were courageous and strong, but this was their first battle. She saw Menelaus in the distance and wondered what he was feeling. A horn sounded, and the Spartans began their march on the city. The bronze line glimmered in the afternoon sun as the army moved steadily forward. The defenders waited until the Spartans were within range and then showered them with arrows. Helen drew her breath. Some of the men fell. Most blocked the arrows with shields. Spartan archers fired. Men screamed and fell of the wall. Officers shouted orders. The Spartans were at the gate with the battering ram. The gate cracked. The back gate cracked. Finally, the gates gave way. Spartans poured into Aphidna from both sides. Helen saw the battle unfold in the courtyard. Swords clanged. Screams and yells of the dying and injured filled the air. Menelaus, Agamemnon, Castor, and Pollux rode chariots through the gate and joined the fighting.

Helen suddenly became aware that she was not alone. Aethra and an attendant had rushed into the room and pulled Helen from the window. "Go, I can handle it from here," Aethra said to the attendant. She then turned and whispered to Helen, "Follow me. I will hide you from the soldiers."

"No! They are my brothers." Helen stepped back.

"Not those soldiers. The other soldiers will be coming to find you and take you to a secret place to hide you from the Spartans. Come with me." Helen hesitated. "Trust me! We must move quickly! We must go now!" Aethra was now shouting. Helen reluctantly followed. What choice did she have?

Aethra led her to a large hall with a huge throne on one side. She removed a small door from the back of the throne to reveal a tiny open space under the seat. "They won't find you in there, quickly!" Helen looked back at the woman and felt uncertain, but obeyed and crawled into the space. Aethra returned the small door to its place.

Helen sat in the cramped space, a slight crack allowed a single ray of light to shine into her hiding place. She heard the sound of armor clanging. Two soldiers rushed in and asked, "Where did she go?"

Aethra's voice was breathless, made to sound as though she had been chasing Helen. "I don't know. I chased her into this room, but I lost her. I think she ran to the back of the building. Go now! Don't let her escape!" The clanking moved toward the back of the building. Aethra loudly whispered, "Stay hidden a while longer."

Amid the battle in the courtyard, Menelaus slashed a soldier's throat. He was surprised at how easily his sword slid through skin. Chills ran down his back. He saw the look on the soldier's face, blood spurting through his hand as he held his neck. He shook his head. Fighting was dizzying. He thrust his spear deep into the stomach of a defender. The man crumpled. Bodies piled in front of him. He stayed in step with Agamemnon.

The two of them helped Castor and Pollux fight their way to the front door of the main house. They left their chariots behind and charged inside. Menelaus glanced behind at the carnage. Some Spartans dragged women and children from their homes while others looted the town. He first glimpse of the ugliness of war. He shook off the images running through his mind and ran to catch up with the rest of the rescuing party.

Helen heard the fighting in the hall, and then she heard her brother's voice. "Check in there! She's here somewhere, and we have to find her!"

A group burst into the large hall, and she heard the sounds of her brothers throwing Aethra to the floor. "Where is she?" Pollux demanded.

Helen immediately came out from under the throne. Her brothers both stood there, Pollux holding a sword to Aethra's throat. "I'm here! Pollux! Castor!" She ran to her brothers, and Castor quickly embraced her.

Agamemnon and Menelaus entered the room. Helen began to run to greet her friends, but Castor stopped her. "We need to leave right away. Take what you want." He shouted to the soldiers. Helen looked around. The soldiers were already plundering the hall.

"What about her?" Pollux asked, nodding to Aethra.

"She is Theseus's mother, but she helped me," said Helen.

"Is that so? Then she will make a good slave and attendant for you. Bring her!" Pollux ordered a group of soldiers that had entered the room. Helen felt relief. She hadn't wanted to watch her brother kill the woman who was the only person to show her kindness through the whole ordeal.

The small group made their way out of the main house and through the courtyard where buildings were now already being set on fire. The army regrouped outside the walls of Aphidna, and Helen turned to watch as the town burned.

General Loiceteus said, "Let this be a lesson to anyone who thinks about kidnapping a Spartan! We will not sit by and let Sparta's people be abducted." He then looked Helen over for injuries. Most had healed by now, but she still obliged the examination.

Menelaus finally turned to her and embraced her. At first, she wanted to slink backwards out of his arms, disgusted by the sensation of touch, but the familiarity of his smell took over and she leaned into him. Agamemnon tousled her hair, and Castor and Pollux embraced their sister. In the background, General Loiceteus ordered a messenger to run ahead to Sparta to inform King Tyndareus they would be bringing his daughter home.

That night, everyone huddled around a campfire and shared their battle stories with Helen. Agamemnon was flush with excitement as he bragged about his kills. "The rush of combat is intoxicating!" he exclaimed.

"Yes," Menelaus agreed, Helen could hear the pride in his voice. "There's a certain feeling of power in one-on-one combat. It's definitely exhilarating."

"I can't wait for my next battle." Castor said. Menelaus glanced at Helen and smiled. She felt a weight lifting from her.

"Me neither." Pollux looked at Helen then said, "So, what happened? We all want to know? Did he hurt you?"

Helen took a deep breath. Everyone looked at her expectantly, and a general hush filled the air. She described how Theseus had surprised her in the night, how he had tied her up, and how she tried to run, but wasn't able to escape. She paused after that for a long moment, and she looked at Menelaus who listened intently. "I couldn't get away. I tried, but he was too strong." Emotion built up within her. "I'm so ashamed. I feel so humiliated." She began to sob and leaned her head against Menelaus' shoulder.

He caressed her head, and the sensation made her feel safe and secure, yet visions of Theseus flashed through her mind. It made her sob harder. Would she ever feel normal again?

"Don't feel bad, Helen," he finally said. "It was not your fault. It wasn't anything you did."

"But why me?" She sobbed softly.

"No one can answer that," said Menelaus.

"He said he wanted a daughter of Zeus." Menelaus patted her head, not responding. His silence told Helen everything she needed to know. He'd heard the rumors, and perhaps, so had everyone else. Before she could say anything else, Menelaus sighed heavily, and she looked up.

General Loiceteus approached the group by the fire. They all respected the seasoned veteran, who was considered a father figure as well as a great general. "Maybe I can explain." Everyone in their small group exchanged glances. "I was there when the three of you and your sister, Clytemnestra, were born." They sat quietly and listened closely.

The general picked up a stick and poked at the fire, causing a huge plume of sparks to rise into the night. He continued, "I saw the great white swan circling the palace. The sight of that swan caused a large crowd to form. It was not unusual to see swans in and around Sparta's ponds, pools, and lakes, but this one was quite a bit larger than even the largest of the swans in the area. It always stayed near the palace. When your father announced that you were born, the swan spiraled skyward in three circles and flew off toward Mount Olympus."

"That is a countryside tale," Menelaus said. A swan has nothing to do with Helen." "Oh, but a swan has everything to do with this bunch. Zeus desired your mother, Queen Leda, so much that while she bathed in a pool behind the palace, he came to her disguised as a swan. He placed her into a trance and made love to her."

"That's quite enough!" said Menelaus. Helen was already sobbing when Menelaus pulled her into him. She tried to speak, but she couldn't get the words out so others could understand her. She thought of what Theseus had done to her and if Zeus had been cruel to her mother in the same way…the sobs continued as she imagined her mother being overpowered the way she herself had.

General Loiceteus continued, waving Menelaus off. "When Leda awoke, she believed she'd had an exotic dream. Later that night, she also made love to Tyndareus, thus conceiving two sets of twins. Your mother named Castor and Pollux before you were born. She named your sister as well, but she waited to name you. Upon seeing your incredible beauty, she named you 'Helen' for 'the shining one' or 'torch'."

Helen looked up, but said nothing, instead leaning in to listen to the general's story.

"As word of your beauty spread, people found it hard to believe you were born to mortal parents. They thought that at least one of your parents must have been one of the gods. That is why people think you are a daughter of Zeus, and Castor is a son of Zeus. And *that* is why Theseus tried to take you."

They all looked at each other, not saying a word. Castor moved to speak, but before he could, the general spoke again, "There is something you should be aware of, Helen. Beauty can be powerful, and extreme beauty can be extremely powerful. There are men who would risk their lives and their nations trying to possess it." With that, General Loiceteus got up from his seat and walked off into the night, staving off commentary from anyone around the fire. Helen stared into the fire in silence for the remainder of the evening, deep in thought before she drifted off into a deep sleep.

When the army reached the outskirts of Sparta a few days later, people poured into the streets to greet them. Shouts of jubilation filled the air, and people waved flags and banners at the party. Helen wanted to hide from the whole show. She'd been ruined for marriage, and yet here were these people celebrating her return. She tried to smile and wave at the people, but it was hard to maintain for long.

When Menelaus caught her eye, she leaned in toward him and whispered, "I feel so embarrassed; everybody knows what happened to me. They all think I'm—I can't wait to get to the palace and be with my mother *and* father." She added the emphasis just in case her friend had his doubts. She then walked closer to him, and the soldiers formed a protective circle around her as they entered the city.

Someone from the crowd shouted, "That will show those Athenians!"

Helen thought about how there had always been an uneasy peace between Athens and Sparta. She knew that those in her city felt as though the Athenians looked down on the Spartan culture. Sparta was a farming community, and Athens, as a trading port, believed they were culturally superior. She couldn't help but smile at the assertion. Playing war with her siblings and Menelaus had been one of her favorite games. They would divide themselves, pretending to be Spartan and Athenian soldiers. A heaviness set into her chest. Those days were over. She could no longer wrestle in the grass with her good friend or her brothers in cheery sport. How would she be able to do that when she couldn't erase the memories of what Theseus had done?

"Yes! Down with Athens!" The general shouted, breaking her from her thoughts. "We have the most beautiful women in the world. The fact that one of their own dirty heroes wanted to steal our Helen from us proves that." The crowd cheered in response. Helen recoiled even closer to Menelaus's shadow.

The army marched to the gates of the palace and then dispersed. The first person running toward her, before she had any time to process anything, was Clytemnestra. She jumped into Helen's arms, and hugged her sister so hard Helen thought it would crush her ribs. The hug brought tears to Helen's eyes.

Her parents were waiting at the door, and Leda embraced Helen tightly. With tears in her eyes, her mother said, "I love you so much. I'm so happy you're home."

The king was next, and he hugged his daughter before nodding in approval at Helen's brothers. He did the same with Menelaus and Agamemnon. Everybody hugged and slapped each other on the back as they made their way into the palace.

Helen found it difficult to look at either of her parents' eyes. Shame filled her, and tears began to roll down her cheeks.

Once her father was out of earshot, Helen's mother turned toward her and hugged her once again. "I know what he did, what men like that do." Her mother's admission only made her sob harder. "You have your whole life ahead of you. You will get over it, but you probably won't forget it. We love you all the same, and you are home, where you belong."

Helen desperately hoped that her mother was correct.

CHAPTER TWO

HELEN'S COURTSHIP

For months after Helen's kidnapping, many of the Spartan people tried to help Helen put the trauma behind her. They often sent small gifts, well wishes, or woven tapestries, all with the hopes of making her feel better. Even after her mother told her of the rumors that Theseus and Perithious were trapped in the underworld by Hades when they tried to kidnap his wife, Persephone, she still struggled. One day, while she was alone in her room, staring blankly out the window with that familiar heaviness sitting with her, one of her attendants entered.

"Your presence has been requested in the front room, my lady."

Helen rolled her eyes and stayed in her seat without looking up. "Probably another diplomat here to see the girl he's heard so much about," she muttered then said, "Tell him I'm busy."

"It is your parents' request, my lady," the attendant said.

"I'm coming," Helen sighed heavily and slid off her seat. She followed her attendant through the hall to the front room where Queen Leda and King Tyndareus stood waiting for her. Many servants and attendants lined the room and watched her approach. Helen had an audience wherever she went. Privacy was a thing foreign to her.

As Helen approached her parents, they stepped aside and revealed a couple standing behind them. Their clean, but plain, clothing revealed to her that the visitors were neither wealthy merchants nor diplomats. A little girl, no more than four years old peaked out from behind her mother's leg.

"We have traveled a long way," said the man.

"We feel terrible about what happened to you when you were kidnapped," said the woman softly. Helen noticed the woman wringing her hands and shaking ever so slightly as she spoke. The woman looked down at the little girl peering out from behind her own leg, and then met Helen's hard gaze, blushing. "Our daughter, Harleopi, felt badly as well and wanted to give you something to make you feel better."

She nudged the little girl forward. Harleopi stepped forward tentatively, with her eyes downcast and her hands behind her back. After a quick glance back to her mother, Harleopi approached Helen, who stooped down to meet the child.

"I'm sorry you got hurt," Harleopi said in a small voice. "I love you, and I hope these make you feel better." From behind her back, the little girl pulled a small basket filled with wild flowers, olives, and some fruit. She presented it to Helen.

Helen took a step back. "Oh my," she said, with her eyes and mouth wide open.

"I picked them myself," said Harleopi. She stood tall and looked up, smiling at Helen.

"You did?" exclaimed Helen. She surprised herself when she picked up the child, hugged her, and twirled her around. The heaviness had lifted from her. "They are the most beautiful flowers I have ever seen."

Tears streamed down Helen's cheeks. The others in the room applauded and cheered. Harleopi giggled, and Helen laughed. She forgot about the stigma for the moment. This little girl saw her for who she was. She invited Harleopi and her family to dinner and asked them to stay the night. She led them on a tour of the grounds and held Harleopi's hand the entire time. She thought to herself, "I'm finally feeling like myself again." She enjoyed seeing the palace through a four year old's eyes, and she finally felt her shoulders and body relax. Helen would always remember what Theseus had done, but she finally felt she could put it behind her.

Helen received marriage proposals on a regular basis from local dignitaries, foreign visitors, and traveling merchants. Six years had passed since her ordeal with Theseus. Helen was now eighteen years old, and although most found it odd that she was so old and still unmarried, King Tyndareus wanted to make sure she was ready and her suitor was truly worthy of her hand.

One day, he and Queen Leda called Helen into their chambers. "My dear child, you know that I love you deeply. I have consulted with your mother, and we both feel it is time for you to take a husband."

"You have overcome some large obstacles and have grown so much in the last few years," added Leda.

"When a daughter of royalty is ready to marry, tradition dictates that word is sent to all eligible bachelors in the area," said Tyndareus.

"Father, I understand the tradition." Helen smiled. She understood the tradition, that didn't mean she liked it. If it were up to her, she knew precisely whom she would choose for her husband. "I hope to take a husband who will make you proud of me."

"I am always proud of you, Helen," her father replied.

"Yes, my darling, I too am so proud of you; we always will be," said Leda.

Helen hugged both her parents and then turned to leave the room. She took only a few steps before she stopped and turned. "Father, if it's any help, there is a man from Mycenae I'm very fond of."

Tyndareus and Leda both smiled. Helen supposed it wasn't a huge secret. "I am sure he will come," her mother said.

Helen's beauty continued to grow with each passing year. Even the goddesses on Mount Olympus recognized that Helen was the most beautiful woman in the world and some began to grow jealous of her. Not only did every eligible Greek man wish to win her heart because of her beauty, but also because Spartan women could own property, whoever married her would be in line to inherit the kingdom through her.

Word that Helen was going to take a husband quickly spread everywhere. The date when everyone was to arrive rapidly approached. There was a parade scheduled for the following weekend. Helen would stand in a wagon as the main attraction, followed by the suitors who would then present their gifts to Tyndareus, Leda, and Helen in front of the reviewing stand. After the presentation of gifts, there would be a large dinner for all the suitors. When thinking about the public display she would have to undergo, that familiar dark and heavy feeling returned. Helen approached her father with a request. "I do not want to be put on display like that. It makes me uncomfortable."

"But my dear child, your suitors and the townspeople want to see you."

"I understand, but I feel like I am being auctioned off like a fine goat." "What do you suggest?"

"If I must be in the parade, then I would like to have my friends by my side. We can walk near the head of the parade, just behind the first group of soldiers."

"If that will make you happy, it will be so." Tyndareus tried to wave her off, but Helen hugged her father before skipping happily down the hall.

While the arrival of the suitors was something special, the people of Sparta had become used to strangers visiting town. Many people came to Sparta in hopes of stealing a glimpse of Helen. She was surprised by the reactions she received from people when they first saw her, because she didn't see herself as they did. She preferred the gaze of the people of Sparta to those of strangers. While they acknowledged her stunning beauty, they were accustomed to seeing her around town and did not gape, point or stare.

Spartans delighted in telling stories of visitors' first encounters with Helen. Some of the stories *were* funny, even though she didn't like all of the attention she received. A favorite story was about the forgettable diplomat who thought he was unforgettable, from a forgettable land far away. As he was walking his horse through the middle of town, Helen emerged from one of the shops with an attendant. The diplomat kept his eyes on Helen as he kept walking, and he did not see the mud puddle in front of him. It was funny enough when he fell face down in the puddle and ruined his expensive clothing, but it was funnier still that his horse stopped before reaching the puddle. Embarrassed and outsmarted by his horse, he left town. Helen tried to blend in among the people when she went into town, often covering her hair with a scarf and wearing plain clothes. Today, she hoped none of the arriving suitors would suffer the same type of embarrassment.

Many suitors had already arrived and were staying at the palace. Helen took the opportunity to greet them, hoping to see a familiar face among the throngs of men. She met some childhood friends who had visited Sparta years earlier such as Odysseus, Ajax and a few others. The parties were beginning, and the servants nervously ran everywhere because most of the guests were royalty. Tyndareus assigned two guards to Helen, and explained to her that he wished to avoid reliving the morning six years prior where he woke up to her kidnapping. Irritated with the constant supervision and the constant reminder of Theseus, she approached her father and said, "Father, must I have these guards with me at all times? I feel like a prisoner in my own home."

Tyndareus finally acquiesced to instruct the guards to keep a certain distance from her in the daytime, but he refused when it came to having them remaining on guard just outside her room at night. He forbade the suitors from interacting with Helen outside of the formal meetings. Helen knew he felt it was safer for her, and it didn't give anyone an unfair advantage. Helen ate with her parents at all dinners as she always did, but the two guards escorted her to all other official functions.

Tyndareus also informed Helen that she would be dancing for their guests the night before the big parade. While she enjoyed dance, it made her nervous. She remembered how she had danced for Theseus the night of her kidnapping. What if her dance was what brought on the—no, no. She told herself it wouldn't have mattered if she had danced or not that night. Her physical body had attracted the attention of Theseus, even at twelve, just as it had caused the diplomat to embarrass himself.

After a long day of attending lessons, greeting suitors and rehearsing her dance, Helen headed for her room. She was the only child left in the palace, and as she lay down on her bed, she thought of Clytemnestra, who married Aegisthus, the King of Mycenae, four years earlier and already had a daughter named Iphigenia. When Agamemnon slew Aegisthus, he regained his family throne and won Clytemnestra's hand. Helen wondered how it felt to be married and have a baby. She wondered whether Clytemnestra's husband, Agamemnon, would accompany her sister when she came for the festivities. She thought about her brothers, Castor and Pollux. They had both left home two years ago. She wondered where they were, how they were doing, and whether they would be home to see her off before she got married.

Then, her mind wandered to Menelaus. She hadn't seen him since he went off with Agamemnon to Phrygia to fight the Amazons three years ago. When last she saw him, he was still a tall, gangly young man with an athletic build. He was a little introverted and shy, but he would put up a bold front whenever he started talking about helping Agamemnon regain the Mycenae throne. She thought back to the night they walked in the garden after an official dinner. The fragrance of flowers filled the air, and the water in the pool was still. Helen and Menelaus were chatting about nothing in particular when he clasped her hands and turned her toward him. He took her chin in his hand, and he kissed her softly on the lips. At first, she tried to pull from him struggling slightly against his embrace, but then, the familiarity of his smell made her collapse into the awkwardness of the first kiss. His lips were warm and smooth, and she felt lightning flash through her body. Her heart fluttered, and her knees grew week. Menelaus smiled at her and kissed her again, this time with a full embrace. She was stunned and elated; she didn't know what to say, so she said nothing. Menelaus smiled at her and said goodnight. The next day, he had left for Phrygia with Agamemnon. The last she heard, he was doing well and living in Mycenae with Agamemnon and Clytemnestra. She hoped he would come to present gifts to her father and try to win her hand. She didn't want to have to kiss anyone else.

Aethra came in. "I wanted to check on you."

"Why can't I just choose who I want to marry?" Helen asked.

"Dear child, this is how it has always been done when royalty is to marry. The process allows you to get more for your family, to provide security, and sometimes to gain power."

"But Clytemnestra married the man she loved! She seems happy with Agamemnon." They both knew that while Tyndareus gave Clytemnestra's hand to Aegisthus, the man who exiled Agamemnon and Menelaus in order to form a powerful alliance, Helen's sister had been in love with Agamemnon.

"Yes I think they are both happy. Clytemnestra is happy with Agamemnon, and he is happy because he regained his throne. Now go to sleep, child. I'm sure your father will make a wise choice for you.

Helen wasn't convinced. She hated the feeling of powerlessness that came with someone else making decisions for her.

The next day, the final suitors arrived. Sparta swelled to ten times its size with all the visiting dignitaries, suitors and onlookers. Street vendors, musicians, dancers, acrobats, and jugglers entertained the crowds. Crimson and gold banners hung from windows and rooftops, and taverns overflowed with patrons. Merchants and visitors lived in tents popping up all over town. Crimson and gold banners, drapes, and curtains decorated the palace banquet rooms and hallways. Food came into Sparta from all over the region. The palace had three fire pits burning simultaneously: one roasted a boar, another had goat, and the last one had half a steer turning slowly on the spit. The laws of hospitality mandated that Tyndareus had to shelter and feed all of the suitors until he made a final decision. Helen overheard her father sending General Loiceteus to narrow down the hundreds of suitors to serious contenders only. When Loiceteus had finished, there were approximately fifty suitors left, most were princes or kings. Hundreds of eliminated suitors viewed the event as the chance of a lifetime to be part of something memorable. Many stayed to see the outcome. Helen was relieved that her father became even more vigilant about her safety.

The day of the big dinner for all the suitors arrived. Helen spent the day rehearsing her dance performance, and she was back in her room resting when Aethra announced that a woman was there to see her.

"Send the woman in," Helen wondered who it could be.

"As you wish, my lady."

Aethra left the room for a moment, and then Clytemnestra entered the room with her four-year old daughter, Iphigenia. Helen was thrilled to see her sister. She jumped to her feet and hugged her, "You made it!"

"The journey was rough, but yes, I am here!" said Clytemnestra.

"Oh, isn't she beautiful!" Helen picked up Iphigenia and gave her a big hug.

"Say hello to your Aunt Helen, sweetheart." instructed Clytemnestra

"Hello," the little girl said in her tiny voice.

"She's adorable," said Helen, "And she's growing so fast!"

"So," Clytemnestra said, leaning in, "What do you think of the suitors you've seen?"

Helen shrugged. "I don't know, I'm so nervous."

"Nervous about what? You have the finest men in all of Greece vying to be your husband. Do you remember the night before I was to marry, how we all gathered waiting for father to make his decision about Aegisthus. It made me so nervous."

"That's why I'm nervous! What if father chooses someone I don't like? The man I'm hoping to marry isn't even here, and I don't know if he will be."

"Father will choose the man who is best fit to be your husband. You have to believe that. If you're speaking of who I think you're speaking of, he is on his way. They sent me early so I could be here for the gathering of the women the night before your wedding."

"You mean…Menelaus?" asked Helen. How does *he* look?"

"And Agamemnon." Clytemnestra laughed. Helen folded her arms. She wasn't trying to be funny, she really wanted to know. Finally, her sister answered. "I think you'll be pleased with his appearance."

"Oh, I can't wait." Helen said, wistfully. Then a thought occurred to her. "What if father doesn't choose Menelaus? Does he have property? Did he acquire treasure from his battles?"

"Not too much, but don't worry. They will come up with something. You need to pull yourself together. You cannot allow the suitors to see your preference of him. Now let's get something to eat and show the little one around the palace."

On their tour of the palace, they saw Cinyras, the king of Cyprus, busying himself about the stable with horses, and the huge Ajax goading Idomeneus, who busied himself with his appearance. When Helen and Clytemnestra passed with Iphigenia, the men froze and gaped. Clytemnestra giggled and said, "I never get tired of seeing the way men stare at you and the ridiculous things they do in your presence."

Helen smiled and shook her head in reply.

When the tour was finished, the women retreated to their quarters to rest before dinner.

That night, suitors jammed the great hall, and the servants bustled about busily. To her surprise, Castor and Pollux arrived before the feast's start and sat at the head table along with the rest of Helen's family. After the jugglers and the acrobats preformed, Helen danced for the crowd. She finished with a solo dance called, "The Majestic Swan," in reference to the myth surrounding her birth. She'd given up fighting the rumors surrounding her entrance into the world, and instead embraced them. After all, if she were the daughter of Zeus, that would give her certain advantages. When she finished dancing, the crowd went crazy. They cheered, whistled, applauded, and gave a standing ovation.

After her performance, and after talking about women's duties in marriage with her female relatives, Helen retreated to her room. She was exhausted from all of the activity of the week, and already she was ready to be married. The attention she received was tiring. While Clytemnestra pointed out often that the attention men and women gave her was something to cherish, Helen couldn't help but feel vulnerable at night and when she was alone. She pushed the fears out of her head, and she worried that Menelaus hadn't yet arrived. "Why isn't he here yet," she muttered aloud. "Tomorrow is the day for the presentation of gifts; he has to be here by then!"

Aethra came in to check on her. "Aethra, I'm worried. Menelaus isn't here. Where can he be? If he isn't here in time, he won't have a chance to present his gifts and I may be given to someone else."

"Dear child, tomorrow is a big day." Aethra sat next to Helen and placed her arm around Helen's shoulders. "You must get some sleep. Menelaus will be here. Don't you worry."

After Aethra left her quarters, Helen tossed and turned for a few hours before sleep finally set in. While she was restless, she kept worrying about whether Menelaus would show up, about what would happen during the ceremony, and about what kinds of gifts the suitors would present.

The next day was perfect for a parade; there was a bright, cloudless sky and a slight breeze. The parade was to begin at the far end of town and conclude inside the amphitheater in front of the reviewing stand. There, Helen would ascend the stairs and sit with her parents and siblings while the suitors announced themselves and presented their gifts.

Helen was nervous and excited; she had two dozen of her friends and attendants in her group, including Clytemnestra, Iphigenia, and Harleopi. They went to the end of town to prepare for the start of the parade. They walked past and lined up behind the soldiers were in front, leading the parade. Next were musicians, jugglers, acrobats, and then handmaidens carrying baskets filled with flower petals to toss in front of Helen and her party. Helen took her place behind the handmaidens, dressed in a golden gown with crimson embroidery and a small tiara with a large diamond in the center. Clytemnestra and the little girls took their place behind her, followed by friends and attendants dressed in crimson and gold gowns with tiaras woven from flowers. Finally, a small cavalry troop fell in line leading the suitors, who were grouped together in no particular order. They all waited, chatting amongst themselves while everyone took their places.

A few minutes before the parade started, Helen wandered around and asked people if they had seen or heard from Menelaus. Finally, the horns sounded and the parade started. Helen thought, "Well, what will be will be," and started walking down the street.

The parade route was crowded with people waving flags, banners, and signs and blowing horns. When Helen passed by, the audience cheered and threw flowers at her and her party. Some people shouted, "We love you, Helen," and a chant of, "Sparta, Sparta!" arose from the crowd. Members of the crowd had banners supporting Ajax, Diomedes, Odysseus, Menelaus, and many others. When a favorite suitor passed by, the crowd cheered loudly. Although part of her enjoyed the attention and playing to the crowd, Helen was uncomfortable with it. She smiled and waved to her friends and fellow Spartans. The parade route covered nearly a mile, weaving all through the town so every Spartan had a chance to see it.

When Helen reached the viewing stand, Tyndareus and Leda remained seated, and Castor and Pollux stood off to the side. Helen climbed the stairs and sat next to her mother, and Clytemnestra chose a seat beside her brothers.

As the suitors approached the stands, they were announced and they presented their gifts. "Ladies and Gentlemen, Cinyras, King of Cyprus!" The crowd applauded, and some Spartans cheered.

A short, pudgy, balding older man bowed before the King. "Good King Tyndareus, I present you with two chests full of gold and jewels along with two barges of grains in exchange for the hand of your beautiful daughter!"

Tyndareus nodded and thanked him. Cinyras bowed again and moved away. A few more suitors presented similar gifts before moving on.

Then, Ajax the Greater presented his gifts. Ajax was a huge man; he stood a head taller than the other men and was very muscular. When he was announced, he was a crowd favorite and they cheered and applauded loudly. Ajax approached King Tyndareus and said, "Your Highness, I pledge that I will give your daughter protection and security. I also pledge the riches of my kingdom, along with all the riches of the Ionian Islands."

Tyndareus looked quizzically at Leda and then Helen before he leaned toward Ajax. "But you don't own the Ionian Islands."

"If I am chosen, I will acquire them!" Ajax bellowed and raised his arms, turning to face the crowd. The crowd laughed and roared its approval. Ajax bowed and descended the stairs in mock triumph. Helen smiled and fidgeted in her chair. She felt as though she were a slave being auctioned off to the highest bidder. Her stomach fluttered and lurched with the announcement of each suitor—not because of each suitor's attractiveness or lack thereof but because although she would try to influence her father's decision, in the end she had no say in which man she would marry.

Idomeneus was the next suitor to approach the king. An extremely handsome man, he approached King Tyndareus and said, "Dear King, I pledge myself! A woman of exceptional beauty should be paired with a man of equal beauty." He bowed and stepped away, tripping over himself as he did. The crowd roared with laughter and then calmed down as he joined the rest of the suitors.

There was a loud roar from the back of the parade route, but it was too far away for Helen to see what was causing it. As the parade moved forward, the roar followed it like a tidal wave.

The next suitor to approach was Odysseus, the King of Ithaca. Odysseus was a short, stocky man, at least a head shorter than any of the others, but he was quite muscular. He stepped forward and said, "Your highness, I have not brought any treasures with me, but Ithaca is a beautiful land with many riches. I pledge that Helen will be well cared for and want for nothing." He then bowed and moved to the side, following the same path the previous suitors had taken after presenting their gifts.

The wave of cheers finally reached the amphitheater. Silence fell over the people inside as they turned to see who was entering through the gate. Helen leaned forward, nearly falling out of her seat as she strained to see who approached. Finally, she was able to see that it was Agamemnon, and walking by his side was Menelaus. Attendants followed them, herding two large bulls. The crowd cheered and jumped to their feet. Helen felt her heart leap—this time in anticipation. Menelaus blushed and smiled as he acknowledged the crowd's cheers. Helen had to fight the urge to fly out of her seat as she tried to get a better look. Menelaus was lean, tan, athletic, and muscular. He'd filled out quite a bit and had grown a well sculpted beard to go with his wavy auburn hair. In all, he was very regal as he approached with his brother.

"Ladies and Gentlemen, Agamemnon, King of Mycenae, and Menelaus, Prince of Mycenae!" Menelaus was the crowd favorite and it shouted its approval. The two men ascended the steps and approached Tyndareus. Menelaus and Helen smiled warmly at each other as their eyes met. Helen felt her cheeks grow hot. Agamemnon stepped forward and said, "Good King Tyndareus, I do not pledge anything on my behalf for I am already married to the lovely Clytemnestra." After a brief pause for applause from the crowd, he continued, "As the King of Mycenae and as representative for my brother, Menelaus, I pledge 100 bulls for the hand of the beautiful Helen." Tyndareus and Leda smiled at each other. The crowd stood up and cheered wildly because bulls were a prized commodity in Sparta. A pledge of 100 Mycenaean bulls was an enormous sum. Agamemnon and Menelaus bowed and joined the rest of the suitors.

Tyndareus stepped forward to address the crowd. "I want to thank everyone for their very generous offers. I will consider all of your pledges and present my decision in a day or two." The crowd dispersed to prepare for the banquet that would be held in the great hall later that evening. Another night of festivities lay ahead.

Helen followed her family down the steps of the platform to greet Menelaus and Agamemnon. She wanted to run to him, but held herself back in a need to keep her composure. Agamemnon was her brother-in-law, so it was not forbidden to interact with him, but it also wouldn't be fair to the other suitors if she hugged one of their competitors and showed affection toward him. Each member of her family greeted Agamemnon and Menelaus, and she did the same. "You look great! How have you been?" Helen asked Menelaus when she took his hands into hers, greeting him.

"You look fantastic!" exclaimed Menelaus, as he looked her up and down.

Helen took a step back and glared at Menelaus for a moment. She hoped he hadn't changed as much inside as he had outside. "Yes, well, thank you for coming. I'm surprised to see you here. You weren't at the parade," said Helen.

"I'm sorry about that. Agamemnon and I didn't travel as quickly as we'd hoped."

Helen gave Menelaus a reserved and tired smile. "I'm glad you were able to make it." Helen was suddenly aware of the other suitors watching her with her old friend, and some had approached her to chat.

"I should go. Will you be at the banquet tonight?"

"I wouldn't miss it for the world," said Menelaus. His smile stretched from ear to ear, and it reminded her of the blind enthusiasm he had when they were kids. She felt his eyes on her as she walked away to join her parents and escorts.

"Is he still watching me?" she whispered to Harleopi, who took a quick glance back at Menelaus.

"Yes!" giggled Harleopi. Helen felt warmth in her heart. Perhaps he was still the same old Menelaus who would let her win at the wrestling games.

At dinner that night, Menelaus sat at the head table with his brother, and Helen sat on the other side of her parents with her siblings. Menelaus and Helen met eyes and grins whenever they could. Even though she felt slightly irritated with him for bringing up her looks, she couldn't help but smile and blush when they'd catch each other staring from across the table.

Tyndareus announced that there would be a series of games and competitions for the suitors the following day for entertainment and stress relief. The suitors were sitting at tables that had been set up in a circle in front the head table so as not to show favoritism. Everyone was having a great time drinking and feasting on the wide variety of wines and foods. After a time it was beginning to get a little too rowdy. One suitor stood up and said, "I have the fastest horses in all of Greece, and I will prove it at the games tomorrow. I wager 100 gold pieces against any horse here."

There was some grumbling, and then another suitor shouted, "I will take that bet!" This opened the floodgates. There were challenges for foot races, chariot races, wrestling, boxing, javelin throwing, weight lifting, and many other games. The room grew raucous and tempers flared. One of the suitors approached Tyndareus and argued, "Noble king, I feel Agamemnon's pledge should be voided because he is part of your family and it was not Menelaus' property that he pledged!" Other suitors agreed and approached Tyndareus to complain about the fairness of considering Agamemnon's pledge.

Agamemnon joined in the argument. "Dear King, a pledge is a pledge. It doesn't matter who gives it, as long as it is fulfilled."

"Yes, but how does he qualify to pledge? It is not Menelaus' wealth he pledges," replied the suitor.

"Menelaus is my brother, my family. What is mine is his. Will you deny me the right to give this pledge as a gift to my brother?" The argument was settled, but the atmosphere remained tense. Tyndareus, fearing a brawl within the palace, ended the party and dismissed everyone by promising that he would give his answer soon enough. He ordered Helen out of the room with her guards in tow.

Helen shuffled back to her room, confused, dejected, and angry. "What if they are right? What if Menelaus is disqualified? Whom will I end up with? Ajax? Diomedes? Oh no! Not Idomeneus!" Helen threw herself on her bed face-down and let out a heavy sigh.

"Helen!" The sound of her name broke her thoughts. She looked around and did not see anyone. "Helen!" She heard it again, although it was soft. "Helen, come here."

It was coming from outside her window, but Helen knew there was a guard there. "Not again," she muttered then walked cautiously to the curtain and pulled it aside while standing to the side of the window to peer out. There she saw Menelaus standing with a huge grin on his face.

She shook her head at him, but couldn't keep her composure any longer. She slid out the window and jumped into his arms. They held each other and passionately kissed. She had missed him so much, but wondered what happened to the guard. "Where is Lurineus?" she asked.

"I have known him for years. He just happened to need a break and will be back shortly." Menelaus winked and jingled a purse, she understood. "I had to see you. I have missed you so much," he said and kissed her again.

"I missed you too, but we must be careful." Helen pushed away from his embrace and climbed back into her room. "Aethra will be her soon to check on me."

"Just a few more minutes," Menelaus said and walked up to the window.

Helen leaned out to allow Menelaus to steal another kiss. "What if my father disqualifies you."

"Don't worry; I will kill whoever he chooses! We will be together, just as we were meant to be." He took her hands, and they shared a long kiss.

"You should go now. Aethra will be here soon."

"I will see you tomorrow," he said and reluctantly disappeared from her view.

The next day, Helen attended the events in the amphitheater. She watched the races and the weight lifting. Menelaus participated in some of the track and field events, including the quarter mile race. Helen admired his muscular, tanned body as he prepared for the race. She tried to turn away before Menelaus caught her looking, but she was always too slow and Menelaus smiled whenever he caught her looking. He did not win the race, but Helen quietly cheered him on all the way to his close third place finish.

Next up was the javelin throw. Menelaus was built for this event; he was tall, lean, and strong. He led the competition until Ajax, the last competitor, had his turn. Ajax was a mountain of a man, and the javelin looked tiny in his hands. With a mighty roar, his throw easily outdistanced Menelaus' best attempt. Ajax was declared the winner, but it didn't matter to Helen. She was thrilled that Menelaus was here in Sparta, trying to win her hand in marriage.

Next came the boxing and wrestling. As she watched the men grappling with each other, it reminded her of male animals in the forest rutting to win the female animals. Helen turned to her father and said, "Suddenly, I feel very uncomfortable. May I return to the palace?" Tyndareus nodded. She caught Menelaus watching her leave, and she hoped that he didn't think it was because she was disappointed with his performance. She'd just had enough of the competition for one day.

A week passed from the time the suitors presented their gifts when Leda came to Tyndareus and said, "Dear husband, what are you waiting for? Why haven't you made a decision?"

"I want to make the right selection for Helen and for Sparta. I fear if I choose one suitor over another, my choice will insult the others, and there will be a fight—if not a civil war!"

"We cannot afford to keep feeding and housing all these people. The servants and the rest of the staff are being run ragged, and our guests are growing restless. There have already been fights between suitors' attendants. Patience runs thin."

Tyndareus felt conflicted. On the one hand, he knew the decision he needed to make. On the other hand, he knew that if he made that decision, he was likely to start a riot over his daughter's hand in marriage. He sighed and finally said, "Give me time to think."

That night after dinner, the suitors were in the garden having drinks and socializing. The party was for suitors only; there were no private servants, weapons, or entourages allowed because of the tension among the groups of people. Menelaus looked around, the garden hadn't changed much since he shared that kiss with Helen three years earlier. The palace servants brought goblets of wine and kept the torches lit. The aroma from the cooking pits hung in the air and mixed with the fragrance of flowers. Menelaus talked with Odysseus and Ajax, and he had his back to another group of suitors including Cinyras, the King of Paphos in Crete. Odysseus spoke highly of Penelope, Helen's cousin. It was refreshing to be part of a conversation that didn't circle around his old friend's beauty. However, it was becoming increasingly difficult to pay attention due to the increasing volume of voices and the offensive way the men behind him spoke about Helen.

"Did you see her legs when she was dancing the other night? So flexible, so strong; the things I could do..." sighed Cinyras. Menelaus rolled his eyes. To him, she was just Helen. Yes, she was a great beauty, but she's also the girl he wrestled with and sparred with in lessons several years ago.

"I agree," another suitor said, "but I really loved her eyes."

"Her eyes?" exclaimed a third. "What do you mean her eyes?"

"I thought they were captivating."

"Are you serious? The woman has a figure straight from Mount Olympus and the part you remember is her eyes? I didn't even notice she had eyes! I never got that far!" The group of men laughed. Menelaus felt heat rising up through his blood. He was having a difficult time focusing on his own conversation.

"I know what you mean," said Cinyras. "Watching her walk away is a vision fit for the gods!" That was it. Menelaus had to get away from this group of men. He turned to walk away when

Cinyras grabbed his arm and said, "Menelaus, wait, we were just talking and we were wondering about something."

Menelaus sighed, "What's that?"

"You lived here in the palace for a few years, correct?"

"That's right." Menelaus could see where this was going, and already, he didn't like it.

"Well, we were wondering…just how well did you get to know Helen?"

"What do you mean?"

"You know what I mean." Cinyras said, his voice now flat and his eyes aflame. "Does she know how to please a man?" Cinyras snickered and looked at the group he stood with.

"I would expect that question from a *pornoboskós*, not a king," snarled Menelaus.

"Well, I hear that Theseus broke her in real well. As a matter of fact, the word is that she likes it rough!" Cinyras jabbed his friend in the ribs, and they began laughing.

Menelaus leapt forward and punched him in the face, knocking him to the ground. "You will not speak of Theseus in this home!" Onlookers grabbed both men and pulled them apart.

Ajax stepped in and bellowed, "All right, break it up."

Menelaus looked around. Already men were taking sides around him. He was sure that if weapons had been allowed that a deadly fight would have erupted.

Menelaus and Cinyras exchanged nasty looks and separated. "Get me out of here," said Menelaus to Agamemnon. "I don't like the company." They pushed their way through the throng of suitors and out of the party.

After the scuffle, King Tyndareus received word that Odysseus had asked for an audience with him. Tyndareus knew that Odysseus had the gift of insight, and that he could read a person's body language, facial expressions, and movement and tell what that person was thinking or feeling. Odysseus' ability gave him the upper hand in negotiations. When Odysseus had inquired about the meeting, Tyndareus felt a sense of relief. Certainly he'd be able to help the king sort through the suitors to choose who was best.

"Good King, thank you for seeing me."

"Odysseus, my friend, what can I do for you?"

"I believe it is I who may be able to do something for you. I know you have a hard decision to make. I am sure that it's a struggle to decide who among fifty men is the best suitor for your daughter."

"Yes, I fear that if I don't choose wisely, I may insult some of the suitors and destroy Sparta in the process." Tyndareus sighed, not only that, but he had noticed the obvious glances between Menelaus and his daughter. Menelaus had already been in the middle of a few scuffles at parties. He had no wish to cause more of a problem than there already was.

"I may have the solution to your problem."

"Oh? And what do you want in return?"

"Very little in terms of treasure, but a great deal in terms of influence. If what I share solves your problem, I would like your help in winning the hand of your niece, Penelope."

Tyndareus thought for a moment about the glances he'd noticed between Odysseus and Penelope over the last several days, then said, "Done. What is your solution?"

"We both know horses are a prized possession in Greece, and the sacrifice of one will not be taken lightly. So I propose that you sacrifice a horse, and cut it into as many parts as you have suitors. Ask each suitor to stand on a piece of the horse and swear an oath to come to the aid of whomever *Helen* chooses as her husband if anyone interferes with their marriage in any way. This way, Helen will do the choosing, letting you off the hook, and Helen gets to marry the man she truly wants."

Tyndareus thought Odysseus' plan was brilliant. He sent out a request for all the suitors to meet in the amphitheater the following day at noon. He had made his decision.

When the time came the following day, Tyndareus ordered a horse slaughtered and the pieces brought to the arena where he,

Leda, Helen, and the rest of the family assembled on the viewing stand. The arena was crowded with people, and all the suitors filed in, dressed in their best clothes, hoping to become Helen's husband. Helen wore a white dress embroidered in gold and crimson. Upon her head sat a gold tiara with a blue diamond in the middle. Tyndareus looked at his daughter and believed she was the most stunning he'd ever seen her. He motioned for her to stop fidgeting with the embroidery on her dress.

With the suitors lined up in front of him, Tyndareus stood and said, "My friends, your pledges have all been very generous. You have made this decision very difficult. I have thought long and hard about my decision. I want the best for my daughter, and that means a solid, loving marriage. Since there are so many men interested in her, I have found a way to ensure that her marriage has a chance to grow and prosper."

He motioned for some attendants to spread out the parts of the horse in the infield. "My friends, behind you are pieces of a horse, an animal we all have great reverence for. I want each of you to stand on a piece of this horse and place your hands on your hearts." The suitors looked at each other as they took their places on small pieces of horseflesh. "Please repeat after me: "I swear this solemn oath on my honor that I will protect and defend the marriage of whoever is chosen as Helen's husband against anyone who would do it harm." Each suitor swore to Tyndareus' Oath. He smiled. So far, Odysseus' plan was a success.

Tyndareus took a deep breath before continuing, nervous that the next step would cause a riot. "Thank you. Now, this was probably the hardest decision I have had to make in a long time, and to be honest, I don't think I am qualified to make it. So, I have decided not to make a ruling at all." A gasp rose from the crowd. Tyndareus looked at his daughter and saw her mouth hung open. He smiled at her, trying to reassure her that things would be okay. The suitors all looked at one another, presumably confused. Tyndareus started again, "You see, I don't have to live with the decision made today, but my daughter does. I have decided to leave the decision in her hands. Helen, please come forward."

Helen couldn't believe what she just heard. Her father was going to let her choose! She took a deep breath to hide her excitement then stepped forward in a daze. She glanced back at her mother and sister, who smiled broadly and nodded. "Father, have I heard you correctly? *I* am to choose?"

"My dear daughter, you have heard all of the pledges; you have seen and spoken with all of the suitors. Who is the man who has won your heart and your hand?"

Helen quietly thanked her father, trying to still her excitement. She looked out over all of the suitors. She swallowed and then said, "I want to thank all of you for your kind words, your very generous pledges, and your patience. I am sure all of you will make excellent husbands and fathers. I agree with my father that this is a very difficult decision, and I do not make it easily." She paused for a moment. She looked out and saw Menelaus, and noticed he had trepidation painted all over his face. She smiled warmly at him. "The man who has won my heart, and my hand in marriage, is Prince Menelaus of Mycenae!" She could no longer publically hold in her emotion, and she flushed with excitement.

The crowd erupted in wild cheering and shouting. Menelaus quickly moved through the crowd and rushed up the stairs. He took her in a huge embrace and kissed her and then he hugged Tyndareus and Leda as Helen's brothers and sister patted him on the back. Agamemnon hugged his brother, and Iphigenia clung to his leg. The crowd surged out of the stands and flooded onto the amphitheater floor to get a closer look, engulfing the remaining suitors. Many of the suitors were disappointed, and some sore losers headed for the exits, including Cinyras. He kicked at the ground and muttered while he shoved people out of his way. Helen felt relief that he would not be her husband.

Tyndareus asked Menelaus and Helen to stand in front of him. He then looked at Menelaus. "Son, I give you permission to marry my daughter."

Menelaus smiled, and Tyndareus handed Helen a wreath. She placed it around Menelaus' neck. He smiled back at her. Tyndareus said to the audience, "I present you my daughter, Helen, and my son-in-law, Menelaus."

Menelaus and Helen kissed easily, turned to the crowd, and Menelaus raised their clasped hands over their heads in triumph and union. The crowd was ecstatic, and the applause was deafening. Even the remaining suitors showed great sportsmanship and applauded. The families congratulated Helen and Menelaus. As was tradition to prove his strength, Menelaus draped Helen over his shoulder. They made their way down the steps, and with the help of an armed escort, they pushed through the cheering crowd. The musicians played and onlookers threw flowers in front of the newlyweds' feet. Before they knew it, Helen and Menelaus had an impromptu parade following them back to the palace for a large feast. Helen smiled broadly. She was thankful that she would marry her dear friend. She knew her father had prepared a massive feast for as many people as could fit onto the palace grounds to celebrate the wedding. What a surprise to choose! Menelaus and Helen dined, danced, and welcomed all the well-wishers. When Ajax spoke to them, he jokingly suggested they should visit the Ionian Islands. After a few hours of merriment, Helen and Menelaus retreated to his room as husband and wife before journeying to Mycenae the next day to tour Agamemnon's kingdom.

Before they left, Tyndareus kept his word to Odysseus and gave his niece, Penelope's, hand in marriage to him. Helen looked back at her fellow Spartans as she and Menelaus set off on their journey. Odysseus had Penelope, Menelaus had Helen and there was great joy among those living in Sparta.

CHAPTER THREE

AGAMEMNON'S PLAN

In the years following Helen and Menelaus's marriage, Sparta fell on hard times. Tyndareus and Leda passed away. Castor and Pollux met their fate at the hands of Idas and Lynceus, and were taken to the heavens. Helen and Menelaus then ascended to the throne. Helen made a natural queen; the people loved and respected her. Though she now ruled Sparta with her husband, she enjoyed many of the same activities she had in her youth. She practiced dancing and weaving, and she helped the people of Sparta when she could. More than anything, though, she enjoyed playing with her nine-year-old daughter, Hermione.

When Menelaus and Helen took the throne, Sparta was enjoying a time of peace. However, a devastating drought marred Menelaus's rule. Sparta was primarily a farming community, so natural disasters such as droughts affected it more than they did ports or trading centers. The people of Sparta struggled to survive. In response, Menelaus dug into the Spartan treasury and bought boatloads of grain and supplies. He was unwilling to sit back and watch from the comforts of the palace. Menelaus knew the Spartan people were supportive when he came to Sparta during his exile, and he was determined to be there for them during their time of strife. He and Helen distributed the grain and supplies to the areas most afflicted by the drought. The couple gave their time, effort, and money to help the people of their polis. They got their hands dirty and tried to help the Spartan people the best they could through the disaster. Those they helped, as they were able to, in order to show their gratitude and repay the generosity shown them, sent gifts and food to the palace. The Spartans weathered the major disaster, but a much larger storm sat on the horizon.

Preparations were underway for a special celebration in Sparta: Agamemnon was coming to visit. The servants were in a flurry preparing the palace for his arrival. Agamemnon had visited many times before, but this particular trip was on short notice. The guest of honor arrived right on time, and Menelaus and Helen welcomed him at the palace door.

"It's great to see you, brother!" Agamemnon said with a broad smile and shook Menelaus's hand before giving him a hug.

"It's been too long! You're looking well," replied Menelaus.

"And of course, there's my favorite sister-in-law. You're looking as beautiful as ever."

Helen rolled her eyes in jest and then embraced Agamemnon. "Thank you, you're too kind. Where are Clytemnestra and Iphigenia?"

"Iphigenia didn't want to make the trip, so your sister stayed home with her. Besides, this is a short visit, planned at a moment's notice. I need to speak to Menelaus about something important."

"I'm disappointed. I wanted to see them. How are they?"

"They are well. Iphigenia has grown into a beautiful young lady."

"Come, you must be hungry," Menelaus interjected. "I hope what you want to talk about can wait until later this evening. I have some emissaries here for lunch, and afterward, we are going on a boar hunt. Would you like to join us?"

"Absolutely! We can talk later," replied Agamemnon.

Menelaus was a good archer, but Agamemnon was excellent. Boar hunting was one of his favorite activities. When the men returned from a successful hunt, the kings gave the boar Agamemnon killed to the emissaries as a gift.

After dinner that evening, Menelaus and Agamemnon retired to Menelaus's private meeting room. The room was large, but appeared even larger due to its sparse furnishings. Sweeping windows provided a view of the mountains beyond. After each servant poured a cup of wine, Menelaus dismissed them. When they were alone, Agamemnon took a drink from his cup and spoke. "Brother, I am not certain how you will react to what I must say."

Menelaus put his hand on his sibling's shoulder. "We have been through so much together. You know you can always speak candidly with me."

"Thank you. We must discuss Troy."

"What about Troy?"

Agamemnon paced around the meeting room, wringing his hands, while his brother sat on the edge of the lone table. Finally, he spoke. "You know that Troy has been gaining power, prosperity, wealth, and influence over the years. The Trojans are also my main competition for trade in the Aegean."

"Yes, I know these things. What are you getting at?"

"Do you remember Priam, the king of Troy? He fought beside us against the Amazons in Phrygia."

"I vaguely remember him. He had a disdain for Sparta and the Mycenaean's."

"Disdain is putting it mildly," said Agamemnon. "He loathes us for what Heracles had done."

"I remember now; Heracles kidnapped Priam's older sister, Hesione, and gave her to Teucer, who brought her to Greece. When Priam sent envoys to ask for her return, they were killed…but that was 20 years ago!" Menelaus watched his brother continue to pace.

"It has been gnawing at him ever since." Agamemnon responded.

"What does this have to do with Sparta?"

"Now that he is powerful enough, I believe he wants war with us. You are soon receiving an envoy from Troy, are you not?"

"Yes. How do you know about this?"

"I have heard from merchants and other travelers." Agamemnon took a sip of wine before continuing. "There is a Trojan prince named Paris who believes that Aphrodite has promised him the most beautiful woman in the world as his bride. Everyone knows that your wife, Helen, is the most beautiful woman in the world."

"But Helen and *I* are already married."

"You know that doesn't matter to the gods. He is accompanying this envoy under the guise of trade and as an emissary to inquire about the release of Hesione. I believe his true purpose, however, is to abduct your wife."

"That's senseless. I will place guards around her."

"He will continue trying because he believes that she belongs to him, that she is his right, that the gods ordained it."

"Then, I will kill him," said Menelaus flatly.

"That may be just what Priam wants. If you kill Paris, Priam will declare war on Sparta."

"Then there will be war."

"Troy is very powerful now, and Sparta alone will not be able to withstand the Trojan army. Of course, I am your ally, and I will declare war on Troy, but I don't know who else in Greece would join us in war. Some will believe the war would be yours to fight alone since you caused it by killing the king's son. Ithaca may remain neutral, and we don't know what Athens will do. The Athenians have not always been on favorable terms with Sparta. Some kingdoms may even side with Troy. Sparta and Mycenae together are not strong enough to defeat Troy." Agamemnon looked Menelaus squarely in the eyes and said, "There is another way."

"What is that?"

"I propose we strike Troy first."

"But, you just said that Sparta and Mycenae are not strong enough to defeat Troy. What about the famous Trojan walls? They say the walls were built by the gods!"

"We are not strong enough alone, but under a united Greece, we can win."

"How are we going to unite Greece? You just said some kingdoms will remain neutral and some will side with Troy."

"We invoke the Oath of Tyndareus." Menelaus sat in silence listening to Agamemnon. "I propose we let this Trojan abduct your wife."

Menelaus could only laugh at Agamemnon's plan. Agamemnon waited a few moments before repeating himself. "The Oath of Tyndareus can unite all of Greece!"

Menelaus began pacing as well. He felt his heart begin to race. "Are you mad? Do you hear what you're saying? You want me to allow Helen, *my wife*, to be abducted by this…fiend! You can't be serious!"

"I am serious. He will keep coming back, and if you kill him, you will have an unwinnable war on your hands. However, if you unite Greece, even the fabled walls of Troy cannot withstand their might. Better yet, I want your wife to seduce him so Paris will believe they fell in love and have a good reason for not returning her to us."

Menelaus stopped. His whole body felt hot. "Seduce him!" He roared." "Now, I know you are mad. No. It won't be done. There has to be another way."

"How hard can it be to seduce this man when he already believes he deserves her? She can take her servants, her attendants, and her treasure with him if she seduces him; if she is abducted, she goes alone. It will be a short war."

"I won't ask Helen to do this."

"For the good of your country, you must!" Now Agamemnon was the one with the loud voice.

"I can't do it. I won't do it."

"I have never asked you for anything, but you owe me much. I am the one who helped you when we were exiled. I am the one who cared for you and trained you; I was the one by your side in battle. I was the one who pledged 100 bulls for Helen on your behalf. You would have nothing if it were not for me. You must do this for Sparta, Mycenae, and all of Greece!" Agamemnon's voice echoed through the hall.

"It is true that I owe you much, but Helen is all that I have. I will not ask her to do this."

"Do not ask your wife to do this; order her to do it. She is your woman. You are the king. Assert yourself. Threaten if you have to. If you command her to make this sacrifice for Sparta, she will obey."

"Perhaps the issue is simple for you, dear brother, but it is not for me. I must ask you to leave me now."

"We will talk more tomorrow." As he walked toward the door, Agamemnon turned and said, "War is coming one way or another. The only choice we have is whether we fight on our soil or on Priam's." Agamemnon left to return to his quarters. Menelaus walked to the window and gazed off into the distance, looking for answers in the moon's shadows.

That night, when Menelaus entered his bedchamber, Helen could tell something was clearly on her husband's mind. Helen stopped combing her hair in front of the mirror, turned, and said, "Menelaus, what's wrong?"

"Ah, one of the servants dropped and broke a jug of wine in the hallway. I had to discipline him."

"I have known you far too long to believe a spilled jug of wine has you this upset. Now, tell me what is troubling you."

Menelaus sighed. Helen knew that was a sign he didn't want to talk, but he would anyway if she remained silent long enough. Finally, he said, "Menelaus speaks of war."

"War? With whom?"

"Troy."

"Why Troy? What would they want with us?"

"Emissaries are coming here. They should arrive in a few days." Helen remained silent, and Menelaus continued. "One of them is named Paris, and he is a Trojan prince. He believes the goddess, Aphrodite, has promised to make you his bride."

"That's silly." Helen turned back to her mirror and continued to comb her hair. "I am already *your* wife. Why would Aphrodite do that?"

"As his story goes, when he awarded her the Golden Apple of Discord as the fairest of the goddesses, she offered him the most beautiful woman in the world as his prize."

"Do you believe this Trojan's story?"

"What I believe does not matter. What does matter is what this prince believes. He will arrive in a few days, and Agamemnon believes he is coming here to abduct you." Helen's blood froze at the notion of being abducted again. Her husband continued, and her heart began to beat faster. "Even if I put more guards around you, he will never give up, because he believes the two of you are destined to be together. If I kill him, Priam will declare war on Sparta. Agamemnon believes we cannot win such a war and that the Trojans would surely destroy Sparta."

"What are you going to do?" Helen asked. She tried to keep the fear from her voice as she knew it would only cause her husband more internal discord. Menelaus walked to stand next to his wife.

"Sparta fears no one. I would rather kill Paris and incur Priam's wrath than see you with another man." Helen leaned in and gave her husband a tender kiss, and they tightly embraced. Menelaus finally said, "Let's get some sleep. I'm very tired. I don't wish to speak of this anymore tonight."

Helen agreed, but they were unable to put the problem out of their minds and had a restless sleep. At lunch the following day, Helen could feel the tension between Agamemnon and Menelaus. Her brother in law kept staring at her in a way he had never looked at her before. She couldn't quite place what was different, but his stares made her feel uncomfortable.

After lunch, Helen went to her weaving to try to forget about her conversation with Menelaus, but it kept coming back to her. How could Aphrodite do this to her? Who was this prince? Why would Aphrodite give a married woman away as a gift? She was furious with the goddess. Would Menelaus really go to war? Would Sparta be destroyed? She believed Menelaus wasn't telling her the whole story. She knew Agamemnon to be ambitious and that he considered Troy a competitor he would like to destroy. She had to gather more information.

Agamemnon had some matters to attend to in town, and Menelaus wandered the grounds alone. He was glad to have some time alone to think. He was torn between his two options. On one hand, he agreed that it was better to take the fight to the enemy, and with a united Greece, success seemed as though it would be assured. On the other hand, he couldn't bring himself to ask his wife to seduce another man. How could anyone who loved his wife do such a thing? And, after everything that happened in her childhood with Theseus? There had to be another way to unite the city-states of Greece, without the oath.

After dinner that evening, Menelaus and Agamemnon returned to the meeting room. Helen was determined to get answers, and so she walked through the hall toward the meeting room door. She could hear their voices, but she couldn't quite hear what they were saying inside. As she got closer, she heard Agamemnon loudly say that Menelaus owed him. She reached the door and opened it just as Menelaus shouted, "I can't ask Helen to do that!"

Both men saw Helen and fell silent. Menelaus finally spoke, softly. "Helen, what are you doing here?"

"I came here to discuss war."

"You shouldn't be here," said Menelaus. He stared at her hard with a look in his eyes she'd only previously seen him have before battle.

Despite his objection, Helen entered the room and glared at the two men, her hands were in fists. "Have the two of you forgotten that I am *Queen* of Sparta? My dear husband, you would not be in a position to lead the Spartans were it not for my inheritance and me. If it involves war and Sparta, then it involves me as well. This is my country, these are my people, and my voice will be heard."

She paused before continuing. "Menelaus, I respect your judgment, but war with Troy is a serious matter. Now, what can't you ask me to do?"

Agamemnon and Menelaus looked at each other, but said nothing. Helen asked again, her voice growing louder. "Answer me! What can't you ask me to do?"

Menelaus sighed deeply, opened his hands, and nodded toward Agamemnon. Agamemnon looked at the floor, before looking at Helen and finally speaking. "There is a man coming here named Paris. He is a Trojan prince, and I believe he is coming here to abduct you."

"So I have heard." Helen crossed her arms. A familiar weight came back to sit on her chest, and a chill ran through her body. Still, she remained firm in her stature.

"I believe that Priam, the king of Troy, is sending Prince Paris in order to start a war."

"Why Sparta?" Helen asked.

"It doesn't matter to Priam which Greek kingdom he goes to war with. Sparta is just the convenient flashpoint for him because his son believes Aphrodite has promised you to him."

"But why does Priam want war with Greece?"

"Priam hates the Greeks because of what Heracles did to his sister. If Paris takes you back to Troy, Priam will feel he has achieved some measure of revenge. If we kill Paris, Priam has a perfectly good reason to go to war with Sparta. I have heard Troy has a large army, and even together, Sparta and Mycenae would be no match for their army's power. This is where you come in. Helen, in your hands, you hold the power of the Oath of Tyndareus. The Oath can provide the army we need for defeating the Trojans." Agamemnon paused as he searched for his words. "I propose that you act first and seduce this prince, make him believe you have fallen in love with him, and let him take you back to Troy."

Helen thought for a long moment, and then she said, "You want me to go to Troy as this Trojan's wife?"

"Don't you see? They will say you fell in love, and we will say he abducted you. Your reputation in Sparta and the rest of Greece will stay intact, and we can invoke the Oath to raise an army of all your former suitors and their followers. They will have to honor their pledge to defend your marriage. We will raise an army consisting of all of Greece. I assure you, it will be a short war; no wall ever built will be able to withstand the might of such a large army!"

Helen was silent for a moment. She looked around the room and watched as her husband paced, visibly agitated. Finally, she spoke. "How do I know you are not just looking for an opportunity to strike Troy? Everyone knows how you despise the Trojans."

"It is true, I would like nothing better than to see Troy defeated, and I believe Priam would like nothing more than to destroy Mycenae, but I have never had the means to accomplish such a feat. Now, Priam has handed me an opportunity, and I don't intend to let it pass. Priam has decided to move first, and the only way to protect Sparta and Mycenae is to invoke the Oath of Tyndareus!"

"And if I decide not to seduce him and I am abducted anyway?" Helen shuddered, remembering the harshness shown to her by Theseus. If she agreed to this, at least she would be in control.

"Then you may be injured in the process, and you won't be able to take your treasure and servants with you. He will say you fell in love with him anyway, so you may as well make it easier for yourself."

"If I agree to this—

Menelaus interrupted her, putting his body between her and his brother. "Wait, I want you to know that I would rather kill this prince than have you do this."

"I know, but I want to learn of all the details of your brother's plan." Helen stepped around her husband and motioned for Agamemnon to continue.

"You will be inside the walls of Troy, inside their palace, so you can send us information to aid in our victory. For example, you can walk on the east wall to indicate the Trojans have strength on the west wall and vice-versa."

"Stop, she is not trained to be a spy! She doesn't know what she's getting into!" Menelaus protested.

"Let him continue," said Helen. Her voice was stern and cold. She had no desire to experience the harshness of another kidnapping. "If this was going to happen anyway, I want it to happen on my terms."

"You must never forget to stick with your story, no matter what. We will go through all the usual diplomatic channels from our side, to keep up the appearance of your abduction, but you cannot send us any messages at all. If they were to fall into the wrong hands, you would be killed as a spy, and the alliance would dissolve."

"And you truly can't see another way?" asked Helen.

"We have no other choice."

Menelaus stepped in and said, "All right, we have heard enough. It's getting late, and I want to speak with Helen in private."

"Yes, this is an important decision. You should discuss it privately. I want to remind you that I leave tomorrow."

As Helen left with her husband, she turned to Agamemnon and said, "Just for the record, Menelaus does not *owe* you. I would have chosen Menelaus with or without your pledge of 100 bulls." They closed the door behind them, leaving Agamemnon alone in the room gazing out the window and wondering what their decision would be.

That night, in their bedchambers, Helen brushed her hair while Menelaus prepared for bed. She could see the issue weighed heavily on his mind. "I know you are torn about the situation you are presented. Talk to me."

"I'm thinking about what was said tonight. Are you seriously considering following Agamemnon's plan?"

"I needed to know what was upsetting you so much. I wanted to know what his plans were. Let me ask you, what would you have me do?"

Menelaus took a deep breath and looked at his wife. To him, she was simply Helen. Yes, she was beautiful beyond all words, but she was mostly the girl he wrestled with, and the woman who now kept him in check. He didn't like any part of the situation. If he let Helen do as he knew she would—play a part in Agamemnon's plan to save the country she loved—he would have to endure her bedding another man. If he forbid her to do so, and he was unable to kill Paris before he abducted her, he would have to live with whatever violence may come of that. Finally, after a long pause where he was deep in his thoughts deliberating, he said, "My dear Helen, that decision is yours. I love you deeply, and I never want to see you with another man. I also would not forgive myself if you were abducted a second time. While it is my desire to kill Paris before he is able to make contact with you, my brother has a point. This is your country. I will let you decide."

"If I choose to go with this man, it is not because I do not love you. It is because I love Sparta, our family, and Greece."

Menelaus felt hot underneath his skin. "The thought of you with another man makes me furious!" Menelaus slammed his fist down into his other hand, hard. "Had Theseus crossed my path again, I'd have killed him. Instead, rumor has it that he spent some time in the underworld with his vermin friend after they tried to kidnap Persephone. The last I heard, he was dead after Lycomedes shoved him off a cliff and spared me the trouble."

Helen flinched at the mention of Theseus. She then shook her head to clear it of the memory, stood up and caressed his cheek with the back of her hand. "You know I am completely yours. The thought of another man touching me makes my skin crawl."

"I would rather kill him than see you in his arms." Menelaus folded his arms and sat with a huff.

Helen felt such deep compassion for her husband. She knew she would make him very angry with her decision. However, she also knew it was her fate to save Sparta and all of Greece from war with the Trojans. She kissed Menelaus lightly, then moved the straps from her gown off her shoulders, and let it drop to the floor.

Menelaus also undressed. They stood naked in front of each other. Helen had well-rounded slender hips, firm ample breasts, and skin as smooth as milk. Menelaus had a strong, muscular body with battle scars across his chest and shoulders. He took Helen in his arms, kissed her deeply, and then scooped her up in his arms and placed her on the bed. He kissed her passionately as he slowly and gently caressed her body. Helen softly pushed Menelaus onto his back. She smiled at him with tenderness in her eyes as they made love, long into the night.

That very night, Paris camped along the banks of the Eurotas River, fifteen miles from Sparta. While sitting by the fire, he asked a merchant about Sparta. The merchant replied, "Sparta is a farming community. It is not as wealthy as Troy, but it is still a powerful military state."

"Well, you can deal with the traders and the merchants; my business is in the palace. I hear their queen is quite beautiful."

"Yes, I have seen Queen Helen, and I can assure you, the stories about her don't do her justice. Her beauty is magnetic; once you see her, it is almost impossible to take your eyes off her. Her smile is magically uplifting." The merchant paused and laughed, "Sometimes people are distracted by her beauty, and they forget how to walk."

"I have seen beautiful women before" scoffed Paris.

"Not like her." replied the merchant. "Her beauty is universal, the best way I can describe it is to tell you about her wedding."

Paris sighed, he had heard a dozen, she is so beautiful stories, he didn't want to hear another.

"Stories about Helen's beauty had spread throughout the many kingdoms of Greece and the surrounding area since Helen was very young. When word spread that Helen was to take a husband many of the young princes and kings were eager to get to Sparta." The merchant sat across from Paris at the fire, smiled and continued.

"Now, my Trojan friend, I don't have to tell you how vivid a young man's imagination can be when thinking of a woman. All these men had different visions of what this woman would look like and they travelled over land, across rivers and some came by sea, some traveling great distances and taking weeks to get to Sparta, all carrying great treasure, to win this woman's hand!" The merchant gazed off into the distance for a moment, and then continued. "You want to know how beautiful Helen is?" After all that, after all that distance and hardship, the suitors arrived in Sparta and when they finally got a chance to see Helen," the merchant paused for a moment, looked straight at Paris, and said. "*Not one* of them complained!" The merchant stared into the fire, nodding. "Now that is beauty."

"We shall see. I will judge her for myself. We will be in Sparta tomorrow," said Paris.

As Agamemnon was preparing to leave the following morning, he said to Helen and Menelaus, "I was hoping to get an answer before I left. I'm sure the answer will come soon enough; Paris will be here soon."

"Sparta fears no one," said Menelaus.

"I know, but that is not the point. I want you to remember that war is coming. We can choose to fight it here, or fight it there." Agamemnon turned his horse and rode away.

"I wish he didn't love war so much," Menelaus said to Helen.

"You love war just as much as your brother."

"Perhaps, but I don't seek it."

The next morning, Paris landed his boat at the Spartan docks on the Eurotas River. He entered the town on his white horse, and his attendants cleared a path through the marketplace for him. Many of the townspeople came out to get a glimpse of the visitor. When there were whispers that he was Trojan, he was met with an eerie silence. Some of the people had heard the tale of the golden Apple of Discord and of Aphrodite's promise. They wanted to see the man who thought he was going to take their queen.

Later that day, Menelaus greeted Paris at the gate. "Welcome to Sparta, Prince Paris." Menelaus sized him up and looked him over, from head to toe. Paris was about a half head shorter than Menelaus. At about forty years old, he had a non-descript body and wasn't very muscular, with dark, curly hair and a well-trimmed beard. It took all of Menelaus's strength not to cut Paris's throat in the same manner as the Aphidnan soldier years ago. He had to remind himself of the wrath that action would incur from Priam and the Trojans.

"Thank you, Your Highness. It is a pleasure to be here."

Helen sauntered in from another room, and Menelaus tried hard to remain cordial. "I would like to introduce you to my wife, Queen Helen."

Paris turned to Helen and froze. He had never seen anyone like her. His words were caught in his throat. Finally, he pulled himself together and said, "It is a pleasure to meet you. I have heard of your beauty, and I must say that you are far more beautiful than I imagined."

Helen had to bite back her urge to grimace at the bumbling idiot before her. She was supposed to convince this man that she loved him? "Thank you for your kind words." Paris turned to his attendant and motioned for him to bring over a small container. Paris removed the lid. "As a token of our friendship, I would like to present you with this gift." He lifted a small statuette from the box and presented it to Menelaus. "I know how much the Greeks revere horses." It was a statuette of a horse in full stride. The body was made of pure gold, the hooves of onyx, the eyes were brilliant blue sapphires, and the mane and tail were made of pure silver.

"Thank you; this is absolutely beautiful," said Menelaus.

Paris replied, "Yes, it is…" as he gazed at Helen. Helen caught his glance and turned away.

Menelaus felt his blood begin to boil. He tried to push down the growing rage at this man gawking and ogling his wife. Finally, he said, "Come, Prince. You must be hungry after your journey."

"I am, but please, call me Paris."

"Paris it is," agreed Menelaus. Helen excused herself and went to her weaving.

After lunch, Paris and his entourage joined Menelaus on a wild boar hunt. Menelaus had to restrain himself and hold back from slaughtering Paris rather than the wild boar they hunted. He contemplated making Paris's death look like a hunting accident, but he knew Priam would never fall for it. The king used a spear on this hunt, but Paris was skilled as an archer. Menelaus wounded a boar with his spear, and before he could kill it, Paris finished it off with two spectacular shots from his bow. This gave Paris enormous satisfaction as they headed for dinner that evening.

A grand banquet was held in honor of the guest from Troy. There were jugglers, musicians, acrobats, and dancers in attendance as entertainment. Menelaus sat between Helen and Paris at the head table, with the golden horse prominently displayed for all to see. Paris tried many times to initiate small talk, but Menelaus wasn't interested and gave one-word answers.

Paris drank the wine, one glass after another, as though it was water. Distracted by Helen's beauty, he turned suddenly and accidentally knocked a jug of wine from a servant's hand. The wine spilled all over Paris' cloak. He slammed down his glass, and then he jumped up and shouted, "You clumsy fool, look what you have done! If we were in Troy, I would have you whipped!"

The servant stepped back and stood there, frightened. Other servants ran over and started cleaning up as quickly as possible. Menelaus dismissed the servant, looked at Paris, and said, "Prince, you are welcome in our palace, but please try to restrain yourself.

You are in Sparta, not Troy. We do not speak to our servants like that, nor do we allow our guests to speak to them in that manner."

"Please forgive me, Your Highness. I believe the wine must have gotten the best of me."

An attendant came in and whispered in Menelaus' ear. Menelaus stood up, excused himself, and left.

After dinner, everyone enjoyed mead and idle conversation in the garden. Paris approached Helen and said, "Your Highness, Sparta is a beautiful place, but it cannot compare to the beauty and richness of Troy."

"Is that so?" said Helen.

"Oh yes, the beauty of Troy is only matched by the sparkle in your eyes."

"It is getting late. If you'll excuse me," Helen said and turned to leave.

Paris reached out and grabbed her arm. "Don't be so quick to dismiss me, Your Highness."

The two guards assigned to watch Helen stepped forward quickly. Helen motioned to them that it was under control, and they stepped back. Helen looked at Paris' hand on her arm and shook it off. "You are quite sure of yourself, aren't you?"

"It is easy to be sure when the gods are on my side."

"What makes you think that?"

"Have you heard of the Apple of Discord?"

Curious to hear what he had to say, Helen replied. "No, I haven't. Why don't you explain it to me?"

Clearly feeling the effects of the wine, Paris proudly said, "Nemesis threw the Apple of Discord into a wedding the goddesses were attending with the words 'To the Fairest' inscribed on it. Hera, Athena, and Aphrodite all claimed it for themselves. Zeus said I should decide which goddess was fairest. That's right, Zeus chose me! Wanting to win my favor the goddesses tried to bribe me with gifts. Hera promised me all of Europe and Asia, Athena promised me the skill of the greatest warriors, and Aphrodite disrobed and promised me the most beautiful woman in the world. I chose Aphrodite!" He paused for a moment, waiting for a reaction from Helen, but her expression remained indifferent. "I call it the 'Judgment of Paris.' Pretty clever, right?"

"Yes, you are a clever man. Now if you will excuse me, I have to leave." Helen could feel Paris's eyes on her back as she left.

When Menelaus returned to their bedchambers, Helen asked, "Where did you go during dinner tonight?"

"We had a problem in the stables that required my attention. How did the rest of the evening go?"

"The night seemed to drag on and on."

"Well, what do you think of our special guest?"

"I find him too old, too cocky, and too ignorant. Plus, he stinks."

"He stinks?"

"Yes. He smells like a foreigner."

Menelaus said, "Good. I'll kill him when I get back."

"What do you mean? Where are you going?"

"I received a message tonight while I was in the stables. My grandfather, Catreus, was killed yesterday. I have to leave for the funeral tomorrow. I'll be gone at least four days."

"Four days? Do you have to go?"

"Yes, I have to sail to Crete to perform the funeral ceremonies."

Feeling suddenly vulnerable, Helen said, "I'll go with you. I don't want to be left alone with the Trojan."

"I can't take you with me. This may very well be a trap set up by the Trojans to lure me away. I will take a troop of soldiers with me, just in case. You have your guards; there is no reason to worry. I don't want to leave, but I have no choice. It is my duty."

Helen regained her composure. "If you have to go, you have to go, but I will miss you terribly." She kissed him lightly, and as she had the night before, dropped her robe to the floor. Menelaus picked her up and placed her on the bed. He kissed her lovingly and they spent the night in each other's arms.

Menelaus left early the next morning, but first, he instructed one of his ministers to serve as Paris' guide. The minister was to take Paris on a tour of the grounds and hunting, if that was what he desired. All day, Helen struggled with the conflicted thoughts in her head. Should she let Menelaus kill Paris and risk having war come to Sparta, or would it be best to follow Agamemnon's plan and seduce the Trojan? She had thoughts of Theseus coming back to her, which caused knots in her stomach. Her hands grew cold and clammy when she thought of being with another man. She tried to calm her mind. She walked the grounds by herself, sat on the edge of the pond, and walked through the stables and palace, just looking at everything. She watched her daughter Hermione playing the same games she enjoyed as a child. Helen wished she could go back to that time in her life, when things seemed so much simpler. She went to the Temple of Athena and sought answers from the Goddess of Wisdom. Here, she received a vision of Sparta burning and Greeks killing Greeks. In her vision, Menelaus was stripped of his armor and lay dead on the ground, her young daughter Hermione was dragged off into slavery, the palace was destroyed, and dead bodies were scattered everywhere. The vision confirmed her fears. She could not let that happen. Giving her body to another man was a small price to pay to save her family and Sparta. She made her decision, even if the idea of being with the Trojan was distasteful, she would do it to save those she loved.

After dinner, Helen sat in the garden with Paris. The other guests had gone to their rooms and Helen dismissed her guards. It was late, so Helen walked Paris back through the palace to his room. He stood in front of his door, looked at her, and said, "It was good to finally have a chance to talk to you alone."

"Yes, I appreciate the company of such a handsome man. And you're so witty; I'm sure all the women in Troy desire you."

"Yes, I have had my share of Trojan women, but I assure you none are as beautiful as you."

"Sparta can be a lonely place."

"You must come to Troy some time. It is so beautiful and opulent, truly a place fitting for a woman such as you."

Helen touched his hand and said, "Thank you. Maybe someday I will make it to Troy." With a sigh, she said, "Sometimes I think Menelaus takes me for granted."

"My dear Queen, I would never do that."

Helen looked into Paris' eyes and said, "No I don't think that you would." She smiled at him and moved in closer.

Paris could feel the warmth of her body and fumbled for his words. "Would you like to see the quarters you have provided for me?" The pair entered his chambers. Like most rooms in the Spartan palace, this one was furnished with a lone table, some chairs, and a bed. A light breeze whispered through the curtains. One small lantern in the corner lit the room.

Paris stopped at the edge of the bed and turned. Helen followed closely behind him. "I have been waiting for someone like you for a long time." She whispered and kissed him softly. Although her stomach was turning in knots, she kept up appearances. She had to. She couldn't allow Menelaus to kill him and bring destruction upon Sparta, and she was not about to become some man's plunder. No, if she had to go to Troy, she'd go willingly if only to save her daughter, husband, and nation.

Paris took her in his arms and kissed her deeply. His hands were all over her as if he were frantically searching for something. Helen tried to slow him down; she gently pushed him away, took off his robe, and let it fall to the floor. She tried to do the same with her gown, but Paris could wait no longer. He took hold of her and kissed her again. He threw her on the bed and fumbled to remove her gown. Finally, he had what he wanted. Helen stared at the ceiling as he satisfied himself. She couldn't wait to get out of there, and was thankful it was over quickly. As soon as he was finished, she made an excuse and got dressed to leave. She practically ran back to her quarters. When Helen reached her chambers, she vomited. She had an attendant draw a bath where she washed furiously to try to get his scent off her. Then, she collapsed in her bed and wept.

The next day, Helen felt dirty. She felt guilty as if she had done something wrong. She had a hard time convincing herself she was doing this for the good of her family. Paris, on the other hand, came to lunch like a conquering hero. When he had a chance to be alone with Helen, he tried to kiss her, but she pushed him away. She knew what she had to do: she had to get out of Sparta before Menelaus came back. She couldn't risk running into him as he returned, she knew what he would do and she couldn't face him after what she had done, so she lied to Paris. "Menelaus will return tomorrow. If he finds out what happened, he will kill us both."

"I don't care. I love you, and want to be with you."

"Well, I care. I don't want to die. What will we do?"

After thinking for a moment, Paris said, "We will run away to Troy. We can be safe there."

"When can we go? Menelaus will be here soon."

"We can leave immediately, my love."

"No, I need some time. We can leave tonight, after dark."

Paris agreed. Helen spent the day gathering the things she would need for her long journey. She called for her attendants, Aethra and Harleopi. "Aethra, I am going on a trip. I want you to pack your things and mine. You will be going with me." She dismissed Aethra, but because Harleopi was still young, Helen didn't want to make the decision for her. "Harleopi, I don't know how long I will be gone, but I am giving you a choice. You may stay here, or you can come with me."

"Your Majesty, you know I will follow you, no matter where you go or how long you are gone."

Helen gave Harleopi a hug. "You have been more than an attendant to me; you are my friend as well. Go and pack your things, and then help Aethra pack mine."

Helen went to find her daughter, Hermione. She struggled to say goodbye to her child. Helen could not hold back her tears as she said, "Come here, my darling." She held Hermione tightly in her arms. "Mommy is going away on a trip."

"Can I come too?"

"Not this time, darling. I promise I will be home as soon as I can." Helen's heart was breaking; she knew she might never see her daughter again.

"Why are you crying, mommy?"

"It's because I love you so much." It took all of Helen's strength to let go of her daughter. She wiped the tears from her eyes as she watched an attendant take Hermione away.

As night fell, Paris met Helen at the back of the palace. They went into the treasury and removed two large chests filled with gold and jewels, and put them on a wagon with the rest of Helen's belongings. Paris' boats waited for them at the docks of the Eurotas River. Helen and her attendants pulled a hood over her heads so they wouldn't be recognized as they rode through Sparta, She knew she needed to vanish into the night so everyone would believe she had been kidnapped. Finally, they boarded the boat and headed down river. They would be in the Aegean Sea by morning.

Two days later, Menelaus returned to Sparta. As he neared the town, he had an eerie feeling something was wrong. He entered the palace and was approached by one of his attendants. "She is gone, sir."

"What? Who is gone?"

"Your wife, the Trojan took her in the middle of the night."

Menelaus ran back to the stables, and then to the weaving room. He didn't know why he was looking; he knew she was gone. The palace seemed empty without her. He walked back to his chambers where he found the note Helen left for him on his bed.

Dear Menelaus,

After much anguish and soul searching, I have made my decision. I feel that giving my body to a man for the safety of my family, Sparta, and Greece is a small sacrifice to endure. You will see me every day on the walls of Troy, so you know that although this man may have me in his bed, he will never have my heart. That place belongs only to you. I do not know what the outcome of my actions will be, but I want you to know that I will love you forever.

I know nothing of codes and secret messages, so I will use Agamemnon's suggestions. If you see me on the West Wall, you will know the Trojans are stronger on the East Wall, and vice versa. If you see me on the walls wearing a red dress, the Trojans are planning to attack.

Eternally yours, Helen

Menelaus crumpled the letter in his hands and grit his teeth as anger boiled inside him. Because he felt her hand had been forced, he wasn't angry with Helen. He was angry with himself for letting this happen. He stormed into the banquet room where he found the horse figurine given to him by Paris. Menelaus picked it up, and with a mighty scream, threw it against the stone wall. He looked at the broken statue for a long moment and said, "I should have known."

Menelaus gathered all his advisors in the great hall. "My wife, your Queen, has been kidnapped by the Trojan called Paris. This is a slap to the face of Spartans and Greeks alike. I assure you he will pay the price for this. I am leaving immediately for Mycenae to form a plan. Our honor will be restored, even if it means war!" He left for Mycenae to discuss the next step in Agamemnon's plan.

CALL TO WAR

As Menelaus made his way to Mycenae, word of Helen's abduction traveled ahead of him. The furious people gathered in the streets and shouted for war. They wanted blood. Helen was an icon, a symbol of their polis; her abduction was a slap in the face. Their honor had been besmirched. Many of her former suitors knew what their obligations were; they just waited for instructions. Even towns that didn't send a suitor clamored for war.

Menelaus found Agamemnon and Clytemnestra waiting when he arrived in Mycenae. "Menelaus, welcome I am surprised to see you so soon after my visit." Menelaus found himself chuckling at the irony of his brother's statement. He knew Agamemnon was expecting to see him.

"Brother, you were right. That Trojan scoundrel abducted Helen!"

"What? Who abducted Helen?" Clytemnestra shouted.

"A Trojan prince named Paris," said Menelaus.

"Oh no, not again! How could you let this happen? Didn't you have guards around her?"

"Yes, but apparently she felt safe enough to dismiss them. You know how she feels about being constantly surrounded by guards."

"Does this mean what I think it means?" His sister in law paused before uttering the word at almost a whisper. "War?"

Agamemnon looked first at Menelaus and then at Clytemnestra before speaking. "Perhaps, we shall see." He then turned toward Menelaus and said, "We were just about to sit down to a meal when you arrived. Let's eat, and we can talk more."

Later that afternoon, Agamemnon and Menelaus retired to Agamemnon's private chambers to discuss how they would proceed with his plan. The palace in Mycenae was not like Menelaus' home in Sparta. Agamemnon preferred luxury. The palace was filled with plush seats, ornate tables and chairs, and woven tapestries hanging from the walls. The servants poured each of them a drink, then Agamemnon dismissed them. Finally he spoke. "So, she seduced him, did she?"

Menelaus felt himself getting hot. Finally he said, "I'll kill him, and I haven't made up my mind about her!"

"Relax, brother. She did it out of love for you and Sparta, not for him."

"That may be so, but it doesn't mean I don't want that fool's head on the end of my sword."

"My plan will work. Have patience. Did you invoke the Oath of Tyndareus?"

"No. I called my ministers together and told them what happened, and then I came here."

"Good. First, we will try to get her back through diplomatic channels; it will strengthen the abduction story. If we just go to war, it may look like a set-up on our part. I would like you to go back to Sparta and write a letter for your minister to deliver to every one of Helen's former suitors. Then, meet Palamedes in Ithaca to recruit Odysseus. He is our best orator, and we'll need him during our negotiations. I want you and Odysseus to go to Myrmidon to persuade Achilles to join us. You and Odysseus will then go to Troy and try to negotiate Helen's release. We both know that Priam will not release her, so your message should ask every suitor to send men, ships, and supplies to Aulis. That is where we will assemble our fleet"

"How soon can we get started?"

"We can start tomorrow. Get some rest and recover from your long journey, then leave in the morning."

"Rest? I keep envisioning her with him!"

I understand, but do not wear yourself out. We are going to war. You'll need your strength." Menelaus conceded to his older brother and agreed that he would leave in the morning.

When Menelaus returned to Sparta, he found that volunteers, young and old, had already arrived in Sparta. They were asking how they could help him to recover Helen. Menelaus went into town where a large crowd formed. He stood on a cart to address his people. "We are doing everything possible to restore our Queen and our honor. All who want to join the crusade to Troy should report to Agamemnon at Aulis."

Menelaus went back to the palace and assembled the Gerousia once again. "I am going to Troy in an attempt to bring Helen home peacefully. However, it appears Paris was sent to us to begin a war, and peaceful negotiations do not seem possible. Therefore, in anticipation of this, I am sending you, my ministers, to locate my wife's former suitors and deliver the following letter:

> *"Paris, Prince of Troy, has abducted my wife, the Queen of Sparta. I now call on you to honor your solemn pledge to defend my marriage against anyone who would do it harm. I will first attempt to resolve this matter through diplomatic means, However, in the event that my negotiations fail, I ask you to send men, ships, and supplies to Aulis, where we are assembling a fleet under Agamemnon, the King of Mycenae. Sail with us to Troy, and help us to restore our honor!*
>
> *"Menelaus, King of Sparta"*

Menelaus then dismissed his ministers and their envoys to deliver his letter to all the suitors. He ordered his generals to report to Agamemnon with troops and supplies, and then wait for his return from Troy. Finished with his business at home, Menelaus left Sparta to find Palamedes in Ithaca.

Many Greek people were incensed over Helen's abduction and were eager for war. There were a few, however, who wanted nothing to do with the war. Palamedes and Menelaus arrived in Ithaca, but Odysseus already knew why they were coming. To avoid going to war, Odysseus feigned insanity by plowing the beach and planting salt. He harnessed an oxen and a mule to the plow, since the animals have different strides, the furrows were crooked. Palamedes saw through his ruse and said, "I have a plan."

He took Odysseus' infant son and placed the baby in front of the plow. Odysseus swerved to avoid his son, thus proving his sanity. Odysseus stopped the plow and ran at Palamedes. "How dare you place my son's life in jeopardy?"

Menelaus jumped between the two men. "Calm down, have you lost your nerve, Odysseus, or are you just refusing to honor your pledge?"

Odysseus felt the anger running through his veins. "Just because a man wishes to live in peace with his family doesn't mean he has lost his nerve. I will honor my pledge." Odysseus turned to Palamedes and said, "I will never forgive you for risking my son's life."

Odysseus and Menelaus arrived in Achilles' hometown of Phthia, and they were met by Achilles' mother. "Achilles is not here. There is only this group of maidens." The men looked at the group of maidens, and Menelaus nudged his traveling companion to point out one maiden larger than the rest.

"Watch this," Odysseus said. He snuck off. A few minutes later, the town's alarm sounded, signaling an attack. The large maiden jumped into action, and grabbed weapons, ready to defend the town, revealing that Achilles had made a very poor disguise for himself.

Menelaus approached the young warrior and said, "My wife has been abducted by a Trojan. I am assembling an army to storm Troy and restore the honor of all of the Greek states. Will you join us?"

Achilles' mother, Thetis, ran to her son. "You don't have to go! The prophecy said that if you stay here, you will live a long life. If you go to Troy, people will remember you forever, but you will die young. Please don't go to war."

Achilles moved his mother aside and took off the dress. "Mother, I wore this at your request, and I know the prophecy. What good is a long life if I feel like a coward for not joining my countrymen in a time of war? If it is the will of the gods that I should die young, then so be it." He turned to Menelaus and said, "I will join you."

Menelaus felt a sense of satisfaction. He looked at Odysseus who said, "The fleet is forming at Aulis under Agamemnon's command. Meet us there." Odysseus and Menelaus then let Phthia and set sail for Troy.

Helen leaned back and watched as Paris docked the ships on the island of Cannae. He repeatedly professed his love for her. He kept telling her how much he looked forward to being alone with her again. Paris had told her that they were stopping for supplies, but she had overheard him sending a ship ahead to rally a welcoming committee to greet them in Troy. She was happy to be back on dry land, but she was not looking forward to being alone with Paris. He was so cocky and headstrong that he was more exhausting than her daughter had been as a toddler.

During the voyage, Helen noticed her attendants had detected something going on between herself and Paris. She felt an obligation to them to explain what was happening. When she was finally able to reach her chambers on the island, she summoned Aethra and Harleopi to her room.

She knew she couldn't tell them the truth yet, because she wasn't sure what awaited their arrival in Troy. When they arrived, Helen sat down upon her bed and addressed them. "I know you are wondering why we are here. I must tell you, I have fallen in love with this man from Troy. The moment I saw him, I knew in my heart that he was the man I was meant to be with. Fortunately, Menelaus was called away, and I had the opportunity to leave with him when I did. I know this comes as a shock to you, but I cannot fight my heart."

The two women stared and blinked at Helen and were silent for a few moments, before Harleopi finally spoke for both attendants. "My Queen, whatever decisions you make, either of the heart or otherwise, they are your decisions. I will stand by and serve you no matter what." Aethra nodded her head in agreement.

"Thank you. It's comforting to know I can rely on you." Helen then dismissed the two attendants.

When Aethra and Harleopi were alone, Harleopi whispered to her companion, "I don't believe her, do you?" Harleopi had seen the love between her mistress and master develop, and she didn't believe anything could come between the two of them. There had been enough hushed whispers and loud shouting matches between Menelaus and his war-loving brother for Harleopi to accept the story at face value.

Aethra finally responded. "No. But she has never lied to us before. Why do you suppose she would do it now?"

"I don't know, but whatever she is doing, I believe she needs us more now than ever before."

"I agree; something is wrong. I hope we can find out what it is soon." Aethra motioned for the young attendant to go to sleep. "We just need to be there for her, in whatever capacity she requires of us."

"Yes, yes." Harleopi muttered, drifting off. "We will be."

As their ships approached the shore, Helen saw the legendary walls of Troy looming on the hills further inland. She caught her breath. It was a beautiful city, surrounded by walls that glistened in the sunlight. On a hill behind the wall sat the citadel and palace, shimmering white in the afternoon sun. Words hadn't done Troy justice, she thought. Nor had they described how impenetrable the walls appeared, even from afar.

When the ship reached the port, Helen could see people scampering all about. The city was bustling. A royal entourage met the ships as they docked. Helen looked at Paris, "Why are we being greeted this way?"

"This is our wedding day," Paris said, smiling.

"What? You can't be serious."

Paris explained that he didn't want to take a chance that she would change her mind or fall for one of his brothers. "Besides, when we left Sparta together, it was obvious that you wanted to be with me. I decided to have our wedding as soon as possible."

Helen thought, "I never considered that I would have to marry this man so quickly. I have to delay this as long as I can."

She then turned to Paris and said, "Before we can be married, I want to know your parents. I want to find out if the Trojan people will accept me." Frustrated, she cried, "I have to put on a better dress!"

"My parents will love you; I don't care what the people think; and the dress you decided to wear today to meet my parents is good enough." Helen looked at him, mouth agape. This was all moving far too fast for her. She needed to slow things down so she could get her bearings.

Helen had hoped she would be able to slip into Troy unnoticed, but it became obvious that was not going to be the case. All the attention took her by surprise. She guessed that the people of Troy had heard about her captivating beauty, and everyone stopped to glance at her. She learned that there was going to be a parade in addition to, apparently, a wedding.

A small contingent of soldiers led the way to the palace, followed by musicians, acrobats, jugglers, and dancers. A chariot pulled Helen and Paris along, and her attendants and more musicians and attendants trailed behind. The parade wound through the small landing area near the beach, through the Scaean Gate, and into the city of Troy itself. People from the surrounding communities and different countries filled the marketplace. The houses and shops were brightly decorated, and people hung out of windows and off rooftops cheering as the parade passed by. The held signs that read, "Welcome Helen" and "Troy loves Helen." Helen looked at Paris, who was visibly ecstatic from the attention they received. Helen, on the other hand, felt like a prisoner being taken to the gallows. All the banners reminded her of when Theseus came to Sparta all those years prior. She looked at the people and felt sorry for them because they did not realize for what they were cheering—war, and the death and destruction that accompanied it.

As they approached the stairs to the palace, Helen's palms became incredibly sweaty, and her breathing was short and shallow. Helen saw King Priam, his wife Queen Hecuba, and a group of Paris' brothers and sisters waiting at the top of the stairs. After they climbed the steps, Priam said, "Paris, you have returned and brought with you a most beautiful woman."

"Father, this is Helen of Sparta."

Priam gave Helen a hug. "I have heard of your magnificent beauty, but the stories don't do you justice."

"Thank you, Your Highness." Helen could feel the eyes of Paris' brothers and sisters looking her up and down.

"I would like to introduce you to my mother, Queen Hecuba," said Paris.

"It is a pleasure to meet you Your Highness."

"Welcome to Troy," Queen Hecuba replied coolly.

Priam said, "Helen, I understand you have agreed to be Paris' wife."

Helen felt as though she had no way out, so she smiled and held Paris' hand, "Yes, Your Highness."

Priam married them on the spot. Paris turned to embrace Helen, who felt herself stiffen and almost pull away. She had to remind herself it was all an act. But when he kissed her, she couldn't help that her kiss was short, cold, and unfeeling. Paris didn't seem to notice. He took her hand, turned to the crowd gathered below, and raised their hands over their heads as the crowd cheered wildly. Aethra and Harleopi stood to the side and shook their heads slightly. The newlyweds boarded a chariot at the bottom of the stairs, and took a triumphant ride through the crowd and around Troy.

The royal family hosted a large banquet that night in celebration of Paris' marriage. Paris was the center of attention, and many of the men patted him on the back as they glanced over at Helen. Helen also drew attention from every partygoer. All of Paris' brothers and sisters came over to introduce themselves. When the evening finally ended, and the newlyweds had retired, Priam and Hecuba withdrew to their bedchambers. When they were alone, Hecuba said, "He came back. You didn't think he would, but he did and he brought her with him."

Priam was clearly agitated. "Yes, I can see that."

"What are we going to do? You know what the prophecy said."

"When I gave birth to Paris, I dreamed I was giving birth to a flaming torch. The prophets at the time said this was a sign that Paris would bring about the destruction of Troy."

"Well the prophecy was wrong! I don't want to hear any more about it."

"I don't like it, I'm worried. You said he wouldn't come back," insisted Hecuba.

Priam remained silent. He had not planned on Paris returning from Sparta with Helen. He was certain that Paris would be killed trying to abduct Helen. The prophecy would be broken, and he would have a reason to go to war against the Greeks and get his revenge. Now he would have to settle for a different kind of revenge, but the prophecy still hung over his head like smoke after a fire. Priam was uneasy but he tried to comfort his wife. "There is nothing to worry about. The walls of Troy are indestructible. Try to get some sleep."

Helen spent her first week in Troy being introduced to the ministers and merchants and taking a tour of the city. Everyone wanted a chance to meet her. She was awestruck by the palace's beauty. Troy was obviously a wealthy city. The floors, walls, and ceilings were made of marble, and the columns had bands of gold inlaid around the tops and bottoms. A small reflecting pool adorned the middle of the great hall. Troy had many courtyards and temples filled with statues of the gods. The main temple paid homage to Athena, and housed the Palladium.

Helen climbed to the top of the four-story walls to marvel at the view. She saw the Aegean Sea beyond the plain, and on the other side, she could see Mount Ida and the Scamander River winding its way to the sea. It was all very beautiful, but Helen was homesick. Every time she saw a child playing, she thought of her daughter, Hermione, and wondered about her. She missed Sparta's mountains and valleys, farms and ranches. It was poorer than Troy, but it was home. Of course, Helen missed Menelaus most of all. She knew that he was in pain, and she regretted hurting him. She wished that she could see him to make him feel better. It seemed like a lifetime since she was home.

A few weeks later, Menelaus stood on the bow of his ship and looked out over the plains of Troy. He saw the citadel gleaming white on the hill behind Troy's infamous walls, and Mount Ida in the distance. Odysseus approached and said what Menelaus had been thinking, "My friend, I hope we are successful in our plea for her return. I don't want to have to breach those walls."

The ship ran onto the shore, and Menelaus and Odysseus made their way to the Scaean Gates. Armed guards met them at the gates and asked what they wanted. "I am Menelaus, King of Sparta, and this is Odysseus, King of Ithaca. We have come for an audience with King Priam."

"Wait here. We will speak with the King."

It didn't take long for rumor to spread that Helen's first husband had arrived to get her back. A small crowd formed around Menelaus and Odysseus. They felt uneasy as the crowd grew and closed in on them. The guards finally returned, and escorted Menelaus and Odysseus through the crowd to the home of Antenor, one of the King's advisors. A buzz went through the city as word spread that two Greeks were in Troy. As they walked the streets of Troy, people came out of their homes and stared at them. Some whispered and pointed, and others just looked on in silence. Menelaus kept his eyes trained on the citadel, hoping to catch a glimpse of Helen. He wondered where she might be. Finally, they reached Antenor's home and were escorted inside. Antenor himself greeted the two visitors and gave them something to eat. "You may wait here while we assemble our council. We will send for you when we are ready."

Helen heard that Menelaus had arrived in Troy. She was excited to see him, but couldn't let anyone see her enthusiasm. She went from one window to the next, but couldn't see him. Paris tracked her down and said, "Menelaus is here."

She regained her composure and flatly replied, "I have heard. I thought he might follow us."

"Don't worry. I won't let him harm you." Paris left to join the council.

Helen missed Menelaus so much; she had to try to find a way to see him. He always made her feel safe, and without him, she felt isolated and vulnerable. Helen tried to join the council meeting, but armed guards prevented her from entering. "We have orders to keep you from this area. Please, Your Highness, don't make this difficult." They led Helen back to her quarters. She was disappointed that she couldn't see Menelaus, but since he hadn't left yet, there was still hope.

Two hours went by before the guards returned to escort Menelaus and Odysseus to the great hall. When they entered the hall, they stood in front of a huge table where King Priam, his five counselors, Paris' older brother Hector, and his younger brothers Helenus and Deiphobus sat. Menelaus learned that Paris was barred from this meeting for security reasons, but was waiting in a back room so he could hear what was being said.

Finally, Priam addressed the two Greeks. "We know why you are here. You may approach and present your case."

Menelaus approached the table as he and Odysseus had discussed while waiting. He felt rage growing inside of him, but he knew he couldn't let the Trojans see it. He was a man of pride, but unlike his companion, he was not known as a great orator. He felt uncomfortable standing before the council and pleading for his wife.

Menelaus breathed deeply and then said, "King Priam, members of this Great Council, I am here today as a husband and father. I come with a heavy heart, seeking justice. I welcomed Prince Paris into my home. I entertained him, fed him, and treated him as an honored guest. When I was called away to perform family duties, he brazenly kidnapped my beloved wife and a large portion of the Spartan treasury. I do not care about the treasure. I come here today to ask only that you return my wife to me, so that my family can be whole once again, my daughter can have her mother, and we can put this matter behind us. Sparta and Troy can be friends in peace and trade." Menelaus stood silently for a long moment looking at the council members then resumed his position next to Odysseus.

King Priam sat with a smirk on his face. He clearly enjoyed watching the Spartan plead for the release of a woman. Odysseus approached the table of important men. His eyes were downcast as he spoke. His voice was soft at first and grew in intensity as he looked up at the council. "Most honorable King Priam and distinguished council, I stand here before you today as a man seeking justice for a friend. My friend accepted Prince Paris into his home. He practiced the laws of hospitality, the same laws that govern all of our societies. The reward for this hospitality was robbery and abduction. Prince Paris robbed his treasury and abducted his wife during his absence. I ask the husbands and fathers on this council to look into your hearts. How would you feel if your wife was taken and your children left motherless? I ask you to feel the pain this man is enduring. His kingdom was robbed and his family torn in half by a man who came disguised as a friend. I humbly ask you to restore this man's family, fortune, and honor. Thank you."

After Odysseus finished, a silence cast over the room like a fog. When King Priam finally spoke, his voice was heavy and hard. "I have listened to you, which is as much as your people did when they received my envoys seeking the return of my sister, Hesione. The Greeks listened, and then they murdered the envoys where they stood! Where was the justice then?" Priam stood up and pointed his finger at Menelaus. "Where is the justice for my sister, who has been stuck in Greece for over twenty years? You have a lot of nerve coming here seeking justice. Your own people don't know the meaning of the word!" Priam stood in silence for a long moment as he tried to calm down. "We are not barbarians. We will discuss your proposal." As he walked away, he said to Menelaus, "Do you know that Helen willingly married Paris right here in this citadel?" The council then adjourned to the back room. Priam's words had their intended effect: they cut through Menelaus' heart like a knife. Menelaus was stunned and glanced over at Odysseus to try to gauge his companion as they stood together. Odysseus motioned for Menelaus to remain silent and wait.

In the back room, Priam said, "Well, what do you think?"

Antenor spoke up first, "I think we should return Helen and her treasure to this man. He obviously loves her very much to travel all the way here to seek her return."

Paris disagreed with the men. "I didn't abduct Helen; she fell in love with me. If she weren't in love with me, why did she come here? Why did she marry me? I will not give her up! I'll give back her treasure, but I'm not giving her up."

Priam glared at his son. The man was foolhardy, but this by far was the most foolish and selfish he'd seen Paris. The conversation continued. Deiphobus said, "I agree with Paris. Return the treasure, but keep the woman."

Hector stepped forward. He was a big man, the same height as Menelaus but more bulky. Hector was Troy's best warrior and their ablest general. He was also Priam's eldest and wisest son. He said, "Father, my advice is to send Helen back to Troy with Menelaus. You will have a war on your hands if you do not send this woman home."

Priam laughed. "A war with whom, Sparta? Maybe Mycenae as well? They are not strong enough to cause us trouble. Let them come!"

"Haven't you heard of the Oath of Tyndareus?" asked Hector. "Nearly fifty kings and princes swore an oath to defend Helen's marriage against harm. I believe that Menelaus will call on those men to fulfill their oath and go to war."

Priam chuckled again. No one would stop the Trojans. Finally, he pulled himself together and said, "That pledge was just a ploy by indecisive Tyndareus to get himself out of a tough situation. Nobody will go to war over such a ridiculous pledge."

"I know many Greeks, and they are an honorable people. They may take their pledge seriously. If you do not return Helen to Sparta, I am fearful for Troy."

Priam thought for a moment. He still didn't feel that there was much to worry about out of Sparta and Mycenae, but he also knew that Greeks were men of their words. "If there is no husband, there is no honor to restore. If we kill Menelaus now, there will be no need to restore his honor, and thus no need for war."

Hector looked at Antenor and nodded. Antenor excused himself from the conference. As he left, Hector turned back to Priam. "We cannot kill Menelaus. I will not be a part of that—morally, and on the grounds that it would surely start a war."

Priam felt himself getting impatient with the whole conversation. "Let them feel the pain I felt! They won't start a war over a woman, especially an adulteress!"

Menelaus could hear the voices getting louder. It was clear that an argument was going on. He and Odysseus remained where they had been, and had remained quiet. They couldn't make out any of the words. They had hoped to, but it was becoming clearer that Priam wouldn't just let Helen go. One of the men from the conference ran out to them. Menelaus remembered him as having introduced himself as Antenor.

Menelaus put his hand on his sword. He wasn't sure what the haste was for, but he was certain that danger loomed. The man leaned in, and whispered loudly, "Hurry, you must leave right now.

You are in great danger. Priam is set on revenge. You must leave now, or you will never see your homes again."

Menelaus looked at Odysseus, who nodded, and they followed Antenor out of the palace and to the stables. Antenor then threw a blanket over their heads, and led them on horseback to the gate. When they got there, Menelaus thanked Antenor. "I will remember this."

Antenor nodded, and Odysseus and Menelaus squeezed his legs against the horse to start it into a cantor with Odysseus right behind him, riding through the gate and along the plains. Behind them, the guards shouted, "There they are!" Arrows whizzed past and struck the ground around them, but they made it to their ship and set sail before the charioteers were able to catch up with them.

Helen heard the commotion, looked out her window, and then ran to the top of the wall. She saw Menelaus riding away from the city with the archers shooting at him. She couldn't show it, but she silently cheered for him, and she was overjoyed when he escaped. She felt mixed emotions at that moment. She missed him, and she was happy that he had escaped unharmed, but she had hoped that the negotiations would work and she could go home. She now knew that Agamemnon was right; Priam wanted war. With war on the horizon, she didn't know whether she would ever see her home or daughter again. Helen bowed her head as a tear ran down her cheek. She suddenly felt very tired, and her body seemed as though it would be too heavy for her legs to carry. Hermoine. What had she done?

It was a long voyage back to Aulis for Menelaus. His thoughts of Helen never left his mind. He envisioned her smiling, talking, and laughing the way she used to with him. He still felt her touch and imagined the smell of her hair. He remembered the way she made him feel and how they made love together. When he pictured doing all of those things with Paris, his heart hurt. He began to have doubts about what she was doing in Troy. "She *married* him?" He muttered aloud to no one in particular. "Maybe she's starting to love Paris."

After a sleepless voyage Menelaus was happy to approach Aulis. He was taken aback by the size of the fleet waiting. He and Odysseus docked their own ship, and looked around. The port was filled with activity. Hundreds of ships were docked in the port, and even more were being built. The two made their way to Agamemnon's headquarters. Someone shouted, "Menelaus is here!" A cheer started softly but grew as more men joined in and started chanting his name. Men slapped him on the back and encouraged him. Menelaus felt himself slightly embarrassed by the welcome, and he was glad when he and Odysseus made it to the refuge of Agamemnon's hut. He didn't like that his private life had become so public.

Agamemnon warmly welcomed Menelaus and Odysseus. "Brother, welcome to Aulis. Odysseus, my good friend, welcome. How did the diplomacy fare? I don't see Helen, so I assume that Priam wasn't too receptive to your overtures."

Menelaus said, "We had a chance to make our plea. I am not good at such things, but we both made an emotional appeal that unfortunately fell on deaf ears."

"That is putting it mildly. If Antenor had not helped us escape, we would not be here today," said Odysseus.

"So, he tried to kill you? It is as I thought. Priam seeks revenge, and he won't stop until he gets it"

"I need to return to Ithaca and prepare my contingent to join your fleet."

"We will be here a while yet. We have many ships to build to accommodate all the men who have volunteered. More men are still on their way!" said Agamemnon.

Menelaus sighed. "I'm glad."

Odysseus said, "I must go and rally my own army. I will be back as soon as I can."

Agamemnon said, "We are honored that you will join us, Odysseus."

Menelaus waited until Odysseus had left, then shouted, "She married him!" He felt his voice shake as the words came out.

"I can hear the pain in your voice, brother. Try to remember that she is alone in the enemy's camp. She is a smart woman. She will do what she must to stay alive. You should be proud of her; she is a very brave woman who loves her country and family very much."

"I am proud of her and I miss her. Every time I think of her there with that…that *dog*, I want to cut his heart out!" Menelaus drew his sword to emphasize his point.

"You must busy yourself with other things to take your mind off her."

"Things have happened so quickly."

"Come, I will show you the preparations we have made. This will help you to take your mind off Helen." Agamemnon led Menelaus around the camp to watch the progress. Ships practiced running up on the beaches and men disembarked the ships as quickly as possible. Soldiers rehearsed different fighting formations and combat motions. There was a buzz of activity as far as the eye could see. They saw ship builders, carpenters, and men making sails. Men practiced hand to hand combat. Fires cooked foods from exotic lands, and the smell of spices and meats filled the air. The sound of men yelling orders and the clang of swords assaulted Menelaus' ears. He was impressed.

Agamemnon excused himself. "I must get back to my headquarters and prepare for more men arriving soon."

Menelaus continued watching the progress, but he couldn't focus. He decided to leave the camp to gather his thoughts. As he walked toward the hills and away from the beaches, he couldn't get the idea of Helen and Paris out of his mind. He saw her face in the trees and the clouds, and he heard her voice in the wind. Menelaus walked until he found a quiet place where he could be alone with his thoughts. "Why didn't I see her when I was in Troy? Did she know I was there? Did she even care? Has she fallen for Paris? Does she miss her home and family? Does she miss me? Will I ever hold her again?" Menelaus looked up at the heavens. "Why did I let this happen?" Menelaus sat down and looked out over the Aegean Sea and the hundreds of ships in the port. In hopeless desperation, he hung his head and wept.

Menelaus spent the night on the hillside. When he returned to the camp the following day, he found Agamemnon busy giving orders and organizing drills, "I thought maybe you went to Troy without us!"

Menelaus replied, "I needed to get my head together. I'm ready now."

"Good. Follow me. I want to show you something. Do you remember Cinyras, the King of Paphos, from Cyprus? Well, he promised fifty ships to the war effort. That ship over there is commanded by his son, and over here are the other forty-nine ships with their soldiers."

Agamemnon pointed at small toy ships made of clay, complete with little clay soldiers, that disintegrated when placed in the water. The brothers shared a good laugh; it was a welcome relief for Menelaus. "Those soldiers dissolved like his manners at the party. At least he sent one ship."

Menelaus was indeed ready to take his place among the leaders of the army. He threw himself into training and planning. Before the fleet set sail for Troy, the leaders of the army held a meeting in Agamemnon's hut to discuss the invasion. The most important men in Greece attended the meeting, including Agamemnon, Odysseus, Menelaus, Ajax, and Achilles. Achilles was about a half head shorter than Ajax. Although Achilles was too young to have been one of Helen's suitors, everyone in Greece knew he had to be involved in the war effort. Achilles was considered to be the greatest warrior in all of Greece. He was a master of all weapons, but was strongest with the spear, and deadly with the sword, the sling, and in hand-to-hand combat. He was lighting fast and very powerful, his muscles were lean and hard. He gave no quarter and expected none. Achilles had developed a large following. The army parted ways when he walked by, and everyone wanted to spar with him. Menelaus chuckled to himself, even he wouldn't mind getting some hand to hand combat practice in with the young fellow.

Menelaus stood with the rest of the leaders. They needed a landing strategy. The Greeks didn't know what awaited them on the beaches of Troy. They decided to split the fleet into three different wings: Ajax commanded the left wing, Achilles commanded the right wing, and Agamemnon, Menelaus, and Odysseus sailed with the rest of the fleet in the middle.

After the meeting, Menelaus, Agamemnon and a group of men went deer hunting in the nearby hills to provide food for the growing army. Midway through the hunt, Agamemnon alerted Menelaus to the fact that he'd spotted a huge stag off in the distance. After a stealthy approach, Agamemnon was within twenty yards of the deer when he released an arrow. The arrow hit its mark; the deer jumped and ran a few yards before dropping dead. Agamemnon was ecstatic; he kept boasting to Menelaus that he couldn't wait to get the animal back to camp to show the others. When the brothers returned with Agamemnon's prize, men gathered around to get a look. It was a beautiful buck with large, well-formed antlers, and Agamemnon said, "I'm a better archer than Artemis, Goddess of the Hunt!"

Menelaus felt his jaw drop and looked around at the other men. Everyone was stunned; no one should compare himself with a god. That was the best way to bring on a god or goddess's wrath and misfortune to their endeavors. Menelaus warned his brother, but Agamemnon didn't pay it any mind.

The fleet had swollen to over 1,200 ships, and each ship carried close to 100 men. Everything was in place, and the fleet was ready to sail, but there was no wind. Menelaus went with his brother when Agamemnon consulted the seer Calchas, who told him that Artemis kept the wind from blowing because of his boast. "What can I do to appease her?"

"The only way to appease Artemis is to sacrifice your daughter, Iphigenia," said Calchas.

Following the meeting, Menelaus turned to his brother. "Are you really going to sacrifice my niece?"

"No. Calchas is full of hot air." Agamemnon said. "Who is he to say who needs to be sacrificed?"

However, after a few more days of waiting for wind to no avail, and much deliberation and struggle, Agamemnon sent a messenger to Mycenae, and asked Clytemnestra to send Iphigenia to Aulis immediately. Menelaus knew his sister in law well enough to know that she would be skeptical of Agamemnon's motives, and he was right. At first, she refused to send her daughter. Agamemnon then sent word that Iphigenia was to be married to Achilles before he went off to war.

Menelaus knew that some thought Agamemnon didn't care for Iphigenia as much as he would have, had she been his own. Many people believed that Iphigenia was actually Agamemnon's stepdaughter, that she was truly the daughter of Clytemnestra's first husband, Tantalus, whom Agamemnon slew to reclaim the throne of Mycenae. He knew that his brother's move would only add to those rumors.

Finally, Menelaus and Agamemnon received word that Iphigenia and Clytemnestra had arrived in Aulis. When they showed up at headquarters, Menelaus was surprised at how much his niece had grown. Iphigenia was a beautiful young woman: tall, slender, full of life, and she walked with confidence and poise. Clytemnestra finally spoke, "Dear husband, we are here as you requested."

Agamemnon gave each of them a kiss on the cheek. "Yes, my dears, I am glad you could come."

Clytemnestra turned to Achilles, who had been visiting with Agamemnon and Menelaus, and said, "I see the groom is here. You must be anxious."

"I'm sorry, Your Highness, but what are you talking about?" Achilles said.

"Agamemnon sent a message saying you wished to marry Iphigenia."

Achilles shouted at Agamemnon, "How dare you use me in this way?"

Clytemnestra was confused. "I don't understand."

"Although she is beautiful, I don't wish to marry Iphigenia. You have been misled, Agamemnon intends to sacrifice her to Artemis to appease the goddess after he had insulted her."

Clytemnestra snarled at Agamemnon and grabbed her daughter tight, "You snake, you liar! I will not allow it!"

Menelaus stepped back from the ensuing argument and watched as Agamemnon tried to defuse the anger in the room. "Listen to me, my love. It was not my idea. I don't want to sacrifice her, but as you can see, we have a huge army ready to set sail for Troy. Artemis stopped the wind from blowing, and demands Iphigenia's sacrifice before she will allow it to blow again. Let's ask her if she is willing."

"Ask her if she is willing? Are you kidding me?"

"If she's willing, then we have her permission to sacrifice her."

"This is my daughter you are speaking of. Not some pawn in your game!"

Achilles interjected, "Iphigenia, before you reply to your father's question, I want you to know I will defend you against the whole army if I must."

"Iphigenia," Agamemnon said, "What say you? We need to defend our lands."

All eyes were on Iphigenia. "Like anyone, I would like to live. However, if it will help the war effort, I…"

Clytemnestra interrupted her daughter, "No, you won't!" Clytemnestra turned to Agamemnon and said, "Please, tell me there is another way."

"I wish there was, but this is what the gods have ordained. Dear child, if you do this, you will live forever."

Iphigenia replied, "I am proud to be Greek. I will show Greek people that our women are as strong as our men, and are willing to do what it takes to restore our honor. I will do it, father."

As Clytemnestra hung her head and sobbed, Achilles hugged Iphigenia. "You are as brave as any warrior."

Anxious to begin his journey, Agamemnon had built a funeral pyre while waiting for the women's arrival. It had a wooden altar at the top. That night, in front of a hundred thousand warriors, respectfully dressed in full armor, Agamemnon led Iphigenia, dressed in her white wedding dress and a golden tiara, to the steps of the altar. Iphigenia hesitated. "Father, I am afraid."

"Don't fear, child. It won't hurt, for the gods will protect you." Agamemnon responded. Menelaus touched his niece gently on the shoulder and embraced her. He held back his emotions to be strong, but he knew had Helen been there, she would have wept.

Agamemnon led her to the top and laid her down on the altar, while Clytemnestra had to be restrained by soldiers. She sobbed loudly. Iphigenia sobbed softly and closed her eyes. Menelaus knew his brother's pain. He'd had enough conversations to know how much Agamemnon dreaded this moment. Agamemnon said a short prayer. "Artemis, Goddess of the Hunt, please accept my beautiful daughter, Iphigenia, as atonement for any discretions against your honor." Menelaus looked away as Agamemnon plunged a knife deep into the girl's chest, and her body slumped forward, blood draining onto the altar. Agamemnon stepped down from the altar and set the funeral pyre on fire. Menelaus wiped his cheek and took a deep, heavy breath.

Menelaus watched as Agamemnon walked by Clytemnestra. She turned her tear-streaked face towards him and spit in his face. With hate in her eyes, she said, "I will never forgive you. You will pay for this."

Artemis accepted the sacrifice; the wind started blowing; and the fleet set sail for Troy.

THE WAR BEGINS

The Trojans knew the Greeks were coming, they just didn't know when. Merchants and travelers brought with them stories about the fleet the Greeks were building in Aulis. The Trojans were on high alert. Men patrolled the beaches, and sentries watched the sea.

At noon on a crystal-clear, early summer day, Helen walked along the top of the walls with her attendants. A warm breeze blew through her hair, and the sun beat down on her face. Sometimes, the people on the street below could see her and would stop to stare. It had only been a few weeks since Menelaus was in Troy with Odysseus, but it seemed like years. She wondered when they were coming and worse yet, whether they would come at all. Helen looked wistfully over the Aegean Sea. She took a deep breath and let out a sigh. She wasn't sure any of this was a good idea. She missed her daughter, she missed her husband, and she missed her people.

When Helen turned to return to her quarters, she heard the horn. Riders sprinted toward the city from the beach, and sentries sounded the alarm, shouting, "Ships! Ships!" Helen hurried back to the wall. Hundreds of ships were appearing on the horizon as if by magic. She was so excited. They came back for her! She concealed a small smile. It was about time. It wouldn't be long at all before she could go home.

Helen saw Hector look up from his work, and he rushed to the top of the wall to see what was happening. By the time she was able to focus her eyes, both he and Paris had joined her. Ships as far as the eye could see filled the Aegean. Hector looked over at Helen and their eyes met for a moment. She had to work hard not to look away first; to do so might have given away her veiled excitement. He then turned and ran, commanding people and yelling at his men to organize as he went. People rushed inside the Trojan walls from the surrounding villages. Inside the city, men ran everywhere. Some got horses ready for combat, and others handed out weapons. Paris finally turned to Helen, "Menelaus has returned! I'd heard there were many ships, but couldn't imagine so many."

"He wants me back. He'll stop at nothing."

"As I told you when we were lying in bed in Cannae, he's no match for me. I am braver and stronger than Menelaus. I am better with a spear and a bow. It was foolish for him to come after you. He will die here, and by my own hands." Paris walked toward the stairs, but stopped to say, "You're mine now. He will learn that soon enough." He left her standing there as he disappeared into the palace. Helen looked at her attendants briefly, and then they all turned to watch what unfolded on the beaches.

As the ships crested the horizon, Menelaus could see Troy gleaming on the hill. The crew watched people run in different directions on the beaches and plains of Troy, and they heard the horns blaring in the distance. Although he was eager to get to shore to begin the war so he could take his wife home, he was again struck by the beauty of Troy. He noticed the crew around him had stopped rowing to look on in awe at the scene. Troy looked like a shining jewel. The other Greek leaders ran up and down the ranks, shouting at the rowers to snap them back to their task. They had been training for weeks, and now Menelaus and his brother hoped they were all ready for battle. On the left flank, Ajax split off with his division of ships. He had been ordered to seize the landing area at the confluence of the Scamander River and the Aegean Sea. Achilles headed the division of ships on the right flank.

Menelaus watched as the Trojans quickly organized and poured through the Scaean Gate. They raced down to the beach, Menelaus presumed, hoping to force the Greeks back off the beach. As the Greek ships neared the shore, the men pulled hard on their oars and rowed to the rhythm of a drum. The closer they got to the beach, the faster the beat of the drum, and the harder they rowed. The idea is that they would build up their speed so the ship would slide up on the beach and they could disembark as close to shore as possible.

The first ships landed, and Hector and a contingent of the Trojan army already awaited them. The combat was fierce from the beginning. As soon as the first Greek soldier set foot on Trojan sand, Hector killed him. Menelaus and Agamemnon fought back to back. Menelaus drove his spear through a Trojan's throat with such force that he pinned him to the ground. He drew his sword, and then he slew two more Trojans. He marveled at how easily his sword penetrated their bodies, and how much satisfaction he got from the act. It was a far cry from the feelings he had as a young man in his first battle. The elation he felt reminded him of that first night after they brought Helen back from Aphidna. He refocused his energy and continued to fight.

The ships landed quickly, but the beach was too small for all of them. Some crashed into oars of beached ships as they tried to get ashore. Men in full armor splashed in the surf and tried to get ashore to join the fighting. The Trojans fought valiantly and killed many Greeks, but Achilles approached with reinforcements on Hector's left flank. Ajax captured the landing area. He moved against the Trojans from Hector's right flank. Achilles and Ajax closed in. They threatened to surround the Trojans. This would trap them on the beach. Before they could successfully do this, Hector ordered a retreat. The Trojan army moved back to their walls. The Greeks pursued until they came within range of the Trojan archers on the wall.

As darkness fell, the Greeks began setting up their camp. They secured their ships on the beaches, set up tents, and built fires. Eager to develop his strategy, Agamemnon called upon the leaders. "I'm glad you are all here. Today went well, but this was just the beginning. Tomorrow, we will test the walls of Troy to see if they are truly invincible." Agamemnon laid out a plan for an all-out, frontal assault on the walls of Troy for the following morning. He was determined to breach the Scaean Gate with a battering ram.

Helen was on the wall in the royal box with Priam, his wife, and the council early the next morning. She saw the Greek army assembled on the edge of the plain, three miles from the gates of Troy. She hoped to see Menelaus. Helen scanned the ranks for the distinctive scarlet crest on the helmet of the Spartan army. However, she couldn't single him out at that distance. On the Trojan side, she watched the Trojan army assemble in their blackened armor. She looked back out toward the sea. The Greeks were a formidable sight as they formed a long line at least one hundred men deep, bronze armor reflecting the sunlight. Helen watched the Greek leaders, including Menelaus, mount their chariots and lead the army slowly forward, like a long wave coming to shore.

As the Greeks came into range, Trojan archers from high on the walls shot arrows down at them. Helen caught her breath. She scanned again, but didn't see her husband. Everyone was in action. Priam looked at her, and she changed her demeanor, smiling at her Trojan father-in-law. "The Trojans will surely win," she found herself saying.

"Of course we will," he replied, and smiled. He placed his hand on his wife's back and turned back toward the action.

"Staying alive," Helen thought to herself, "will mean I have to cheer for the side I want to lose."

Helen didn't have much time with her thoughts. A loud roar interrupted them. The Greeks burst into a full charge. The Trojans held their ground as a hundred thousand Greeks slammed into them. There was an explosion of sound as armor clashed against armor. Men screamed and cursed. Arrows and spears filled the air. The dead and the dying piled up on the battlefield. Men slipped in the blood and gore around their feet. Achilles mowed through the Trojans. He killed scores of men. Ajax pummeled the enemy on the opposite flank. Hector rallied his troops. He forced the Greeks to back off, regroup, and prepare another attack. As the Greeks regrouped, Hector called for a full retreat behind Troy's walls. Helen started to get the feeling that the fighting would go on longer than anyone anticipated.

On the ground, Menelaus scanned the walls, looking for Helen. He spotted her on a balcony, high over the main gate, in the royal box with Priam and his council of elders. He knew that this distraction could cost him his life. He returned his mind to fighting, determined to put her out of his mind.

A six-foot deep by eight-foot wide trench surrounded the walls of Troy. Menelaus knew when he saw this that the Greeks would not be able to use siege machines to strike. Thinking the Scaean Gates may be a weak point, the Greeks organized. They brought out a huge battering ram to knock the gate down, but it was too strong. They lost many men in the attempt. The Trojans assaulted the men pushing the battering ram with a barrage of arrows, hot oil, and grease.

Menelaus and Agamemnon had already determined the Scaean Gates would not burn. They were three stories high, and covered in ornate bronze. They were impossibly heavy but were so equally balanced that a single man could open them from inside. A large wooden beam lay across the inside of the gate and secured it against being broken through. Menelaus watched his brother order the men to withdraw. They were losing too many men and not getting good results.

That evening, it became clear to Menelaus that they were in for a longer war than originally thought. To protect their ships, the Greeks built bulwarks: walls made of sand, lumber, and stone. Although they had a very large army, Agamemnon and Menelaus didn't have enough men to completely surround Troy, and they needed to protect their ships and supplies.

Agamemnon turned to his brother. "Help is pouring into Troy from the surrounding communities."

"This is bigger than we thought it would be, brother."

"So it is. We must call a meeting of our leaders and devise a solution."

When the men had gathered, Agamemnon began speaking of the coming day's strategy. "Today's battle went well, but we learned that it is impossible to knock down the gate. We are going to have to try a different strategy. The Trojans are receiving men and supplies from the surrounding towns and villages. We need to cut off their supply lines, but we also need to protect our ships, since they are our only way of getting home." He stopped at a large table with a map. "Ajax, I want you to take ten thousand men, go around the right flank of the city, and destroy all the towns and villages on that side. Achilles, I want you to take ten thousand men and destroy all the towns and villages around the left flank of the city."

"When do you want us to leave?" asked Achilles.

"As soon as possible." Said Agamemnon.

"I can start in the morning," said Achilles. Ajax concurred.

Agamemnon continued with his plan. "Menelaus, Odysseus, and I will continue to attack Troy to keep them gated up and unable to help the others. The Trojan defenses are stronger than I expected, but no wall can withstand the might of our army. I am certain that we will prevail." The men all agreed and headed to their respective camps to execute the plan.

Every morning, Menelaus rode his chariot to the plain, just outside the range of the archers on the walls, and waited until he saw Helen walk along the top of the walls. He hoped to get some sign that she was safe, but Helen just kept walking. She stopped occasionally and looked at Menelaus, but she never waved or gave any signal. Every day, Menelaus watched for a few moments and then rode back to camp. He began to wonder if Helen had indeed fallen in love with Paris. Why didn't she give him information, as she promised?

The evenings were filled with reports of the battles by the ranks. Ajax had led his force around the right flank of Troy destroying everything, including the Thracian peninsula. He killed the Phrygian King, Teleutas, and carried off his daughter, Tecmessa. The Greeks could not feed the thousands of men in the invasion force for long, so they had to find food and supplies on site. Ajax hunted the Trojan flocks on Mount Ida and in the surrounding countryside, and brought meat back for the troops.

Meanwhile Achilles and his force conquered eleven cities and twelve islands. Achilles and Ajax were great warriors, and the Greek army was too powerful for the small armies of the surrounding towns. The Greeks easily over ran the smaller forces. They showed no mercy, they killed all the men and children they could find, and took the women as slaves. The soldiers looted and plundered all the treasure, and then burned each town to the ground. Every day, Priam watched smoke billow up from one town or another. Those who managed to escape the Greeks made their way to Troy, where a large group of refugees gathered. The marauding armies shared the spoils of war with the other leaders when they returned.

Menelaus watched over the days of the battles, which began to run together. It was a stream of waking, checking to see if Helen was giving him a signal, fighting, receiving reports about Ajax and Achilles, sleeping, and repeating.

Menelaus tried to steer Agamemnon correctly. When his brother took a daughter of the priest, Chryses, as a concubine, a plague fell on the Greeks. Seeking answers, Agamemnon once again consulted the prophet Calchas, who told him to return the girl to Chryses if he wanted to eliminate the plague. Agamemnon said, "If I have to return my prize, I will take treasure of equal value from someone else. I will not be left empty handed."

"The treasure has already been shared. How can you take what rightfully belongs to another?" asked Achilles. Menelaus could see Achilles growing nervous. During the young hero's mission, he captured and fell in love with a young woman named Briseis. Since returning to camp, the camp knew Agamemnon lusted after the woman.

Agamemnon replied, "It is not right that I should have nothing while you have your treasure. I will take your woman to compensate for my loss."

Achilles shouted, "You selfish dog! I do the brunt of the fighting, and you take the greatest share of the plunder. If you take my woman, I will not fight for the Greeks. I would rather sail home than pile up treasure for you!"

"Then go! We don't need you; we have enough brave men to win this fight without you!" Achilles gathered his men and left for his ships, vowing not to fight.

Inside Troy, nerves were beginning to fray. One night, the royal family sat down to dinner to discuss the events of the day. Paris' sister, Laodice, said to Helen, "Why did you come here? Did you think you would be a queen here as well? Did you think your Greek friends would put you on the throne?"

Laodice's comments caught Helen off-guard. She remained silent, and Paris made no effort to defend his bride. Hector stepped in and said, "My dear sister, it is not Helen's fault that we are in this situation." Turning to Paris he said "It is because of you that the sounds of war surround our city!"

Paris got up from the table and left the room in silence. Hecuba said, "Helen you were a queen in the back woods of Sparta, but here you are nothing more than an adulteress and a harlot."

Helen rose to her feet. "Your Highness, it is true that Troy is more opulent than Sparta, but the natural beauty and the love, respect, and courtesy of the Spartan people is something you could never have."

Hector continued to defend Helen's honor. "Mother, she is now a member of our family. You should treat her with the respect accorded to all family members. Come, Helen. I will escort you to your quarters." They left the room and Hector said, "Please forgive them. They are under a great deal of stress. I, for one, don't blame you for our situation; it is what the gods have ordained."

"Thank you, but aren't you under a lot of stress as well?"

"Yes, I am, but I am more accustomed to it. Being under stress doesn't give me the right to lose my manners and become accusatory."

They reached Helen's quarters, and she said, "Thank you Hector. You are a good man."

"Please try to understand, they are good people. Give them time."

Helen just nodded and entered her room. Inside, Paris was sulking. She looked at Paris. "Good people," she thought. She almost snorted to herself, but had to stop. Theseus was a "good man," but he had ravaged her and taken what wasn't his. Here was Paris, another "good person" and her in-laws, yet they wanted war against her people. All Helen wanted was her husband—her *real* husband. He was a real good man, Menelaus.

"Can you believe he blames me for this war?" Paris interrupted Helen's thoughts.

"Who?"

"Hector!" Paris yelled. Helen knew that Paris could feel his influence slipping away. When he brought her to Troy, she made him into an important man; people finally paid attention to him. With the war underway, the mounting casualties made Helen feel guilty, and she'd pulled away. She knew Paris felt like a scapegoat. "I don't care what they say. You are staying here with me. I have heard some people suggest that I return you to the Greeks and end this war. Well, that is not going to happen. I will die first."

Helen walked past Paris and gazed out the window. Without Helen in Troy, she knew Paris was nobody, just a wayward man at the end of the line to inherit the throne and who as an infant his mother wanted to leave to die from exposure,.

Helen followed her regular routine, but began to notice that people reacted to her differently. As she walked through the marketplace, she was met by whispers and angry looks. Some people turned their backs when they saw her coming, and others just glared at her without saying a word. Finally, she heard it. "Whore!" Someone standing on the street shouted it as she passed by. She felt very uncomfortable as people gathered around and started following her. For the first time in her life, she was grateful for the two bodyguards Paris had given her. Even with them flanking her, Helen decided it would be best to cut her walk short and return to the palace.

Once she and her attendants were safe inside her quarters, Helen dismissed the Trojan servants. She checked to see that she was alone with Harleopi and Aethra and closed the door. She turned to the women and asked them to sit. "How have the Trojans treated you here?"

Aethra spoke first. "When we arrived, I was treated well. I thought because I was older, they wanted to be respectful. Lately, however, I have been met with more and more hostility."

Harleopi said, "Yes, at first it was good. They wanted to help me, but now everyone is cold and distant. May I speak frankly, Your Highness?"

"You know you may."

"I have been approached by several men who asked if I was a whore like you. I have even overheard others calling the three of us whores."

Helen slowly paced the room, wrung her hands, and searched for the right words. "I am sorry this has happened to you. You have both been with me a long time, and I feel I can trust you. There is something I need to tell you. As long as we are here, our lives are in danger, and you deserve to know why."

Your Highness, it doesn't matter why we are here. We are with you," said Harleopi. Aethra nodded in agreement.

Helen gave them both a hug and said, "Dear ones, you are so faithful, which is why I feel I can trust you with the truth. This information will jeopardize your life if it is shared with anyone. You must swear an oath to remain quiet." Both women pledged to protect the secret. Helen turned and whispered, "Agamemnon and Menelaus felt that Priam planned to start a war with Sparta. Priam sent Paris to Sparta to spark tensions. I was asked to seduce Paris in order to bring the Greek cities together to conquer Troy."

The two attendants looked at each other in disbelief. "I knew you couldn't be in love with that obnoxious fool!" Aethra finally said.

Harleopi chimed in, "We knew something was wrong. You were too quiet and unhappy. You would send us away, but we knew you were weeping when you were alone. We have known you a long time, we can tell."

"What a relief. I feel as if the weight is off my shoulders."

"What can we do to help?" asked Aethra.

Helen started to sob. She was so relieved to have someone to talk to, and she couldn't hold back her tears. "I am frustrated. I was supposed to send information to Menelaus from the walls about the strengths and weaknesses of Troy, but there are none that I can see. I haven't sent him any messages, and I worry that he thinks I may have gone over to the Trojan side."

The two women were energized by this new information. They now saw things differently and wanted to help. Harleopi asked, "What kind of strengths and weaknesses?"

"I need information about the army, where they plan to position their men on the walls, or if they are going to attack, any information that could be useful to the Greek army."

Harleopi said, "We want to help. How can we gather this information?"

"Just listen to people, especially soldiers, and watch what they are doing."

Aethra added, "Don't ask too many questions. Better yet, don't ask any questions. It may raise suspicions."

Helen said, "You're right. The Trojan people are not fond of us. We don't need anyone questioning our motives. Agreed?"

They all agreed. Harleopi would try to gather information outside of the palace. Since she was older, Aethra would stay within the palace grounds, where her main duties were. Helen would try to collect information wherever she could. The three of them agreed to meet every day, and share what they had learned.

That evening, Priam and Hecuba discussed the war effort. Hecuba said, "I don't like this. We have to send her back."

"That is out of the question. We are not sending her back."

"The prophets said Paris would bring the destruction of Troy. You agreed to expose him on the side of Mount Ida. What changed?"

Priam grew agitated, "Nothing!"

Hecuba said, "Do you know what Helen's name means? Torch! The name 'Helen' means torch! Paris has brought the torch that will destroy us into Troy, just as the prophecy said! You have to send her back!"

Priam shouted, "I can't send her back, I won't send her back!" Priam pulled himself together and calmly said, "Can't you see? I have the eyes of the world on me. I can't send her back, especially after what they did to my sister. I would be the laughing stock of the world, of my allies. The Greeks would go home and mock me."

Softly, Hecuba said, "Better to be mocked than dead."

That morning, Menelaus watched as the Trojans poured out of their city and formed a long line in front of the gates. On the other side of the plain, the Greeks advanced in silence. The plain was badly beaten and barren in places from the horses, soldiers, and chariots running across it. Periodically, a dust cloud flared up from the worn surface. When the Greeks were within a stone's throw of the Trojan lines, Paris stepped out from the ranks. A panther skin on his back, a bow slung over his shoulder, and twin spears in his hands, Paris shouted, "I challenge the best of the Greeks to one-on-one combat."

Menelaus thought, "This can't be happening. The man who caused all my heartache has issued a challenge for one-on-one combat. I can kill him in front of both armies, and get Helen back all in one fight." He quickly stepped forward before any other Greek could accept the challenge. "I accept this challenge," Menelaus shouted.

When Paris met Menelaus' eyes, and saw who accepted his challenge, Paris turned and ran back to hide amongst the Trojan ranks. Menelaus laughed. He watched as Hector turned to his brother and said, "Paris, you are embarrassing us in front of the Greeks. Your looks and your charm won't help you now. You sailed across the sea and brought this man's wife back here while he was away attending to family matters. Now, you are afraid to face him in combat? You're lucky we have gotten soft, otherwise we would have stoned you to death before we let you shame us in this way."

Paris replied, "Hector, you are right to rebuke me. I will come forward to fight Menelaus. Let he who wins take Helen and all her treasures with him, and we can call an end to this war."

On both sides, the men were quiet. Finally, Menelaus spoke. "I agree. Let this fight be between Paris and I. My heart is the one that has suffered most. Let one man die for this cause, and the rest of you can go in peace." The Trojans and Greeks alike were overjoyed to hear him say this. It would mean the end of the war.

Helen was in the palace, weaving a tapestry of battle scenes she witnessed between the Trojans and the Greeks when Laodice came running in. Before Helen could speak, Laodice said, "Come quickly. The warriors have all put down their arms, and are watching a single combat between Menelaus and Paris."

Helen ran toward the Scaean Gates. She was fearful for the outcome of this fight. She could be going home, or she could be stuck in Troy forever. Aethra and Harleopi also wanted to see the fight, and followed her to the gates. Priam and his council of elders were already watching the fight from atop the wall. When he saw Helen, Antenor said, "No wonder men fight over her; she is like an immortal goddess. Still, I think it would be best if she were sent back with the Greeks, to end this war."

"Dear Helen, sit with me and look upon your former husband and your dear friends. I do not blame you for this war. It is surely the will of the gods that caused me to wage war against the Greeks. Who is that great warrior, there?" Priam pointed to Helen's brother-in-law. "He is a head shorter than others, yet he carries himself in such a regal manner."

Helen remembered that Priam knew Agamemnon from the wars in Phrygia, and wondered why he would pretend otherwise. She thought that he intended to test her loyalty, so Helen said, "Dear father-in-law, I have much respect for you. I wish I had died instead of causing this war by coming here with your son and leaving behind my daughter and my childhood friends, but I didn't. To answer your question, that warrior is Agamemnon. He was once my brother-in-law, in a life that seems so far away."

Looking out at Agamemnon, Priam said, "So he is the leader of all these Greeks. I remember him from Phrygia, and the thousands of soldiers fighting the Amazons, but there are more Greeks here than were there. Now tell me, who is that Greek over there? He is a head shorter than Agamemnon, but he has a broader chest and shoulders."

Helen replied, "That is crafty Odysseus, King of Ithaca. He is a master of deceptive strategies and tricks."

Antenor said, "Lady, what you say is true. I remember when he and Menelaus came to us as ambassadors in your affairs. I received them in my home. When they spoke on your behalf, Menelaus was eloquent and right to the point. He said few words and did not deviate from his purpose. When Odysseus rose to speak, his eyes were downcast. He gripped his scepter tightly, like some ignoramus, but when he spoke, his voice bellowed and no man alive could match him."

Priam spotted Ajax and asked, "Who is the big, burly Greek over there? He is head and shoulders above the rest."

Helen replied, "That is mighty Ajax, one of the strongest of the Greeks. Menelaus welcomed him in our home whenever he visited from Crete."

Helen watched as on the battlefield, Odysseus and Hector marked the ground where Menelaus and Paris would fight, then cast lots to see who would throw the first spear. Paris' lot was drawn. Chariots came to a halt, horses were reined in, and all the soldiers on both sides took off their armor, laid down their weapons, and sat down to watch the fight.

As soon as Paris and Menelaus entered the fighting grounds, Paris threw his spear. Helen held her breath. It struck the middle of Menelaus' shield, but didn't penetrate all the way through. With a mighty groan, Menelaus threw his spear. It easily pierced the center of Paris' shield, but Paris swerved and it merely wounded him. Menelaus drew his sword and swung wildly at Paris. He struck Paris' helmet and his sword broke into four pieces. Menelaus could not believe it. "Almighty Zeus, I finally get a chance to kill the man who wronged me, and my sword breaks on his helmet!" Menelaus jumped on Paris, grabbed him by the helmet, and dragged him toward the Greek lines. Paris choked on the strap under his chin. Suddenly, a strong wind kicked up a cloud of dust into Menelaus' eyes. He covered his eyes just as the strap on the helmet broke, and Paris ran away through the ranks of the Trojans. The Trojans shouted, "Coward! You're a disgrace! Come back and fight!" Paris didn't look back and ran all the way to his chambers.

An old woman Helen used to know in Sparta approached Helen. "Funny," Helen muttered to herself, "She's the last person I'd expect to see here."

When the woman reached Helen, she said, "My lady, Paris waits for you in his chambers."

The woman walked with Helen, not saying a word. When finally they were alone, the woman revealed herself to Helen as Aphrodite. Helen finally had a chance to talk face to face with the goddess, whom she blamed for all her trouble. "Goddess, Menelaus has beaten Paris and wants to take me home. Why don't you let him? Or would you have me follow you to some other city, to be the lover of some other man you favor? Why don't you go yourself? Forget about Olympus, go to Paris, and pamper him. You can be his wife, or better yet, his slave! I won't go. The women of Troy would scorn me even more."

Aphrodite held up her hand and angrily replied, "Woman, don't anger me or I will hate you as much as I love you now. I will bring Greek and Trojan hostility onto you, and then we will see how you feel!" Realizing things could be worse Helen silently followed her to Paris' quarters.

Helen walked in to see Paris sprawled across the bed. She could feel the anger building in her chest. "So now the goddesses fetch me for you like some whore or slave? I see you have run away from Menelaus. You used to say that you were stronger and faster than him. Go back now and fight Menelaus, if you are not afraid of dying on his spear!"

"Yes, woman, it is true. Menelaus has defeated me. Next time, he won't be so lucky. Now come, lie in bed with me."

Helen turned her back, and walked to the window. "I won't lie with you. I wish you had died today."

Paris got out of bed and took her shoulders in his hands. "Get in bed. I want you now more than I wanted you when we were on Cannae."

Helen whirled around and looked at him with contempt. "I could never love you. You are a coward and a weakling."

"Do you think I don't feel the coldness in your touch or see the distance in your eyes? Whether you love me or not is of no concern to me. I have your body; your heart and mind will follow!"

"I could never love a coward. You talk big, but really you are a little, cowardly boy. Do you think having Menelaus' woman will make you a better man?"

Paris grabbed Helen's face, his fingers pushing her cheeks in as he menacingly whispered, "You are *my* woman." He turned his head to kiss her neck, but Helen punched him in the ear. When he threw her on the bed, she jumped up and punched him squarely in the face. Her resistance only fueled his rage. He grabbed her arms, threw her on the bed, and jumped on her while tearing at her clothes. Helen fought back. She slapped, punched, and kicked Paris, but he pinned one of her arms down with his knee and punched her in the face. She was stunned and could resist no more as Paris satisfied his lust. When Paris was finished, Helen got up to leave. "Hear my words and be warned, Prince. You have to sleep sometime."

Paris knew he crossed a line. He thought, "She is serious. I should make different arrangements." He went to Queen Hecuba and said, "Mother, I have a request. Although I love her dearly, Helen was accustomed to having her own quarters in Sparta. I would like her to have the same privilege here."

"Of course, Paris. To be honest, I really don't care how she feels. But if that would make you feel better, it will be done."

Back on the battlefield, Menelaus rubbed his eyes as he ran through the ranks of Trojans holding Paris' helmet. "Where is he? Where did he go? Come out and fight, you coward!"

A Trojan soldier said, "We're not hiding him. We despise him, and want him to fight just as much as you do. He keeps your wife here against our wishes. He thinks only of himself! One of the gods must have carried him to safety behind the walls."

Hector shook his head and approached Menelaus. "He has run away. I am embarrassed and ashamed for myself and all the brave Trojan soldiers here today."

Agamemnon shouted, "Menelaus clearly won this fight. He should be given Helen, all her treasure, plus retribution!"

The Greek army shouted its approval, but Hector disagreed. "The fight never ended. No man was declared the winner." Seeking fame, glory, and the end of the war, a Trojan named Pandarus restrung his bow and fired an arrow at Menelaus. The arrow passed through Menelaus' belt buckle and corset, and pierced his skin wounding him near the hip.

Agamemnon shouted, "The truce has been broken! Let the battle resume. Men, form your lines!" Agamemnon and Menelaus both knew that Menelaus' death would break the Oath of Tyndareus, so he ushered Menelaus to safety behind the lines. "Brother, how foolish of me to allow you to stand up to the Trojans by yourself. If you die here, the Greeks will demand to sail home, and Helen will be stuck in Troy. Men would forever mock me for not finishing what I started."

"Oh brother, shut up. It's a scratch. It would take a lot more than that to kill me."

Agamemnon called for a healer to care for the wound and take Menelaus back to his camp.

The Trojans advanced on the Greeks, and Agamemnon ran about ordering his men to pick up their weapons, put on their armor, and fight. The battle raged back and forth across the plain, with one side gaining the advantage, and then the other. It went on like this until nightfall, when both armies retreated to their respective camps.

Across the plain, Agamemnon and Menelaus discussed plans for the upcoming battle. At night, there were hundreds of fires and tents strewn along the three miles of beach. Some men cooked meals for the hungry battalion, some repaired equipment, and others relaxed by playing long wooden flutes. As they strolled by his recuperating army, Agamemnon shared his thoughts about the problems the army faced. He wasn't sure how to overtake the Trojan walls, and although Ajax and Achilles conquered all of the cities and towns surrounding Troy, supplies were still getting into the city at night. He sent out patrols, but couldn't interrupt every supply line. Agamemnon said, "We have been mercilessly attacking, but we aren't getting anywhere. We are just losing men."

Menelaus replied, "This may take longer than we thought."

"Tomorrow, we will try again. Come, I'll show you what I have in mind." They walked a little farther down the beach, where the men were building ladders. "We will attack the main gate, and meanwhile, we will put the ladders up and try to scale the walls. We must be able to get into that city!"

The two leaders walked back to Agamemnon's hut. When they had privacy, Menelaus said, "I don't know what is happening with Helen. I haven't received messages or any kind of response from her."

"Well, you said she wasn't trained as a spy. Maybe she doesn't have any information to share."

"I see her every day on the walls, and she doesn't even acknowledge me."

"We don't know her situation. She may be being watched and can't give herself away."

"I can't stand the thought of her being in there. I should have killed that little coward when I had the chance."

Agamemnon gave Menelaus a cup of wine. "Brother, if it is up to me, you will have another chance to get at Paris."

Menelaus sat in a large chair. His brother liked comfort and opulence, so his hut was well furnished and hanging curtains partitioned the space into three sections. There was a sleeping area, a dining area, and a large meeting room. He put down carpeting on the floor, and his bed was piled with furs and blankets. Menelaus had to admit, it was quite cozy. Agamemnon said, "I'm hoping for great success tomorrow. I think we will finally break through."

"I hope so." Menelaus finished his cup of wine and walked to the door of the hut. "I don't know what it will take, but I'm not leaving Troy without her."

Back in his hut, Menelaus tried to get some rest, but he could only stare at the ceiling and think about Sparta. He thought about the day when he first met Helen. Although she was young, she was so confident and mature for her age. He was immediately smitten. He had never seen anyone so beautiful, and the more he got to know her, the more beautiful she became. Those were happy times;

they would run and play, fall and laugh. He felt on top of the world the day she chose to marry him. Menelaus closed his eyes and tried to sleep. He would need his rest for the upcoming battle.

The next day, the Trojans assembled in front of the gates and put up a ferocious fight defending them. The clash of armor and the clanging of swords echoed through the city. Men were screaming and crying, and the dead piled up in heaps near the heaviest combat. The Greeks attacked the walls with their ladders. The Trojan archers picked off the men as they tried to climb, and then pushed the ladders over, causing them to land on the soldiers below. Any time the Greeks managed to get a few men on top of the walls, they were quickly thrown back. When the Greeks were about to break through, Hector joined the battle and rallied his troops to stop them. The Greeks were forced to pull back and regroup.

Hector felt that the Trojans were in trouble. While the Greeks were regrouping, he left Aeneas in charge, and went into the city to ask the women to give prayers to Athena and Zeus for a Trojan victory. Hector then went to Paris' chambers, where he found him relaxing and polishing his bow, while Helen instructed her attendants in weaving. Hector said, "Paris, you are worthless. You would fight any man you saw running from battle. What are you doing sitting here, while we fight your war outside the gates? Go and get your armor!"

"Hector, I am not sitting here out of spite or anger. I am grieving our losses. Just now, Helen has urged me to join the fighting. Now wait here while I put on my armor, or go and I will catch up with you."

Helen *had* urged Paris to join the fighting in hopes that he would be killed, and she would be free. Helen knew Hector was a great leader and the Trojans needed him in battle. She respected and cared for Hector, but thought that if she delayed him, perhaps his absence would help the Greeks. Helen turned to him and said,

"Hector, you are like a brother to me. Sit by my side. I feel terrible about this war, and I wish I had died before any of this happened, but since the gods have ordained this, I wish I could have been the wife of a better man. A man who would stand up for me when others insult me, someone like you. Paris doesn't have any sense. He is a coward who won't even stand up to my Spartan husband. He should send me back to Greece, but he won't do that now, and I don't think he will any time soon. I'm sure he will pay the price for his stubbornness. Please come in and sit down. I know this war is weighing heavily on your mind. The gods ordained this war, so you and I will forever be linked in men's songs and tales."

"Thank you for the offer to sit. You are kind, but I must get back to the battle. Please tell Paris to hurry. I'm stopping by to see my wife, for I don't know if I will ever see her again." With that, Hector took his spear and left.

Hector turned to see Paris in his full armor behind Helen. He said nothing to his wife as he hurried out of the door to catch up to Hector. "Hector, I am slowing you down," Paris shouted.

"Paris, once you are in battle, you fight as bravely as anyone, but when you deliberately keep yourself out of combat, it hurts me to hear what others say about you. Hurry, we must get back to the fight."

Menelaus and his Spartans had opened a gap in the Trojan lines, and were threatening to break through. Menelaus had just captured a wounded Trojan when Agamemnon shouted, "Why are you sparing this man's life? You treated the Trojans well in your own home and look where that got you. Don't let any of them escape, not even the baby in the womb. Let everyone in Troy be slaughtered without pity or leaving anyone to grieve!" Agamemnon jammed his spear into the captured man's side, killing him as he fell to the ground. He placed his heel on the dead man's chest and pulled the spear out.

Nestor, one of the Greek elders, cried, "Let no man plunder or loot in a hurry to take it back to the ships. This is the time to fight! There will be plenty of time to strip the dead." Inspired, the Greeks fought with more intensity.

They were close to overpowering the Trojan line when Hector returned. He shouted, "Men, stand your ground and fight! Don't run back to your wives. The enemy would jeer us if we did so." Hector cleared a path through the Trojans by swinging his spear from side to side. Agamemnon did the same on the Greek side. Hector announced, "I challenge the bravest of the Greeks in one-on- one combat so we can stop this battle now."

The warriors from both sides fell silent and crowded in to see who would accept the challenge. No one stepped forward. Finally, Menelaus said, "If there is no one among us courageous enough, I will accept the challenge to fight Hector."

Agamemnon knew that Hector was a better warrior than Menelaus and Menelaus's death would end the war. "Brave brother, there is no need for you to sacrifice yourself. Even Achilles, our best warrior, hesitates to fight mighty Hector. Let someone else take up this challenge." Menelaus reluctantly agreed and removed his armor.

Nestor said, "I am ashamed that no one has taken up this challenge. If I were a younger man, I would fight noble Hector."

With that admonition, nine Greeks stood up, including Agamemnon, Ajax, Odysseus, and Diomedes. They decided to draw lots to see who would fight Hector. Ajax's lot was drawn, the two warriors put on their armor and prepared to fight. Ajax said, "Now, Hector, you will see what Greek generals are made of."

"Don't try to frighten me with your words like I'm a small child. I know how to fight and kill as well as you."

Hector was the first to throw his spear. It struck the middle of Ajax's shield and penetrated seven layers of leather, but was stopped by the eighth layer of bronze. Ajax hurled his spear at Hector and pierced his shield, but Hector moved to the side and it missed him, only piercing his tunic. Both men grabbed a second spear and lunged at each other. Ajax thrust his spear through Hector's shield and wounded his throat. Hector's spear bounced off Ajax's shield, so Hector threw a jagged rock, but Ajax blocked it. Ajax, too, grabbed a large stone and threw it at Hector, breaking his shield and knocking him to his knees. As both men drew their swords, two heralds placed their staves between them to end the battle. "Both of you have fought well, but darkness is coming, and we should declare a draw."

Ajax replied, "Hector issued the challenge. If he agrees to a draw, I will also."

"I agree with the heralds. Ajax, you have fought well. Let us depart as friends and fight another day." The two men exchanged gifts. Hector gave Ajax his silver handled sword and scabbard, and Ajax gave Hector his crimson belt. Both armies retired to their respective camps.

When the Trojans got back inside the city, an angry and noisy crowd had formed outside the doors of Priam's palace. Inside, the council of elders met once more. Antenor rose to speak. "Trojans, let us send the woman back to Greece, along with the worldly goods she came here with."

Paris interjected, "Antenor, what you have said displeases me. I will give them back the treasure I took from Sparta and some of my own, but I will not give up the woman."

"I agree with Paris. Send a messenger to Agamemnon with our offer, and suggest a truce until we have gathered and burned our dead in funeral pyres," said Priam.

At dawn, a messenger approached Agamemnon and the Greek war council. The men listened to the offer. Diomedes said, "Let no one accept the Trojan offer. Even if Helen were returned, one can clearly see that we are about to destroy the Trojans."

Agamemnon realized that the war was starting to take on a life of its own. Agamemnon and all the Greeks agreed that the offer would be rebuked, but a truce to gather the dead would be honored.

CHAPTER SIX

HECTOR AND ACHILLES

That evening, after the fight between Hector and Ajax, Helen heard of the Trojans offer, the Greek's reply, and Diomedes' declaration. She knew that her only way home was if Troy was conquered. Priam and Paris would never give her up. Helen felt helpless. She needed to do something to help the Greek war effort. Later that night, she met with her handmaidens to discuss what they heard throughout the palace and the city.

Aethra said, "I know the attendant of Priam himself. She and I were washing clothes and I overheard her say to another attendant that she was worried about the next few days because the Trojans were either going to drive the Greeks into the sea or die trying. She hoped the war would be over soon."

"That is good information. Now we need to know what they plan," Helen said.

Harleopi added, "I was walking past the stables and I heard a soldier say that Hector's plan almost worked. I pretended to need a rest and I sat near where he was talking. The soldier said that Hector challenged the Greeks to one-on-one combat so he could kill one of their champions, demoralize them, and make them more vulnerable to attack."

"Very well done, both of you. We just need to know when they plan to attack." Helen turned away and started to pace slowly about the room. She made her way to the window and then out to the balcony. "They have called a truce for now to burn the dead. The day following the truce seems the most likely for an attack, because they will be rested. Agamemnon may not think the Trojans are capable of an attack, and wouldn't be expecting one so soon after the funeral pyres. Hector planned to demoralize the Greeks today and attack tomorrow, but his plan has been delayed by the truce. They may strike as soon as the truce is over." Both attendants nodded in agreement. Helen said, "Aethra, I want you to go to my wardrobe and set out that dress I was saving for a special occasion. I think I may want to wear it tomorrow."

The next morning, Helen put on her special dress and made her way to the walls, accompanied by Harleopi. Paris stopped her along the way and asked, "Why are you wearing such a brightly colored dress on such a dreadful day?"

"I am wearing it to honor the many heroes who have given their lives in this awful war."

"It is early to be moving about. Where are you going?"

"I am going to the walls to see for myself where these brave men have given their lives because of me. I feel so awful and wish I was never born than to come here with you and see this." Helen pushed past Paris and continued to the walls. As she climbed the stairs, she could see the flocks of vultures circling the great plain in front of Troy. She saw the bodies strewn all over the battlefield, the patrols gathering firewood, and the men piling their dead on the wagons. Helen's heart grew heavy. She bowed her head and began to weep.

Harleopi tapped Helen on the shoulder and said, "Look over there." Helen looked out over the plain and saw Menelaus in his chariot watching her. Helen's heart immediately lifted. She was happy to see him alive and unhurt. She desperately wanted to call out to him, but she restrained herself.

Menelaus went to the plain in his chariot and was met by a gruesome sight. There had been many battles, but after the current battle involving three days of continuous fighting, hundreds of bodies littered the plain. Some bodies had been laying there for three days, and vultures and other scavengers feasted on the corpses. The stench of death was everywhere. Because a truce had been declared, Menelaus watched as the crews sent by the Trojans and Greeks set about the grisly chore of chasing away scavengers and washing the bodies for identification. To avoid showing weakness to the enemy, there was to be no wailing or lamentations, only quiet weeping and tear-stained faces. Slaves and servants were sent to gather the thousands of arrows, spears, and shields scattered across the plain for reuse. Others gathered firewood for the pyres. The body wagons kicked up huge swarms of flies as they made their way to the blazing funeral pyres with a heavy load of stiff bloated corpses. The acrid rancid smell of burning flesh permeated the air as smoke blanketed the area like a fog.

Menelaus scanned the Trojan walls as he did every day, and that was when he saw her. He wiped his eyes to get a better view. Yes, it was Helen and she was wearing a red dress! She was wearing a red dress? She had never worn that before. What was the meaning, if any? Then he remembered her note; she said if she wore a red dress, an attack was coming! For Menelaus, this meant everything. It wasn't just that the information was valuable, but that Helen was finally giving him a sign! He knew her heart still belonged to him and to Greece, and she hadn't fallen in love with Paris. Menelaus smiled and felt a weight lifted from his shoulders. He wanted to give her a sign, anything to let her know that he understood. He whipped his horses and they reared up on their hind legs, and Menelaus rode back to his camp, his heart a thousand times lighter.

When Menelaus returned to camp, he searched for Agamemnon. Menelaus found him in his hut on the beach, having his breakfast and preparing a campaign strategy for the day after the truce. Menelaus said, "I have some confidential information I need to share with you."

Agamemnon heard the urgency in Menelaus' voice, so he dismissed his servants. "What have you brought me?"

"Helen has finally contacted me."

Agamemnon looked surprised. "How?"

"Remember I told you she left me a note when she left Sparta? When I saw her on the wall today, she was wearing a red dress." Agamemnon just looked at him and raised his eyebrow quizzically. "In her note, she said if I see her wearing a red dress, it means the Trojans are planning an attack."

Agamemnon hesitated for a minute then replied, "Okay, then we will be ready."

As doubt crept into Menelaus' heart, he fell silent, deep in thought. After a moment he said, "How do we know she isn't wearing that dress to cause us to go on the defensive, and allow the Trojans more time to recuperate?"

Agamemnon said, "I believe her. I *have* to believe her. Even if she did fall in love with Paris, she would not betray her country. She would not betray those who rescued her from Theseus. Dear brother, I know your heart is torn and full of pain. Don't let the pain plant doubt in your heart."

Menelaus took a deep breath and sighed. "You are right. The pain in my heart deceives me, but I know Helen's heart as well, and it is Spartan through and through. She may be inside Troy and married to a Trojan, but she is 100 percent Spartan! If she says there is going to be an attack, I believe her. Let us make preparations!"

Agamemnon put his hand on Menelaus' shoulder, "That's good enough for me."

"How do you think we should prepare?"

"In the morning, we will strengthen our ramparts, and then I propose we attack first. For today, we are at peace and must devote our attention to honoring the dead. We will drink wine and eat heartily because we will need our strength when the war continues."

Later that evening, Agamemnon gathered his generals together to discuss the next day's battle plan. Agamemnon said, "Everything points to a Trojan attack. The truce has given them time to rest, and since they have been fighting in front of their walls, I think they will want to test our defenses. I believe they will attack at dawn, the first morning after the truce. To defend ourselves, I propose that we widen the trench in front of our ramparts and fill it with wooden spikes. We should make the gates through the bulwarks just wide enough for a single chariot to pass through, and then build a wall from the funeral pyre on one end of the ramparts to the other end to protect our ships."

Ajax asked, "Are we to become like the Trojans, bottled up behind walls and afraid to fight? What's next, running from combat like that cowardly Trojan who began this whole mess?"

"Brave Ajax, I also propose that we attack the Trojans first. We should reinforce our own defenses anyway. It is the prudent thing to do, for no one knows how the tide of war will sway," said Agamemnon. The others agreed. "Now go and enjoy wine and meat with your men, for only the gods know what tomorrow will bring."

The next day, the Greeks were up before dawn building the wall, planting stakes in the trench, and strengthening the bulwarks. Before the sun came over the horizon, the Greek warriors came through the gates with their chariots and infantry, and began assembling on the plain. They were too late. The Trojans and their allies were already streaming through the Scaean Gate and were on their way across the plain. The two armies ran at each other in full gallop, their bronze armor dulled by the dim pre-dawn light. The field was soon engulfed in a huge cloud of dust kicked up by the chariots. A great clash of armor filled the air, followed by the cries of the wounded and dying mixed with the shouts of the victors. Men and horses ran in all directions and arrows and spears penetrated the air. Hundreds of men lay dead on the plain stripped of their armor as men claimed their glory. Nestor and Diomedes led the Greeks in a fierce attack and forced the Trojans back to the Scaean Gate. As the Trojans faced defeat, Hector led a counterattack that pushed the

Greeks across the plain and back to the edge of their own bulwarks. The battle raged back and forth all day. The dead lay everywhere, and were trampled by horses, chariots, and infantry until they were unrecognizable and covered in a mixture of blood and dust. The Greeks had their backs to their ramparts when darkness set in and the battle was called to an end for the day.

That evening, the Trojans and their allies camped on the plain within shouting distance of the Greeks. They had the advantage when night fell. Hector addressed the warriors. "Trojans and allies, I had hoped to destroy the Greek ships today, but night fell too soon. Now unharness your horses and post your sentries, so the Greeks will know we are here. Keep watch over the Greek camp in case they try to get in their boats and sail away like cowards in the night. Send a messenger to Troy and command that the young and old should man the battlements incase the Greeks try to attack our city while we are here. Make your fires, cook your meat, and drink your wine." Hector raised a cup of wine and shouted, "In the morning, we will drive the enemy from our soil!" The Trojans let out a tremendous roar of approval and set about feasting with high hopes for the coming day.

Across the field in Agamemnon's hut, his war council desperately searched for a solution to the dire situation they faced. Their backs were to the sea, the Trojans and their allies were camping on the plain just short of their bulwarks, and they had heard a great cheer among the Trojans as if a god had descended among them. Agamemnon placed sentries and troops on the ramparts to warn the Greeks of any Trojan movement toward them. Menelaus knew his brother was under great stress. He had never given up or run away from a fight before, but he could not see a solution to his problem.

Agamemnon approached his generals and said, "Friends, I am filled with great sadness as I say we should abandon our attempt to conquer Troy. I think we should load our ships and sail for home."

Diomedes said, "Agamemnon, you are a great leader, but I thought you knew us better. You may get in your ship and leave for home, but we are not going to run from these Trojans. We will stay here and fight. We will either sack Troy or die here among our own ships."

Menelaus said "The Spartans will not leave without our Queen."

The men in attendance all agreed with Diomedes and Menelaus. Nestor was adamant, "Agamemnon, you have led us well, but you have been blinded by your own pride. We have the greatest warrior in Greece on our side, and he hasn't seen battle because you have taken what was his. Let us reconcile with great Achilles and bring him back into the fold."

Agamemnon said, "Nestor, you are right. I have been stubborn and prideful. I will send messengers to Achilles and present him with many gifts, including the lovely Briseis. I swear to the gods I have not taken her to bed nor slept with her."

The reconciliation was so important that Ajax and Odysseus asked to take the message to Achilles themselves. Ajax and Odysseus walked along the beach to where Achilles beached his ships and found him playing a lyre, while Patroclus was opposite him playing a flute. When Achilles saw them approaching, he got to his feet and said, "Welcome my friends, because it is you that have come here, your message must be of great importance." Achilles welcomed them into his hut and gave them food and drink.

Odysseus said, "Friend, we come here because the Trojans are camped not far from our walls and ships, and we fear what the morning will bring. Agamemnon has realized that he made a grave mistake and wants to set things right. He is willing to return Briseis, whom he swears to the gods he never took to bed. He also pledges more gifts than any man has ever given to another man in compensation for his actions."

Achilles listened and sat motionless for a moment considering the offer. "What is the point of fighting? The coward is rewarded the same as the brave man. I toiled and conquered many cities, but it was Agamemnon who sat back and took the lion's share of my labors, leaving me only a small portion. Then he gives the treasures I have won to princes and kings, and still I get nothing. He takes the woman I love and lies beside her. Why are we here? Are Menelaus and Agamemnon the only men who love their women? Every man loves his own, as I love Briseis with all my heart. Now brave Hector threatens to destroy Agamemnon's army, so he comes to me and wants to make amends. He has shamed me in front of the other warriors. In the morning, I will sail home. You will see me at dawn as my men toil on the oars, and hopefully the gods will grant me a safe voyage. Give Agamemnon my message in front of all the Greeks, so that they will know who they are dealing with the next time he chooses to cheat someone."

Ajax stood and said, "We should go, Odysseus. We are wasting our time here. Achilles is angry, we can offer him twenty times what we have, and he will not change his mind. Achilles, you are my friend and I never thought I would say these words, but you are using Agamemnon's insult as an excuse to act like a coward."

Achilles stood quickly and responded, "If another man said those words to me, he would be dead now. However, you and Odysseus are the two Greeks I honor the most, and because of our friendship, I will wait until noon to decide whether I go or stay."

Menelaus accompanied Ajax and Odysseus on their way back to report to the war council. Ajax said to Agamemnon, "Achilles is still angry and wants nothing to do with you or your gifts."

The council fell silent; the outcome of the coming battle looked grim for the Greeks. Diomedes said, "Let Achilles leave. He hasn't been fighting for our cause anyway. I say we should eat and rest, for we will need our strength in the morning." All agreed, so they drank and went back to their respective huts to sleep and wait for the dawn.

Menelaus couldn't sleep. He was restless, he left his tent and walked on the beach among the ships. There he was met by Agamemnon, who also couldn't sleep with too many thoughts about the morning running through his head. The two leaders decided that they needed to do something. They woke the other members of the council, and then went to make sure the troops guarding the walls were awake and prepared against a night attack by the Trojans.

As Odysseus and Diomedes walked through camp, Odysseus spotted someone approaching from the enemy base. Odysseus whispered to Diomedes, "Someone is coming from the Trojan camp, either to strip the dead or to infiltrate our ranks." The two men lay down on the side of the path, among the corpses, and watched as a Trojan spy ran past them. Odysseus and Diomedes let him go for a while and then they gave chase. The spy saw them and first thought it was another Trojan coming to bring him back, but soon realized it was two Greeks on his tail. He tried to outrun them, but a spear whizzed past his ear. "Stop or die," Diomedes shouted.

The spy stopped running, and the two men captured him. He shook with fear. Odysseus said, "Who are you? Why are you here? Tell the truth or you will feel the wrath of my spear."

"My name is Dolon. Please don't kill me! I will tell the truth. Hector offered a bounty of gifts for information about your guards and whether you were preparing to set sail in the night."

Odysseus said, "Tell me about the Trojan camps. Where is Hector, where do they keep their horses, and where are their guards?"

"Hector stays in the main camp where the guards are alert, but the outlying camps don't have guards and the men are sleeping. Many horses are tied there. You can bind me as tightly as you wish and go to find out if what I say is true."

Diomedes replied, "Tie you up, so you can escape and spy on us again? No, you will die now!"

Dolon tried to speak, but Diomedes drew his sword, and with a single swing, cut through the man's neck. His head fell onto the dirt at his feet. Armed with new information, they crawled into an outlying Trojan camp. Diomedes crept down the line of sleeping warriors, stabbing them as he went, while Odysseus followed him and pulled the bodies out of the way. When they were done, they stole a dozen horses and retreated to camp. When they returned, there was great rejoicing. Their foray into the enemy's territory instilled much needed confidence into the Greek army.

Before dawn, the Greeks charged out on chariots from behind their walls, with the infantry close behind them. With their advantage of surprise the Greeks drove the Trojans all the way back to the walls of Troy. Just when victory seemed within their grasp, a spear passed through Agamemnon's arm and pierced his side. It was not a life-threatening wound, but he could no longer fight. Agamemnon fell back, but called to his men as he left, "It is now up to you to continue the fight. I am done for the day."

Hector seized the opportunity and rallied his troops. With Hector leading the way, the Trojans fought with more ferocity, energy, and purpose. They pushed the Greeks all the way across the plain, right up to their ramparts. Paris fought with the other archers, using the many mounds on the battlefield as cover. Like snipers, they fired their arrows and then ducked behind a mound for cover. From this vantage point, Paris sent an arrow through Diomedes' foot into the ground. Paris shouted, "My arrow has struck your foot, but I wish it had killed you."

"This is only a flesh wound! Come down here and fight me like a real man, with real weapons, instead of fighting like a woman from behind cover!"

Odysseus ran to aid Diomedes as he tore the arrow from his foot and provided cover as he fell back to the ships. Odysseus now stood alone and found himself surrounded by Trojans. Quickly, Ajax and Menelaus ran to his aid and helped fend off the attack. The Trojans kept up the pressure, and although the Greeks put up a spirited defense, they eventually gave way. Just before noon, the Trojans stormed through the trench and assaulted the Greek walls. Hector threw a huge anchor stone, which broke a gate and allowed the Trojans to pour through. Heated fighting broke out all along the beach and in front of the ships. Blood spilled onto the sand and ran into the sea; the waves broke with a crimson crest. Ajax was defending a ship against dozens of Trojans when his pike broke and he was forced to retreat. Hector threw torches on board and set the ship on fire.

Across the beach, Achilles watched as the smoke and flames rose into the sky. Patroclus pleaded with him. "Lord, I know your heart is hardened toward Agamemnon, but as you can see, the Greeks are overwhelmed and the Trojans burn our ships. If you do not wish to fight, allow me to wear your armor and lead our Myrmidons against the Trojans."

Achilles replied, "I said my heart would soften when Hector threatened to burn our ships, our only means of escape. Now I see the smoke rising from our camp. Go and put on my armor while I assemble our men, but heed what I say: do not chase the Trojans all the way to their walls. Stop when you have given the Greeks some breathing room, and let others lead the chase after the fleeing Trojans."

Patroclus put on Achilles' armor and Achilles assembled his men. The Myrmidons had been kept from battle, and were fresh and eager to join the fight. The Greeks and Trojans had been fighting all day and were nearing exhaustion. Patroclus and his assembled warriors marched along the beach, sweeping the Trojans in front of them. When the Greeks saw Achilles' armor, they thought he had joined the battle and fought with renewed energy. Soon, the Trojans fled across the plain toward the safety of their city walls. Hot on their heels, Patroclus killed as many Trojans as he could catch. The Trojans reached the gates of their city and had their backs to the walls when Patroclus was wounded in the back with a spear. He withdrew into the Greek ranks for protection, but seeing an opportunity, Hector fought his way to him. He speared

Patroclus in the belly and mortally wounded him. Patroclus was bent over with the spear in him when Hector stood above him and shouted, "Patroclus, you thought you would destroy our city and take our women as slaves, but I am here to protect them. I'm sure Achilles told you not to come back until you have killed me, but the vultures will have you instead!"

With his dying breath, Patroclus said, "If I fought twenty men like you one-on-one, I would have killed them all. Now your death is fast approaching at the hands of Achilles."

Hector pulled the spear from Patroclus' gut and pushed him over on his back into the dirt. Hector stripped Patroclus of Achilles' armor and wore it himself. The Trojans tried to drag Patroclus' body back to Troy, where they intended to display his head on a spike. Unwilling to allow them to desecrate Patroclus' body, the Greeks fought the Trojans over the corpse for the rest of the day. With Ajax's help, the Greeks eventually prevailed, and Menelaus carried the body back to the ships, with the Trojans on his heels all the way. Achilles saw the Greeks being pushed back to the ships, and feared that something was wrong. He went to the walls without his weapons and shouted encouragement to inspire the Greeks to stop the Trojan onslaught. The Greeks rallied and the Trojans retreated to their camps to regroup for the next day.

The Trojans met in an urgent assembly. Polydamas said, "My friends, we have fought all day and we have still not destroyed the Greek ships or their army. Now it appears that Achilles has ended his quarrel with Agamemnon and will enter the fight. He is too ambitious to fight only on the plain; he will attack the city. It is not safe for us out here. We must retreat to the safety of our walls and let Achilles attack us there."

Hector disagreed. "I will not go back to the city. We will make camp here, near the ships. In the morning, we will destroy the Greeks on the beaches. If Achilles joins the battle, it will be all the worse for him. I will not run, but I will fight him and see who the gods favor." The Trojans listened to Hector and made camp once again on the Trojan plain, just a stone's throw from the Greek ramparts.

In the Greek camp, the leaders gathered around Patroclus' body. Achilles was overcome with grief. With tears streaking his face, he said, "Dear friend, I will not hold your funeral rites until I bring the head of your killer, Hector, back to the ships." Achilles ordered his servants to boil water so he could clean the blood from the wounds of Patroclus' broken body. He covered it in soft linen and placed it on a brier to await the funeral pyre.

Agamemnon knew it was time to apologize to Achilles. He had to remain seated, due to his wound, but with great conviction, he said, "I have been blinded by my own selfishness and pride. I should not have taken the girl from you, and I swear I never took her to bed. Let me now grant you all the gifts and the girl I promised you just two days ago."

"The gods must have blinded both of us, for you would not have taken her from me without their will. Now is not the time to give gifts, but a time to fight," said Achilles.

Odysseus intervened and said, "Achilles, we are pleased that you are eager to fight, but we have been fighting all day. Let Agamemnon bring you his gifts, and then let your men eat, drink, and rest, for men can't fight without food to sustain them."

Achilles relented, and Agamemnon sent Odysseus to retrieve the gifts promised to Achilles. The gifts included seven tripods, twenty gleaming caldrons, twelve horses, seven women skilled in handiwork, twenty talents of gold, and of course, Achilles' love, Briseis. Achilles agreed to wait until morning to resume the fighting. He returned to his hut with his gifts and waited for the dawn.

Walking through the marketplace, Helen noticed an increasing number of refugees. Her heart went out to these people; she felt responsible for their suffering. She went to Priam and said, "Your Highness, there is much suffering in Troy. I feel I am the cause for much of this, and I would like to do something to help."

Priam responded, "My child, you are not responsible for the war. Is a leopard responsible for its spots? No, child, it is not your fault that you were born beautiful. Just as gold strikes a fever in men's minds, so does your beauty create desire in men's hearts."

"Thank you for the kind words, Your Highness."

"What is it you would like to do?"

"I see so many old and homeless refugees. I would like to distribute food and water to them. I have brought much treasure with me from Sparta. I could use some of it to pay for the supplies."

"That may be a dangerous thing for you to do here."

"Do you think these refugees care who gives them aid? Besides, your son has put guards around me to protect me from harm. These people need help and food. It wasn't their fault that war came to Troy."

"Go, then. I will give you the gold to pay for their food, and you may clear an area near the stables to distribute it. They can get their own water from the fountains and pools inside Troy."

Helen replied, "Thank you, Your Highness. You are truly a generous man."

She hurried back to her quarters and found her attendants. "We have been given permission to help the refugees." The three of them went to the stables and cleared out an area to distribute food. The people of Troy came by to stare at Helen, and some lent a hand. They were not accustomed to seeing royalty doing such work. When they saw Helen, a princess, giving out food to the poor, they began to wonder if their assessment of her as nothing more than a whore was premature. Many Trojans decided to withhold their opinion for the time being.

After Helen readied her area, she sent her attendants and slaves around the city to tell the homeless and the aged where they could find food. Many people took advantage of her generosity, and very few publicly blamed her for the war. A homeless old woman said, "I lost my family when Achilles ransacked our city. He took everything we had. I was spared because I am old, and there is no glory in killing me. I don't blame you for this war, Miss Helen. I blame Paris for not sending you back to your home and ending all the killing."

Helen didn't reply. She just smiled slightly and gave the woman a bowl of grain. She did this through most of the evening, and when she no longer had grain to distribute, she left and went to the walls. Helen looked out over the plain and watched a thousand fires burning. The plain looked like a reflection of the night sky in a clear calm lake; there seemed to be as many fires as stars in the sky. Gripped by sadness upon looking at all the fires, Helen turned to her attendants and said, "I fear for Menelaus and the rest of my friends when the dawn comes. I came here in hopes of sparing Greece the destruction of war, but now many of my friends lie dead on the plain. I have brought misery to countless families."

She looked at the Trojan camp and could smell the scent of meat and spices, but this time it was blended with the rancid smell of death. Neither side called a truce, so the dead lay roasting in the summer sun. In the places where the most fighting took place, they were piled in heaps of twisted agony, awaiting burial or the flames of the funeral pyres. Helen gazed on the scene below and tears welled up in her eyes. "I am so distraught. I feel horrible. My friends and fellow Spartans are dying in front of me, and on my account. Agamemnon and Menelaus would say it isn't my fault, but if I hadn't come here, many of these men would still be alive."

Harleopi tried to comfort Helen, "Please don't blame yourself, these men are here for their own honor, as well as yours."

"I feel like all of this is in vain. The Trojans appear to be on the verge of victory. I would have rather died fighting in my home of Sparta." Helen bowed her head and cried.

Aethra put her arm around Helen in a motherly embrace. "My dear, do not give up hope. Sometimes things are not as they appear."

Harleopi put her arm around Helen's other shoulder and said, "My Queen, I have been with you for a long time. I know you are strong, and must not give up hope. The Greeks still control the beach and haven't given up. We have many great warriors left. We haven't lost this war yet."

Helen replied, "This is such a nightmare. I long for the peace and beauty of Sparta. If only that weren't an impossible dream. I fear that even my death will not end this war."

"My Queen, please do not talk of your death. You are scaring me," begged Harleopi.

Helen looked at the battlefield, then longingly out across the sea, and wished it were all a bad dream. She felt the streak of a tear down her face, took a deep breath, and pushed back the emotion. It still wasn't the time. She still had to be strong until the Greeks won. The three women looked silently over the scene below them before returning to Helen's quarters.

Achilles donned his new armor, made by the god Hephaestus, as the sun chased the stars from the sky. He walked along the beach, exhorting his men to fight and readying his chariot for battle. With a war cry, Achilles mounted his chariot and led the Greeks to battle. He mowed down soldiers by the dozens as he burst through the Trojan lines. He seemed to be everywhere. The wheels of his chariot bounded over bodies and shields as he killed men from one end of the plain to the Scamander River on the other side. The Trojans fled for the safety of the city, and the Greeks killed all the stragglers they could find.

Without explanation, Hector lingered outside the Scaean Gates while others hurried past him seeking shelter. When Achilles saw Hector outside the gate, he dismounted and ran toward him, his armor glistening like fire. Priam and Hecuba pleaded with him to come inside and fight another day, but Hector shouted, "Let Achilles come! I am not afraid to fight him."

A crowd formed on the walls as the people called out to warn Hector. When Achilles came to within spear throwing distance, Hector turned and ran away, but Achilles gave chase. It looked like a hound chasing a rabbit as they ran three times around the walls of Troy. Achilles took the inside track so Hector couldn't get back into the city, but he was unable to close the gap between them. Unable to distance himself from his pursuer, Hector finally stopped running. Delirious from the effort, he believed that his brother, Deiphobus, was beside him, "Deiphobus, my brother! You have come to stand by my side. Together, we can defeat Achilles.

The two sweaty and blood splattered warriors faced each other. Achilles threw his spear at Hector, but missed. Hector threw his spear, and it bounced off the shield the gods made for Achilles. Hector felt defenseless. "Deiphobus, give me another spear."

But Deiphobus was not there. He was only a mirage. It was then Hector knew he had been fooled by the gods into thinking he had help against Achilles. Hector quietly said, "So, Athena, you have deceived me and led me to my fate."

With a loud war cry, Hector drew his sword and rushed at Achilles. Achilles' heart was filled with anger. He met Hector with all his savage power, and knowing the weak spot in his own armor, drove the spear through Hector's throat, but missed his vocal chords. "You killed Patroclus but forgot about me. Now I have laid you low!"

In a weak voice, Hector replied, "Don't let the dogs eat my flesh by the ships. Allow my parents and wife to give me a proper funeral pyre."

"Don't talk to me, dog! I wish I could carve you up myself. No man will stop the scavengers from eating your flesh."

"Your heart is made of stone, Achilles. Beware that the gods don't turn their back on you in my name."

Achilles pulled the spear from Hector's throat. "Now lie there, dead. I will meet my fate when the gods ordain it."

As Achilles stripped the armor from Hector and placed it in his chariot, the Greeks started to gather around to look at Hector's body. One soldier shouted, "Hector doesn't look so tough now," as he plunged his spear into his body. Helen winced as she watched the violence against the only member of the Trojan family who had been kind to her. Other Greeks joined in defiling Hector's corpse, until Achilles stopped them.

Achilles cut a hole in each of Hector's heels, threaded a rope through, and tied it to the back of his chariot. In a show of triumph, strength, and brutality, Achilles dragged Hector's body around the walls of Troy. It seemed as though the whole city watched the grisly sight from atop the walls, including the army, which had retreated inside. In shock and sorrow, Priam and Hecuba could only watch and wail loudly. Helen could no longer stand tosee the body of her protector being dragged through the dirt. She dropped her head and sobbed. Paris felt remorse and responsibility for his brother's death and vowed revenge. Many shouted curses and obscenities at Achilles. Achilles dragged Hector's body behind his chariot back to the Greek camp.

Inside Troy, Priam was overcome with grief as was the whole city. Citizens mourned the loss of their champion and best warrior. Priam was beside himself with thoughts of his son's body being dragged behind Achilles' chariot and eaten by dogs. He decided to retrieve Hector's body, so he boldly set out for the Greek camp.

Achilles prepared for Patroclus' funeral by building a huge funeral pyre. It was a wood pile one hundred feet wide, twenty feet high and Patroclus' body rested in the center. Horses, sheep, dogs, and twelve young Trojans whose throats were cut were thrown on the pyre with him as a sacrifice to the gods. Before he lit the fire, Achilles decided to hold games and competitions. Both armies were exhausted and overcome with grief, so they welcomed a break from battle. The Greek soldiers participated in chariot races, boxing, wrestling, and running. Achilles handed out the prizes to the winners. After the competition and as tears rolled down his face, Achilles lit the funeral pyre.

Priam walked into Achilles' hut unnoticed, as the warrior was eating. To Achilles' surprise, Priam took his hand and kissed it, then wrapped his arms around Achilles' knees. "Brave Achilles, please think of your father when you look at me. I am much like him, except he still has the hope of seeing his son again. I once had fifty sons, but I have watched as many of them have died in battle before my eyes. I came here because the bravest of them has met his fate at your hands. I beg you to return his body in exchange for a handsome ransom. I have done what no other man would do: I have kissed the hand of the man who killed my son."

Achilles' heart softened and he was moved by the King's words. He picked Priam up and said, "You are truly courageous to come here, pleading for your son's body. I could easily kill you as well."

"Death would be a blessing to end this suffering in my heart."

"Surely, the gods helped you to come here unseen by my guards. I will not go against what the gods ordain." Achilles decided to release Hector's body. He ordered a few of his slave women to boil some water, clean the body, and wrap it in linen. Then, he sent two attendants to gather the ransom Priam brought from his wagon. Achilles himself placed Hector's body in Priam's wagon. "You can look at his body when you get back to Troy. First, you must join me in a meal."

Priam was relieved by Achilles' gesture and he sat down to eat with him. Achilles and Priam agreed to twelve days of peace while the Trojans gave Hector his funeral rites. When Agamemnon heard of the truce, he was upset because Achilles was not in a position to negotiate with the enemy. Soon, however, Agamemnon realized it was a wise move. His army needed to rest, and he didn't want to start another argument and risk losing Achilles again.

It was dawn when Priam returned to Troy with his son's body. The sentries at the gate called out. "Priam returns with Hector's body!" The whole city came to life and rushed to the gates to see the body of their fallen hero. They could have gazed on him all day, but Priam said, "Let me take him into the palace and prepare him. Then, you can share your grief."

The following day, Hector's body was displayed on a marble bed in the palace. The first to speak was his wife, Andromache. "Hector, you have died too early, leaving me a widow and your young son fatherless. You fought to defend this city and its inhabitants, but I fear Troy may soon fall without you as its protector and leader. I will become a slave to some soldier in a foreign land, and your son may not survive. This city may fall because of revenge for some brother, father, or son you killed, for you killed many of our enemies. My grief is multiplied because I didn't have a chance to hear your last words to me."

As Andromache collapsed in her seat, Queen Hecuba rose. "Achilles has taken many of my sons and sold them in faraway lands as slaves. Yet you, who are dearest to me, he has killed with his bronze spear. My heart is torn with grief."

Although she was not Trojan, Helen was allowed to address the crowd. She was nervous, but she had an opportunity to honor Hector, a man she admired. She also had the chance to tell the Trojan people what it was like to be in her shoes while she was in Troy. "Hector, you were the dearest of my Trojan brothers. I wish I had died before I came here, so that you would still be alive. Never did you have an unkind word or a harsh remark for me. Whenever your brothers, sisters, or even your mother would say harsh things, you rebuked them with kind words and actions. Now, I stand here and grieve for you as much as for myself, for there is no one left in Troy who will be as kind or gentle to me as you were. They all turn their heads and shudder when they see me coming."

Helen took her place behind the rest of the family. The people wailed and lamented in grief. Priam ordered the soldiers to gather wood for eight consecutive days. They didn't need to worry about an ambush by the Greeks, for Achilles gave his word there would be no fighting until after the twelfth day. The Trojans built a huge funeral pyre outside the walls of Troy, placed Hector's body on top, and lit the fire.

CHAPTER SEVEN

DEATH OF ACHILLES

In Hector, Troy lost their best warrior, their ablest general, and their main source of inspiration. Priam knew the tide of battle had turned, especially since Achilles joined the fighting. However, the Trojans were made of more than just Hector. They still had a powerful army, and Aeneas was a skilled warrior and a capable leader. Troy received reinforcements and supplies on a regular basis from surrounding cities, and although the Greeks destroyed the cities immediately surrounding Troy, they didn't have the manpower to completely shut off every supply route.

As wine extinguished the last embers of Hectors funeral pyre, Priam sought direction and answers. The truce would be over in the morning, and he didn't have a plan of action. The funeral pyres on both sides of the plain had burned for four consecutive days to deal with the massive casualties. Priam knew the citizens of Troy were disheartened, his soldiers were disheartened, and the leaders of Priam's war council were disheartened. All across the city, women wore black, and the whole population was in mourning. He needed to do something to rally everyone.

When the atmosphere in Troy couldn't get any bleaker, Penthesilea, the Queen of the Amazons, arrived with a dozen of her warriors. When she reached the Scaean Gate, the guards blew the trumpets to announce her arrival. The whole city came out to catch a glimpse of the legendary female warriors they had heard so much about.

The Amazons were a war-like race of women from the Thermodon River valley, to the north of Troy. Penthesilea came to Troy's aid because she recently killed her sister, Hippolyte, in a hunting accident and was haunted by her sister's memory. Since she no longer cared for her own life, Penthesilea intended to purify herself by dying gloriously in battle.

Penthesilea and her warriors rode into Troy on horseback. Trojan escorts led them directly to the palace, where Priam greeted them warmly. The Amazon women were impressive; they were tall, statuesque, and muscular, walked with purpose, and exuded confidence. Priam said, "You are the answer to our prayers. We are overjoyed to see you."

"We have heard of your loss, and are deeply saddened over the death of brave Hector."

"Thank you, but let's not talk of that now. Let us welcome you to Troy with a great feast."

The horses were taken to the stables, washed and fed, and the women were led to the great hall were a huge feast was prepared for them. With Penthesilea's arrival, the Trojans were hopeful for an end to the war, for they had heard many stories about her prowess in battle.

Penthesilea enjoyed herself at the celebration, but was eager to attend to business. "We could see the smoke rising from the funeral pyres miles away. At first, we thought we were too late, that you had already burned the Greek ships."

"There have been many battles and countless are dead. My son, Hector, had the Greeks with their backs to the sea and even burned some of their ships, but he sadly met his fate at the hand of mighty Achilles."

"Tomorrow, you will see the Greek ships burning in the bay, and I will slay Achilles myself."

There was a slight gasp from those in attendance, followed by cheers. Hector's widow, Andromache, was skeptical. "What makes you think you can kill Achilles, when Hector, who was a much greater warrior than you, failed to do so?"

"I am the daughter of the war god, Ares. Achilles is no match for me." Again, the crowd cheered and confidence was restored among the Trojans. That evening, Penthesilea and her bodyguards slept on couches in the great hall to wait for morning.

After the feast, Helen returned to her quarters and confided in Aethra. "I have met the Amazon Queen and her warriors. They are an impressive group. They are confident and fearsome, and look as formidable as any of the men on the battlefield."

Aethra replied, "My son fought against them years ago, and he found them to be a difficult foe and very much the equal of the strongest men."

"I remember when Menelaus and Agamemnon fought against them at Phrygia. Many men were lost. Now I hear they plan to attack in the morning, and I can't get a message to Menelaus in time to help."

"There are only twelve of them. How much harm can they do?" asked Aethra.

"It is not their numbers I fear, it is the confidence they instill in others that will do the most harm. Now, it is time to sleep. I want to be up before dawn to walk along the wall."

During the truce, the Greeks reinforced their battlements, built lookout towers, rebuilt the wall, and replaced the spikes in the trench. They, too, received supplies from other countries; they bought wine from Thrace and livestock from the surrounding islands. Behind their walls, they gradually built a small town with huts and pens for sheep, cattle, and horses. The one commodity they weren't able to replenish was men.

Agamemnon met with his war council to discuss his battle strategy. "We have had a chance to repair our defenses and heal our wounds. Like me, many of you have sustained some type of injury in the last battle. Menelaus was wounded in the upper leg, Odysseus and I in the hip, Diomedes in the foot, but now we are ready to start a new campaign. Recently, we have been on the defensive, but it's time to take the war back to the Trojans. They are leaderless, and I am certain that they will fight a defensive war from this point on. We should build the ladders once more and storm the city walls, concentrating the bulk of our efforts on the front gates."

The council agreed. Nestor said, "The Trojans are disheartened and weak after Hector's death. Now is the time to finish them."

The next morning, Penthesilea awoke early and donned her armor. She grabbed two spears, a sword, and slung her bow over her back, then went to join her warriors. The Amazons wanted to strike the Greeks before they knew what was coming. The Trojans rallied behind their new leader and came pouring out of the Scaean Gates like a torrent just as the sky was turning blue. Wearing her red dress, Helen watched the last of the infantry leaving Troy to start the day's battle. She hurried to the walls hoping to warn the Greeks. She got there just in time to see Menelaus turn his chariot and ride back, as he saw the flood of warriors pouring out of the city. She was too late. Helen watched as Penthesilea and her warriors led a charge across the plain. The dust from their horses rose like a storm cloud and covered the Trojan chariots and infantry charging behind.

The Greeks had been planning an attack of their own, so the approaching army took them by surprise. A Greek soldier shouted, "Who is this leading the Trojans, like Hector himself?"

Agamemnon knew he had to change tactics. "Drop the ladders and form your ranks!" The Greeks quickly moved into position in front of the trenches, and prepared to meet the onrushing Trojans. With desperation and anger, Agamemnon cried, "Charge!" and the two lines moved toward each other like great waves. The clash of armor was deafening as it echoed off the walls of Troy. Many warriors fell in the initial assault, and Penthesilea mowed down Greeks like a sickle mows down wheat. Her horse trampled those in front of her, and her spear pierced flesh to the left and right. In mere minutes, the plains ran red with blood, and the horses and chariots ran over the dead and dying.

Although a few of her bodyguards died during the attack, Penthesilea kept the pressure on and forced the Greeks to retreat. She shouted, "Where are Ajax and Achilles? They are supposed to be the best of the Greeks. Are they afraid of my spear?"

Helen and the warriors' families gathered on the walls and watched as the Amazons and Trojans pushed the Greeks back over their wall and threatened to burn their ships. Ajax and Achilles were mourning at Patroclus' burial mound when they heard the sounds of battle get closer to the ships. Ajax said, "It sounds as though the Trojans have started to rout the Greeks once again. We must arm ourselves for battle before it is too late."

They hastily strapped on their armor and joined the fight. Ajax slew two Amazons with his sword, beheading one unfortunate warrior as she rode by so cleanly that the headless body continued to ride for a few more yards before falling to the ground. Achilles took down four others with his spear and sword and moved through the ranks like a wild animal. When Penthesilea saw them, she threw her spear at Ajax and shouted, "I am the daughter of Ares!"

Ajax deflected the spear, laughed, and moved on to fight the Trojans. Penthesilea threw her other spear at Achilles, which just bounced off his shield. She became so enraged that she attacked Achilles with her sword. He countered with his spear and drove it into the right side of her chest. Wounded, Penthesilea slumped over her horse's neck. Achilles withdrew the spear, then plunged it through the horse's chest and into her stomach. Penthesilea and her horse fell as one, skewered on a single spear. Achilles pulled the spear from horse and rider, stood over the body, and removed her helmet. He admired her beauty and found himself very attracted to her. He felt angry that a woman would have the nerve to challenge him on the battlefield, but as he stared at her peaceful face, his contempt waned. Feeling a compassion for his foe as he had never felt before, he knelt next to her body and embraced her for a few long moments before letting her lie on the ground.

When Penthesilea and the rest of the Amazons were dead, the Trojans turned and fled back to the safety of the walled city. The crowd on the wall dispersed as the archers took up their positions to cover the returning soldiers. The Greeks did not give chase. Instead, they gathered around the bodies of Penthesilea and the fallen Amazons, and admired their skill and courage in battle. Thersites, considered the ugliest of the Greeks, said, "Look at Achilles, a woman chaser who forgets all about glory in battle when he sees a pretty face. Aren't we here because of a woman chaser? Achilles should be ashamed. "Filled with rage at the accusation, Achilles walked over and punched Thersites in the face so hard that the soldier's teeth flew out of his mouth. Thersites fell dead in the dust. When Achilles checked him, he realized he had crushed the man's skull.

"As a show of respect, do not strip the Amazons of their armor!" Agamemnon ordered. Instead, the Greeks placed the women's bodies on a brier and sent it to Troy for funeral rites. The Trojans then burned Penthesilea and her bodyguards on a funeral pyre outside the city walls. Later that evening, the Greek council convened to decide Achilles' punishment for killing another Greek. After a private discussion with the other council members, Agamemnon said, "Achilles, we understand that emotions run high in the heat of battle. Still, your attack was intentional. You clearly knew you were hitting a fellow Greek, and perhaps you didn't aim to kill him, but nonetheless, that was the result. What do you have to say?"

"It is true I did not mean to kill Thersites. I ask forgiveness from his friends and family. The council is wise, and I will abide by their decision."

"It is the decision of this council that you will leave for the island of Lesbos in the morning and perform purification rites. When the rites are complete, you may return." Achilles agreed to their terms and left the assembly. Agamemnon continued the meeting of his war council. "Once again, we were driven back to our walls. The Trojans have been the aggressors for the past few weeks, and I'm unsure how much more we can withstand. We need to repair the ramparts and take stock of our army."

Odysseus replied, "Agamemnon, we are still strong and have the will to continue the fight."

"Our men are focused and determined. They are hardened by the fighting and eager to finish Troy," said Nestor.

Menelaus agreed. "The Trojans have been considerably weakened by Hector's death and our victories on the battlefield. They cannot last much longer." The council agreed with Menelaus' assessment.

Agamemnon remained unconvinced. "We will maintain our defensive position until Achilles returns and we have a better battle plan. Tomorrow, I will send out small scouting parties to reassess the weaknesses of the Trojan defenses, cracks in the wall, ideal times to strike, and methods of attack. I am open to all suggestions. For now, go back to your men, get a good night's rest, and come up with some new ideas."

Menelaus sighed. They could certainly use new ideas. After all, the plan was not working, so many died for this war on each side. He looked longingly at the wall that separated himself from his love. A lonesome pain crept up inside him and he shuddered. He couldn't believe he'd honestly thought it would be quick. Instead, years had passed that he'd never get back with his wife or his daughter.

Behind the walls of Troy that night, Priam also addressed his war council. "The Amazons have died a heroic death, but they demonstrated that the will of the Trojan people is still strong. We cannot give up hope. When the Greeks first attacked our walls, I sent a message to my nephew asking for his help. Today I received word that he will arrive soon with an entire army. We can still win this war."

His optimism was not returned. Antenor pleaded, "Priam, we are weary of war. Many of our sons, brothers, fathers, and husbands have died. Haven't we paid enough to keep the Spartan Queen here? Now another army comes to our aid, and many more will die. Let us send her back to her home with her treasure."

Deiphobus said, "I say we keep the woman. Our men will have died in vain if we send her back now. I believe the Greeks will be satisfied with nothing less than the total destruction of Troy."

Priam agreed with his son. "The Greeks have come to our land, to our home, to wage war. We will not submit to them or anyone else who thinks they can come here and take what they want. No, Troy will not back down!" Priam thrust his sword into the air, eliciting a cheer from his council.

Two days later, a Greek scouting party came rushing back across the plain. As the chariots sped past, flocks of vultures rose from the corpses, and packs of dogs barked and growled at the disturbance of their feast. The men repairing the ramparts stopped their work to watch as the charioteers made their way immediately to Agamemnon's hut. The first charioteer said, "There is a large army just to the east. They will be here within the hour."

Agamemnon asked, "Whose army is it?"

"The army belongs to a man from Ethiopia named Memnon. We couldn't begin to count how many men he brought with him."

Agamemnon's gaze drifted far away. "Go to all the camps and tell our leaders to have their men form ranks on the walls and prepare for an attack."

The call went out and the entire Greek army took defensive positions on the ramparts. They watched in awe as the huge Ethiopian army made its way into and around Troy. It was so large that the colossal city of Troy could not contain it.

The Trojan people welcomed Memnon and his army with cheers and shouts. Some people hung banners from their windows and others shouted from rooftops. Priam and Hecuba met Memnon on the stairs to the palace. King Priam was overjoyed to see his nephew. Memnon was a large, thickly muscled man of imposing stature. His skin was the color of night because he was from Susa, a land to the east where the sun was extremely bright and hot all year long. Priam greeted him with an enthusiastic hug. "Welcome, Memnon! I am elated that you have come."

Memnon said, "Your Highness, it is with great pleasure that I have come to your aid. Queen Hecuba, you are as lovely as I have been told."

Hecuba smiled. "Thank you, you are so kind. I have been told of your charm."

Priam introduced the rest of the royal family, and when he introduced Helen, Memnon said, "You must be the woman they are all talking about. Your beauty is capable of stealing a man's soul. It is as if you are a living jewel." Helen bowed in appreciation as was custom. Priam escorted Memnon to the top of the stairs, and looked out over the crowd of waiting Trojans. With the polished shields of Memnon's men reflecting the light of the sun onto them, the two leaders thrust their swords into the air and shouted, "For Troy!" The crowd went wild. Then they walked back into the palace to prepare for the feast.

The celebration was just what the Trojan people needed to boost their confidence after their recent losses. At the feast, Memnon told Priam of his journey to Troy. "King Priam, I have traveled a great distance, I have been in many battles, seen many lands, and defeated all the armies in my way."

Priam was impressed with Memnon. "Your arrival is like a ray of sunshine breaking through the clouds." He lifted a golden chalice filled with wine and said, "I honor you with this wine and wish you glory and honor when you do battle tomorrow."

Memnon took the chalice in his hands. "Thank you for your blessing, but I will not make any promises about the battle to come. A man's worth is not judged by words or promises, but by his actions, which you will witness for yourself." Memnon took a drink from the chalice and handed it back to Priam. "Now, I must excuse myself. To drink the whole night without rest would dull my fighting spirit." He left the feast to prepare for the coming battle. Priam's heart lifted, and he beamed with confidence that the answer to his prayers had arrived.

Agamemnon was concerned about the gigantic army camped in and around the city of Troy. When everyone was in attendance at the council meeting, he said, "We are faced with a new enemy. You have all watched the army arrive, so you know the size of the problem we face. We have been fighting for many years, and our forces are tired and dwindling in number. Meanwhile, our opponents have just received thousands of fresh troops."

Always a hawk for war, Diomedes said, "We have all seen the fresh troops, but we haven't seen them fight. We have endured and overcome many obstacles and defeated great warriors. We can overcome this as well. There is not a man here who would turn away from battle. Let the Ethiopians regret the day they joined this war."

Nestor, the wise elder, agreed. "I have heard of the Ethiopians. They are good fighters, but they are not better than we are."

Menelaus' faith was not shaken. "I know I speak for Sparta and the rest of the Greeks when I say that we fear no one." His confidence drew a rousing cheer.

As the cheer inside the hut died, the war council could hear another cheer rising outside and getting closer. To their delight, Achilles came through the door, looking fresh and rejuvenated. "I have completed the purification rites as proposed by the council. I am here to fulfill my duty to my fellow warriors and countrymen."

Everyone he passed welcomed him back with cheers and slaps on the back. Clearly relieved to have Achilles back, Agamemnon said, "Brave Achilles, welcome back! You are just in time. The Trojans have just received thousands of reinforcements and we are trying to devise our battle plan." When the council members were seated, Agamemnon said, "I propose that we take the battle to them. We must continue to be aggressive. We have been fighting within a spear's throw of our ships, but it's time for us to take the initiative. I'm sure they will expect us to hide behind our walls."

Some of the leaders were skeptical of this tactic. Odysseus asked, "Do you think it is wise to expose our army in the face of such overwhelming numbers?"

Agamemnon replied, "The enemy will not anticipate it. If we are overwhelmed, we can always withdraw to our walls. However, if we start fighting from our walls, there is nowhere to fall back to but the sea. Ajax and Achilles, I want you both to continue to be aggressive, but be cautious with the men in your flanks. Because of their large numbers, the enemy may split their forces, try to lure us into thinking they are retreating, and then swing a force in behind us. Menelaus, Nestor, and the rest of the army will join me in front of our ramparts. We will attack, and then fall back to the protection of our walls if necessary."

The council agreed to put the plan into effect the next morning. When the meeting was adjourned, Ajax and Achilles went to get their men into position for the coming battle. Menelaus sat at the edge of the plain to study the Ethiopians' camp, and was in awe of what he saw. The campsite took up a third of the plain and surrounded Troy. Hundreds of fires made Troy look like a moon in the middle of a starry night. He heard the faint sound of music and celebration.

Menelaus thought, "I don't know if Agamemnon's plan will work. There are so many Ethiopians, and we have been fighting for so long and are very tired." He looked over his shoulder at the Greek camp. "We have come so far and many have died. We can't turn back now. All we can do is fight with every ounce of courage we can muster." Menelaus believed that the coming battle would be the key in deciding the war.

The next morning, Memnon put on his armor and a rousing cheer greeted him as he emerged from the palace. So many soldiers were inside Troy, it was hard to move through the streets. The people waved banners and cheered for their heroes as Memnon boarded his chariot and led his men out of the city. His legions of soldiers were so massive that it looked as though a parade followed him out of Troy. Aeneas, who was now the greatest Trojan warrior, joined Memnon on his march and led the Trojans to fight alongside Memnon's company in an attempt to overwhelm the Greeks. Outside the walls, the combined army moved forward like a flooding river, kicking up huge clouds of dust that enveloped the whole plain.

The Greek army watched with dread. Their foe spread in front of their walls like a bronze curtain. Agamemnon wasted no time; he didn't want to fight by his ships, so he attacked immediately. The Greek army let out a roar as the men moved in unison, the sun glistening off their polished shields and armor. The two armies met with a thunderous clash. The Greeks fought bravely for a few minutes before the sheer weight of numbers started to weigh against them. Agamemnon felt his line beginning to break, so he shouted, "Back to the ships!"

The Greeks immediately turned to retreat, and Memnon sensing his opportunity shouted. "The cowardly Greeks are running like women! After them! Destroy their walls and burn their ships." The Greeks reformed ranks at the edge of their walls, as hidden archers rained arrows down on the pursuing Trojans. Achilles and his men were holding solid on the right flank, while Ajax and his men held firm on the left flank. In the center of the action, Memnon led the Trojan attack like a spearhead, cutting his way through the Greeks, killing and wounding dozens of men.

Nestor saw Memnon effortlessly slaughtering Greeks. "I must stop him!" he thought. He turned his chariot to confront Memnon, but Paris popped up from behind a mound and fired an arrow toward Nestor. The arrow struck one of his horses in the head, killing it instantly. Nestor dismounted his chariot to cut the dead horse free, but Memnon spotted him and charged.

Nestor's son, Antilochus, rushed to his father's aid. "Father, I'm coming!" He hurled his spear at Memnon, but Memnon dodged the spear and continued his attack.

Antilochus shouted, "This will stop you!" He picked up a huge stone and threw it at him, but it clanged off Memnon's armor and didn't slow him down.

Memnon laughed. "It takes more than stones to stop me." He drove his spear through Antilochus' breastplate, killing him instantly. Memnon stood astride the body and started stripping the armor from Antilochus.

Horrified, Nestor shouted, "Memnon, you have slain my son. Now see if you can handle the spear of a more experienced warrior!"

Nestor approached Memnon with fury in his eyes, but as he got closer, Memnon could see he was an older man. "I am not without honor. You are an old man, and I cannot fight with you. Leave now; because I am the better warrior. What purpose would it serve for you to die by your son?"

"How dare you insult me in this way? If I were a younger man, I would have killed you by now." Memnon paid him no mind and continued to strip the armor from Antilochus.

The other Greek soldiers were afraid to confront Memnon. Nestor climbed into his chariot and rode away with desperation and tears in his eyes, as he sought out Achilles. "Achilles, Memnon has slain Antilochus and stripped him of his armor. In life, he was your friend. Now that he is dead, will you help me recover his body?"

Achilles looked across the battlefield and could see Memnon creating a pile of dead Greeks. He left his own mound of dead Trojans and made his way over to Memnon. When Memnon saw Achilles coming, he picked up a huge stone and threw it at him. Achilles deflected the stone with his shield and advanced with his spear ready. He wounded Memnon's right shoulder, but Memnon retaliated and cut Achilles' left arm with his sword. "Ha, this is the day you will die! You have killed many Trojans, but now you meet a better man!" shouted Memnon.

"You don't know who you're fighting. Enough with the words— our swords will decide who lives or dies!" Their swords flashed like lighting, and the sound of them hitting shields boomed like thunder. Like two horn-locked bulls, they kicked up the dust beneath their feet as they stepped over the heaps of dead warriors. Both armies stopped to watch the two giants do battle. The sweat and drying blood of their victims mingled on their bodies as the fight grew more intense. Each searched for an opening in the other's defenses. In an instant, Achilles plunged his sword beneath Memnon's breastplate. He stiffened, and then slumped over to reveal that the blade had gone clean through his body. Achilles stood him up, pulled the blade from his body and pushed Memnon to the ground in a thunderous clang of armor. Achilles stepped over the corpse and started to advance on the rest of the Ethiopians, while Achilles' men stripped the dead man of his armor. Having seen their king killed, the Ethiopians fled as quickly as a flock of birds scared out of the brush.

The Trojans and the Greeks stood stunned. They had never seen an army disappear so hastily. Finally, the Trojans fled back to their walls, and the Greeks were left standing alone on the battlefield. Their cheers of joy were tempered with the cries of anguish for the death of Antilochus and many others. Antilochus' body was taken back to the ships, and that evening, it was placed on a funeral pyre and turned to ashes.

Inside the great city, Priam and all the Trojan people were distraught. Priam gathered his war council. "We have watched great warriors fall time after time at the hands of Achilles. There seems to be no way of stopping him. I fear we are facing the destruction of Troy."

Antenor said, "Once again, I call on you and Paris to return Helen and all of her treasure, plus some of our own, to save our city from certain annihilation."

"I will not give into their demands. There must be another way."

Antenor only shook his head. "All of this death because of a woman."

There was a long silence in the council chambers as the members searched for an answer. Finally, Priam spoke. "If the love of a woman started this war, maybe the love of a woman can end it. Achilles sat out of many battles because of Briseis. Perhaps we can make a deal. I have information that Achilles is quite taken with one of my daughters. I will offer him my daughter Polyxena's hand in marriage in exchange for peace."

Antenor replied, "But it is not Achilles who leads the Greeks. It is Agamemnon."

"Yes, but Achilles holds a great deal of influence in that army. Maybe he can convince Agamemnon to go along with the pact."

"If it will bring peace and save Troy, I have no argument with that," said Antenor, and the rest of the council members agreed.

Priam went to Polyxena's quarters and hugged his daughter. "Hello, dear one." He turned his back and stared out the window. "The war goes badly. Many brave men have died, and I fear Troy may not stand much longer."

"You didn't come here to tell me that."

"You may be our last chance to save Troy."

"Me? How?"

"You can rescue our great city by marrying Achilles."

Polyxena turned from her father and remained quiet for a long time. Finally, she said, "You want me to marry the man who has killed so many members of our family and our people, the man who murdered my brother and dragged him around the city walls?"

Priam put his hands on her shoulders. "I know what he has done, and I know what I ask of you. I have met Achilles, and he is a man of honor."

"Do you honestly believe that if I marry him, we can have peace?"

"I wouldn't ask such a thing of you if there were any other way."

Polyxena turned to her father with doubt in her eyes, but said, "Yes, father if you believe this, I will do it."

Priam hugged her tightly as his confidence and optimism began to return. "I will send word to Achilles immediately."

The next day, the Greeks were regrouping after the death of Antilochus and the surprising disappearance of the Ethiopians. The archers on the watchtower saw a lone chariot approaching. As it neared the walls, the charioteers shouted, "Don't shoot! We come with a message for Achilles from King Priam." The guards blindfolded the messenger and led him to Achilles' hut.

Achilles said, "What do you have for me?"

The messenger said, "Lord, please have mercy on me. I am only the messenger. I do not know what the message bears."

"You have come at a bad time. We are in mourning over the death of my friend. Your fate will be decided by what the message contains."

The messenger's hands shook as he handed the note to Achilles.

Noble Achilles, whose glory is above all the Greeks,

I have a proposal for you. I offer you the hand of my beautiful daughter, Polyxena, in exchange for your help in negotiating a plan of peace and a withdrawal of all forces. I propose that you meet with Polyxena at the Temple of Apollo tomorrow at noon, just inside the walls of Troy. Come in peace and I give you my word that you will not be harmed.

Achilles laughed. "Tell King Priam that I respect and honor him. I will go to the Temple to meet with his daughter, and decide if I want her hand in marriage. You may return, with my answer."

The messenger was blindfolded once again, led to the other side of the walls, and released. Achilles met with Agamemnon and the other Greek leaders, to discuss the note and their options. Agamemnon looked at the message and said, "Priam's plan is to split the loyalty of our army."

Achilles replied, "Yes, I agree. I can assure you I did not encourage this plan. I came here immediately to show that I am not trying to subvert your authority."

"Priam baits a trap for you with a beautiful woman," said Menelaus.

Achilles said, "I thought that as well, but I have met this man, and I believe his request is sincere."

"I am still concerned that it may be a trap. You must not go alone; I will go with you," offered Ajax.

"Agreed, I will take Ajax with me, but not because I fear any Trojan trap."

Agamemnon said, "Regarding a plan of peace, I am still the leader of this army. There will be no peace until Helen and all her treasure is returned, along with compensation for our trouble."

"I will give Priam your message," said Achilles.

Ajax, Odysseus, Menelaus, and Diomedes all volunteered to go with Achilles into Troy, but Agamemnon decided that he did not want so many of his leaders in one place. He asked Diomedes to remain in camp.

That night, Paris went to Polyxena's chambers to discuss her agreement to marry Achilles. He hugged her and said, "Dear sister, I have just talked to Priam. I hear Achilles is coming to the Temple of Apollo, and you are willing to marry him. Is this true?"

"Yes, it is true."

"How can you marry the man that killed Hector and so many of our people?"

"You married the woman who started this war. Father believes that our marriage may lead to an end of the war."

Paris was unable to control his anger. "I have watched this man slaughter my friends and family. I saw him mock all of Troy by dragging Hector's body around the city behind his chariot! I have a better way to end this war. When Achilles comes to the temple, we will ambush him. He will not leave Troy alive!"

Polyxena protested. "Father has given his word…"

"Priam really wants Achilles dead, but he doesn't know how to do it. This is our chance. Don't you see? Without Achilles, the Greeks have no chance of victory. If we kill him, the detestable Greeks will go home, no more Trojans will die, and we will have won!"

Polyxena said, "That sounds wonderful, but how do you plan to kill Achilles? No one else has been able to."

"When he enters the Temple, you will be waiting for him at the altar. I will hide behind a statue of Apollo at the rear of the Temple, and when he goes to you, I will shoot him with an arrow dipped in aconite. The poison is fast acting, and he will be dead before he can walk out the door."

Polyxena thought carefully about her role in Achilles' murder. "I will help you with your plan and I will not tell anyone about it, but I want my involvement kept between us."

Paris hugged his sister and said, "This will be our secret. Thank you, dear sister. You may have just saved Troy."

At noon the following day, four chariots carrying the Greek leaders approached the walls of Troy. The Scaean Gates opened slowly, and the four chariots stopped just outside the wall. The drivers waited by the gate as the Greek leaders entered the city. Fully armed with spears, swords, and shields, they were met by an armed guard who escorted them through the streets to the temple of Apollo.

Word quickly spread that Achilles was in Troy, and the people came pouring out of their homes and shops to see him. At first, they just whispered, but when someone yelled, "Murderer!" they all started shouting insults at him. "Butcher! Monster!" The Trojan people pressed against the guards to get closer.

The men walked up the stairs, and into the Temple. Standing at the altar, in a beautiful white gown and a small golden tiara was Polyxena. Aside from the Trojan escorts, she appeared to be the only person in the building. Menelaus waited by the door as the others approached the princess.

Struck by her beauty, Achilles said, "You are as exquisite as I have heard."

"Thank you, brave Achilles. You are as handsome as you are courageous."

Paris crept out from behind a curtain and drew his bow. Just as he was about to let the arrow fly, Menelaus shouted, "Archer!" Surprised by the shout, Paris lost his aim. The arrow fell far short of Achilles, but it must have been guided by a god, because it skipped across the marble floor like a flat rock on water and struck him in the heel.

Achilles screamed in pain and feel down on one knee. He grabbed the arrow and snapped it off at the head. "Who is the coward that attacks me from behind? Come forward and fight me like a man!" Achilles got to his feet and started toward Paris, but the poison was taking effect. He stumbled after only a few steps, and Ajax caught him.

Paris and Polyxena ran out of the back door of the Temple as soldiers filed in. The soldiers surrounded the Greeks, but stayed just out of reach. Achilles was weak, but like a wounded animal, he was still very dangerous. He lashed out with his spear and killed three Trojans, before he succumbed to the poison. The soldiers wanted to show Achilles' body the same disrespect that he had shown Hector. They jumped on him and tried to drag him away, but Ajax and Odysseus stayed steady and fought them off. Ajax picked up Achilles' body and draped it over one shoulder. As Odysseus fought back the Trojans, the two men ran out of the Temple. The crowd moved out of their way, and the chariots came to pick them up. The fighting was brutal. Menelaus and Odysseus held off the Trojans as Ajax loaded Achilles' body onto the chariot. The Trojans tried to surround them, but the men courageously fought their way out of Troy.

The Trojan people celebrated. They had killed Achilles! Surely, the Greeks would give up and go home. The people wanted to know who was able to end Achilles' reign of terror against the Trojans. Who was the hero? When they found out it was Paris, and that he had attacked Achilles from behind, their enthusiasm was tempered with a degree of apprehension. The Trojan people knew the Greeks would seek revenge for such a cowardly attack. Immediately after the attack, Paris raced to meet with Priam. "Father, I have killed Achilles!"

"You did what? He came here in peace!"

"He's dead. I got revenge for all of us, especially Hector!"

"Don't you see? I gave him my word that no harm would come to him if he came here!"

"What difference does that make? He is dead, and there is no Greek strong enough for us to fear now. They will have to give up and go home."

"The Greeks entered our city under a truce. I gave my word, and now it was broken. I fear they will be more determined than ever before."

"I don't care what you fear. The Greeks have lost their best warrior, and I killed him!" Annoyed by his father's reaction, Paris stormed out the door and headed for Helen's chambers. He found her weaving a large purple tapestry embroidered with battle scenes. Paris said, "I suppose you've heard?"

Helen replied sarcastically, "I heard that Achilles came here under the guise of a truce and was wounded from behind by a coward. I assumed it was you."

"It *was* me, and I am no coward! Achilles is dead. I killed him!"

"In Sparta, when a man attacks another man from behind, he is considered a coward."

"You will give me the respect I deserve. I will kill more leaders, and Menelaus will be next!" Paris slammed the door as he left. Helen just looked at the door, shook her head, and went back to her weaving.

The Greeks were furious when Ajax returned with Achilles' body. The entire Greek army gathered around the three men as they unloaded his body and told the tale of his death. Agamemnon said, "I knew he shouldn't have trusted Priam."

Menelaus replied, "It was that coward, Paris. He set a trap and shot him from behind a curtain."

Covered in blood from the fight, Ajax shouted, "The Trojans have shown once again that they have no honor. We will teach them with the end of our spears!"

The army cheered and shouted, "Revenge!"

Able to see the bigger picture, Agamemnon stepped forward. "The time for revenge is near. First, we must honor the great warrior and our brother, Achilles."

The Greeks sent men to gather wood for Achilles' funeral pyre. They built a pyre one hundred feet wide, one hundred feet long, and fifty feet high, placed Achilles body on top, and lit the fire. When the fire died down, they gathered his ashes and put them in an urn, then placed it next to Patroclus' remains. The two old friends were buried together.

After the funeral, Ajax approached Agamemnon and Menelaus. "I would like to be awarded Achilles' armor.

Odysseus also approached them and said, "I believe I should be awarded the armor."

Agamemnon gathered his senior leaders to help decide who should get the armor. "Tell us why you think you deserve to be given Achilles' armor."

Ajax said, "Achilles was my cousin. I carried his body from the Temple while the Trojans attacked me."

It was Odysseus' turn to state his case. "I fought off the Trojans by myself as Ajax carried the body from the Temple. Even a woman can carry a body after it is on her shoulder."

The leaders discussed the issue amongst themselves and were unable to come to a decision. Agamemnon said, "Both are deserving of the armor, and because we honor and respect both of you, we cannot decide. We will ask someone who doesn't know either of you who is the better warrior."

The Greeks called upon a dozen Trojan prisoners and told them to decide who should get the armor. The prisoners heard both arguments and decided that Odysseus was the better warrior, Ajax was furious. He drank heavily that night, and after he was thoroughly drunk, he decided he would kill Agamemnon and Menelaus. Fortunately for them, Ajax thought he was attacking the two leaders, but he actually slew two large rams. When he awoke and saw the slaughtered livestock, he was embarrassed and ashamed. He could not face his men after what he had done, so he took the sword he won from Hector, propped it up, and fell on it. When Odysseus heard of Ajax's death, he said, "If I knew the armor meant that much to him, I would have let him have it."

CHAPTER EIGHT

PARIS AND THE PALLADIUM

The battles continued to be as ferocious as any so far in the war. Furious about Achilles' murder, the Greeks made a push to end the war. With Achilles gone, the Trojans thought they had a great chance for victory. Chariots from both sides, with their wheels covered in blood and gore, bounced over the corpses that piled up among the ranks of the men. Emboldened by his victory over Achilles, Paris went to Priam and said, "I want a chance to prove that I am a warrior. Let me lead an attack."

Paris rode his chariot in front of the Trojan lines, firing arrows as he sped back and forth. The battle was nearing a stalemate as the armies tired and the fighting diminished. Philoctetes fired an arrow at Paris that wounded his left hand, but Paris fought on. Philoctetes' next arrow was poisoned, and hit Paris' hip, near the groin. He cried out in pain and fled back to the safety of Troy.

Paris sought medical aid in Troy, but none of the available salves or treatments were of any use to him. The slow acting poison was taking its toll. Paris limped to Helen's chambers. "You have never given me any respect. Today, I have led the attack like a great warrior."

Helen looked at Paris and saw the blood running down his leg. "Leading an attack does not make you brave. Any crazed fool can do that. One-on-one combat with an enemy, looking him square in the eye—that is what makes for a brave warrior."

Rebuffed again, Paris replied, "My days may be numbered, but you will never leave Troy."

Paris limped out the door. He was in extreme pain, but remembered there was still one person who could help him. When Paris was a young man living on Mount Ida, he married a woman skilled in the art of medicine and healing named Oenone. He left her to go to Troy and seek his heritage, but now he had to face the woman he left behind. Paris took one of his servants as a driver, climbed into the back of a wagon, and slipped out of Troy just before daylight to make the long trip up the mountain to Oenone's home.

Paris finally arrived at Oenone's cottage, but the poison and the blood loss had left him very weak. Oenone's home was on the outskirts of a small village, set in a valley high on Mount Ida. It was an average shepherd's hut made of stone, with a thatched roof and a small ribbon of smoke spiraling out of the chimney. It was late in the afternoon when his wagon approached the home of his former wife. Paris hobbled to the front door on a crutch. Oenone heard the wagon coming up the hill, and watched it come closer from her window. She was a small, wiry woman with long red hair. She stood by the fireplace as Paris limped through the door. When she turned to face him, he hovered in the doorway and leaned on his crutch. "Hello, Oenone."

She turned her back to him without saying a word. He limped toward a chair, groaning with every painful step. "Oenone, I have come to beg your forgiveness. I know you are angry with me, and I know I have made a huge mistake. I never should have left you. I know now that this is where I belong, with you. I have been such a fool. The riches of Troy and the beauty of a woman have blinded my heart to my true feelings."

A prolonged silence lingered between them, and Paris grew more desperate. As tears welled up in his eyes, he said, "Oenone, I have been seriously wounded and need your help. Please find it in your heart to forgive me. I promise I will make it up to you. You can have anything you want: treasure, livestock, jewels. You are my last hope!"

Oenone paused for a moment, then faced him and said, "I have been waiting a long time to see you again, and this is how you have come back to me, crawling in here wounded and begging for forgiveness. Now that you need me, I am important to you! You broke my heart when you left. Go to Helen now. Maybe her beauty will heal your wound and stop death from taking you."

"Oenone, please. There is no one in Troy willing to help me."

"Yes, I have heard. They call you coward and worse. Can you blame them? You have caused them so much misery with your selfishness and stubborn ways! No, Paris. I will not help you. I loved you once, and you turned your back on me. Now, it is my turn!" Oenone could feel the pain in her heart as she said those words, but time had hardened her toward Paris. "Go back to Troy. Maybe you will find peace in death!"

Oenone turned her back to him and stared into the fire. Out of options, Paris bowed his head, took a deep breath, and limped to the door. He looked back at her one last time and said, "I know you won't believe me, but I want you to know that I never stopped loving you."

"Your charms won't work here anymore. Go!"

He limped outside to the waiting wagon, climbed in the back, and painfully lay down before they rode away. The full moon lit up the road for Paris' trip back to Troy. He could feel the poison taking control of his body. His breathing became shallow and labored, and his legs were growing numb. He felt the sadness well up as he closed his eyes, he knew death was near.

Oenone heard the wagon roll down the road, and she began to weep. That night, Oenone tried to sleep, but couldn't get Paris out of her mind. Her heart was troubled. She still loved him deeply, but felt justified in turning him away. Still angry, she told herself,

"He abandoned me the first chance he got, didn't he?" She got out of bed and paced around her room. Her anger was starting to wane, replaced bit by bit with compassion. "I wanted to hurt him, I wanted revenge, but I don't want him to die!"

When morning came, she was distressed. "What have I done? The man I love finally came back to me, and I turned him away! Now he will die if I don't get to him in time!" Oenone grabbed some supplies and potions, and headed for Troy. She traveled by foot, and ran most of the way. She reached Troy by nightfall, but her heart sank when she saw a large pile of wood outside the Trojan walls. Her heart raced as she ran toward the funeral pyre. She stopped a stranger and asked, "Who is the fire for?"

"It is for Paris, of Troy."

Unfortunately, she was too late; Paris died on his way back to Troy. The funeral pyre had just been lit, but the flames had not yet engulfed Paris' body. Oenone was tired, worn, and dirty. She took a deep breath, steeled herself, and walked onto the funeral pyre. As tears fell from her eyes, she reached Paris and embraced him. No one stopped her, because there was no one there to weep for Paris. There, the two lovers were consumed by the flames. Their ashes would be mingled together forever.

That night while the funeral pyre burned, Antenor sensed an opportunity to end the war. He approached Priam, who sat alone in his quarters. Priam knew why he was there and before he could speak Priam said, "I know what you are going to say, but Helen stays here."

"But..."

Priam stood up and said sternly, "I said, the woman stays here."

"But, Priam we..."

"The woman stays here!" he screamed as his eyes flashed and his fist slammed the table.

Antenor stared at him for a moment and turned to leave. Now he knew the war was about much more than Helen.

The next morning, before his ashes cooled, Paris' brothers were already vying for position to see who would be Helen's next husband. Deiphobus and Helenus were the two remaining senior sons, and both approached Priam to present their cases. Deiphobus said, "Father, what are your plans for Helen? I don't feel as though I need to prove myself. I have proven myself in battle many times over, and I am the oldest son. I feel I should be awarded Helen."

Helenus said, "Dear father, I have proven myself just as many times as Deiphobus in battle. Plus, I possess the gift of prophecy, which allows me to be even more useful to you. The Spartan beauty should be mine."

Priam replied, "This woman has caused so much trouble, and now she is going to pit the both of you against each other. Is this really what you want? I'm going to let you decide who gets Helen through a no holds barred wrestling match."

Deiphobus happily agreed to the plan. Helenus was disappointed because he knew his brother was the better warrior, but he was determined to try. With little hope, he said, "That's fine with me."

Helen's hopes were high. Now that Paris was dead, surely Priam would let her go back to Greece and her family. She heard a knock at the door, and King Priam walked in. "Your Highness, it is good to see you."

Priam said, "Yes, my dear, it is good to see you as well. I came here to tell you what has happened since Paris' death."

"Yes it was a tragedy, in a war filled with tragedies."

"Two of my sons, Deiphobus and Helenus, have expressed an interest in your hand in marriage."

Helen turned away, so he couldn't see the disappointment in her eyes. "Both are very brave and worthy warriors.

"They will have a contest this evening to see who will be your next husband. Due to the uncertainty of war, you will marry the winner tonight."

"I understand, Your Highness. However, I don't think it would be appropriate for me to attend the event so soon after the death of my husband. I would like to await the outcome in my chambers."

"You don't need to attend the match. The outcome will be what it will be, whether you are there or not. We will send for you afterward." Priam put his hands on Helen's shoulders for a moment, then turned and walked out the door.

Helen collapsed in a nearby chair, put her head in her hands, and sobbed. "Is this ever going to end?" Aethra and Harleopi entered the room and tried to console their weeping friend.

That evening, Deiphobus and Helenus squared off in a wrestling match in the great hall. The brothers faced each other in the center of the floor, surrounded by dozens of fellow soldiers and politicians. Finally, they lunged at each other like two rams fighting for the right to mate with a female. Deiphobus was larger than Helenus and dominated him early in the match. Sly and wiry, Helenus used Deiphobus' weight to turn the tide of the fight. It looked like he was going to win, but Deiphobus hit him with an elbow to the chin and knocked him unconscious. Deiphobus was declared the winner. When he finally recovered, Helenus was distraught and angry over the outcome. He left Troy in shame and went to live on Mount Ida.

Deiphobus celebrated with wine, food, and song with the rest of the guests. Priam sent for Helen and her attendants. She entered the hall to great fanfare, and the musicians and dancers led her to the head table. Helen looked like a goddess in her sparkling golden dress and white gold tiara with a large ruby in the center. Deiphobus had too much wine and couldn't wait to be with the woman he secretly craved all this time. As Helen walked toward him, he leaned forward and whispered to Priam with a smile, "Father, can we get this over with quickly?"

The crowd was hushed when Helen reached Priam and Deiphobus. Deiphobus grinned broadly at her, but Helen could only manage a slight smile. Deiphobus took her hand and they turned toward Priam. Priam said, "Helen, because you are a widow, and I am your king and father-in-law, I have the right to give you away in marriage. I now give you to my son, Deiphobus, as his wife."

Deiphobus spun Helen toward him and kissed her hard on the mouth. This took Helen by surprise, and she tried to push him off, but she failed. Finally, Deiphobus stopped, and the newlyweds took a seat at the head table, continued the feast, and watched the entertainment. When the party was over, Deiphobus took Helen to his chambers. As he disrobed, he said, "I have dreamed of this night for a long time."

Helen coldly replied, "You may have my body, but you won't have my heart."

Deiphobus laughed aloud and tore off Helen's robe. "Do you think I care if I have your heart? All I want is your body. *I* am going to enjoy this. Whether you do or not is of no concern to me." He then threw Helen on the bed and forced himself upon her trembling body before passing out from the wine.

Helen shoved him off of her, rolled to the side, and cried silent tears. When would this end? She took in a deep breath. She should have never gone along with Agamemnon's plan. The war was never going to end, and she was never going to be in Menelaus's loving arms again. It was just time to accept it.

The Greeks were optimistic when they heard of Paris's death and saw his funeral pyre. Many of the soldiers thought the war would be over since there was no longer any reason for Helen to remain in Troy. Many believed that Priam would give her back to Menelaus and they could finally go home. Menelaus hurried to Agamemnon's hut. "Have you heard the news? Paris is dead."

Agamemnon replied, "Yes, brother, I have heard. We have cancelled our attack until we have more information."

"Surely Priam will give Helen and her treasure back now. There is no reason for her to be there any longer."

"I agree, but we need to wait for more information."

"Odysseus and I will go and speak with him." Menelaus was becoming increasingly impatient with his brother's unwillingness to take action to get Helen back from the Trojans. He felt his face start to heat up.

"No, you won't. I can't afford to lose two more leaders. Don't you remember that poor Achilles went there under the guise of peace? No, we will send a herald with a message."

"Then, I will compose the letter." Menelaus returned to his camp. As he walked, he could feel and hear the optimism in the air among the men. He heard some say they couldn't wait to get home, and that they hoped to set sail in a week or so. Menelaus entered his hut and sat to write his message.

> *Your Highness, King Priam,*
>
> *Please accept my condolences on the loss of your son, Paris. His death, while tragic, may present us with an opportunity to end this war. There is no more reason for us to continue this fight. The man who dishonored us is dead. I ask that you return my wife and all of the treasure that is rightfully mine, and we will return home. Troy and Greece can heal and start on the long road to a peaceful and prosperous friendship.*

The next morning, Menelaus took his usual ride to the edge of the plain, hoping to see Helen on the wall. He waited as long as he could, but she never appeared. Menelaus took the note to Agamemnon for his approval, and then he sent it with a messenger to Troy. Menelaus and the rest of the Greeks spent the day shoring up their defenses and repairing weapons while they awaited Priam's reply. Early that evening, the messenger returned from Troy and took his note to Agamemnon's hut. Menelaus was excited, and he snatched the note from the man as soon as the he entered the tent.

> *Most honored Menelaus,*
>
> *I have received your note and carefully considered your request. Many brave men have died on both sides during this war, including many of my own sons. I don't want them to have died*

in vain. I still feel we have done nothing to cause this war. Your wife fell in love with a Trojan once, and I must tell you she has done it again. She married my son, Deiphobus, last night. It is obvious she loves Troy and her people. Now it is my turn to make a request: give up your lost love and return to Greece. There is no honor lost because a woman's heart has changed.

Menelaus crumbled the note and pressed it hard into his brother's hands without looking Agamemnon in the eye. Then he walked away, his back to his brother.

Agamemnon sighed after a moment. Then, he said, "It looks like we have more work to do."

Through gritted teeth, Menelaus said, "He pats me on the head and tells me to go home, like a child. I will kill him with my bare hands!"

"Try to keep a cool head, brother. Don't let this anger get the best of you and cause you to do something foolish."

"And why has she married another Trojan? Deiphobus, no less… that braggart!"

"We don't know the situation within the walls. She may have had no choice."

"That may be the case, but it doesn't make it any easier."

The two men called a meeting of the war council. All the leaders arrived except Odysseus, who was encircling Troy to look for weapons, deserters, and a way into the city. Agamemnon stood before his men with the grim news. "We have received a response to our overture to Priam. With Menelaus' permission, I will read you the response." Menelaus nodded, and Agamemnon read the note aloud. "Now, I know all of you had hopes that this was our opportunity to sail home, but I ask you to stay with us a while longer. Troy's leadership has been devastated. They can't fight much longer."

Diomedes said, "Priam insults us all with his message. I will go back and tell my men that it isn't over yet, but I can't guarantee they will fight much longer."

"I agree with Diomedes. Priam doesn't understand why we are here. But the men are tired, hungry, and homesick; they don't have much fight left in them," said Nestor.

Agamemnon said, "Do the best you can. We will prepare our battle plan tomorrow. Tonight, let your men rest."

The following morning while the leaders were discussing the war plan, hundreds of soldiers gathered outside Agamemnon's hut. Finally, the council of leaders came out and faced the men. Before the leaders could speak, a soldier stepped forward and said, "We have lived on these beaches for a long time. We have done our duty."

A second soldier stepped forward and chimed in. "We have wives and families, too!"

"Achilles, Patroclus, Ajax, and countless others have died. We have fought for years. How long are we bound to our oath?"

The soldiers were starting to get riled up. "Menelaus, we have fought to restore your honor, as well as our own. Now, Helen has married another Trojan. Consider our oath fulfilled, so we can go home!"

Ever the calm, collected leader, Agamemnon addressed the crowd. "Men, I understand your frustration, and none are more frustrated than we are. Troy is going to fall. It is inevitable. I ask that you stay a while longer; our task is almost finished."

While there was still some grumbling from the crowd, Menelaus came forward and said, "Men, I know we have fought long and hard, and like you, I have lost many friends during this war. I honor all those who gave their lives to defend and restore my honor, and the honor of all of Greece. Now, many of you feel the work is done, that you have honored your oath, and want to go home. I will not force you to stay. I release you from your oath. Those who want to leave may do so, but I cannot. I will not leave! What is a home without honor? I will stay as long as it takes to win this war, even if I have to fight it alone!"

The soldiers stood in stunned silence, and then Diomedes shouted, "Menelaus is right! What good is your home if you have no honor? Many have died here, and I will not let their deaths be in vain! I, too, will stay and fight by his side!"

The men cheered, raised their swords, and chanted, "Menelaus! Menelaus! Menelaus!"

Agamemnon raised his arms to quiet the crowd. "Okay, men! Everyone return to your camps, and we will design a battle plan."

Later that afternoon, while Menelaus was going over maps and plans with Diomedes and Agamemnon, Odysseus pushed a Trojan prisoner, bound and blindfolded, into the hut.

Agamemnon greeted Odysseus. "Welcome back, old friend." He then turned and grabbed the Trojan by the chin to lift his head. "Who do we have here?"

Odysseus said, "May I present, Helenus, a son of Priam, and more importantly, an oracle. I found him on Mount Ida."

Diomedes said, "I have heard of this man. You were a good warrior, Helenus. I don't believe you deserted your countrymen in a time of war. What was a son of Priam doing on Mount Ida?"

"Thank you," said Helenus. "Maybe you should tell my father that. Apparently, I wasn't good enough for him. After Paris died, Deiphobus and I asked Priam for beautiful Helen's hand in marriage."

Menelaus immediately grabbed him by the throat and shouted, "I'll kill you right now!" Odysseus and Agamemnon pulled him off the prisoner.

Agamemnon said, "Calm down, Menelaus. Hear what he has to say!"

Helenus regained his balance. "Priam decided we should fight for her, like two animals. Being the better warrior, Deiphobus won. Priam never appreciated my talents. He knew Deiphobus would win, why didn't he just award her to him and save me the embarrassment?"

Agamemnon said, "We may appreciate your talents. I understand that you are an oracle. Can you tell us Troy's weakness?"

"Troy means nothing to me now, but I still can't betray my family."

Before anyone could react, Menelaus pulled his sword and placed it under Helenus' chin with enough pressure that the cold blade sliced his skin and a trickle of blood ran down his neck. Through clenched teeth, Menelaus said, "I want you to understand this: you mean nothing to me, and I would like nothing better than to cut off your head right now!"

In a terrified, squeaky voice, Helenus asked, "What is it you want to know?"

"What is the key to conquering Troy?"

"Troy will not fall as long as the Palladium is in the city. The Palladium is a statue created by Athena to honor her friend Pallas, whom she accidently killed while they were children, practicing the art of war. When Troy was being built, it fell from the heavens and landed in the Temple of Athena. The rest of the city was built around it."

Menelaus asked, "How big is it? What does it look like?"

"It is a three-foot tall wooden statue of Pallas. Her feet are joined together, she holds a spear in her right hand, a distaff and a spindle in her left, and has an aegis wrapped around her breast."

"Is it heavily guarded?"

"Only lightly, some priests pray to it every day, but there is no need to guard it. All Trojan people have respect for it."

Satisfied with Helenus' answers, Menelaus asked the rest of the leaders, "Are there any more questions for him?"

Agamemnon said, "Put him with the rest of the prisoners." Diomedes took him outside and gave him to two soldiers, who put Helenus in a holding pen.

After Helenus was gone, Odysseus asked, "Do you trust him?"

Menelaus did not. "I made the mistake of trusting a Trojan once, and look what has happened. Paris even gave me a beautiful, golden statuette of a horse that turned out to be gold-plated lead and hollow."

Odysseus wondered, "How did you know it was hollow?"

"It broke open when I threw it against the wall in anger."

Agamemnon said, "I don't know if we can trust Helenus either, but nothing else seems to be working. We must take the chance. We need to find a way into Troy to steal the Palladium."

Pulling out the strategy maps, Odysseus pointed to an area near Troy. "On my scouting mission, I found what looks like some sort of sewer system near the Scamander River. It is very small, maybe big enough for one person to get through."

Agamemnon asked, "Are you sure it goes all the way into Troy?"

"No, but it is our best hope of getting into the city. Our other efforts have failed."

"I will ask the men for a volunteer to explore the tunnel."

Odysseus replied, "No. I found it. I can't ask someone to go when I'm not sure what they will find. Besides, I'm small enough to fit through the tunnel."

Diomedes volunteered, "I'll go with him."

"No, I can't afford to lose the both of you if something goes wrong," protested Agamemnon.

Odysseus said, "Diomedes can wait outside the tunnel until I return."

Menelaus asked, "How do you plan to move around inside Troy without being recognized?"

Odysseus thought for a moment. "I will go dressed as a filthy beggar. I will leave tonight at midnight, when most of the people are asleep."

Agamemnon said, "Stop by my hut before you go. Now, go and get some rest." Diomedes and Odysseus got up to leave. Agamemnon stopped them and said, "Odysseus, good job today!" Odysseus smiled in response.

Alone in the hut, Menelaus asked his brother, "Can we give Odysseus a message for Helen?"

"It may blow her cover. Are you sure you want to take the risk?"

"From the prisoners we have captured, we know she hands out food to the refugees each day. If Odysseus enters Troy as a beggar, he can meet with her and perhaps she can help him."

Agamemnon said, "We can trust Odysseus. I will tell him before he leaves tonight."

That evening, at the strategy meeting, Odysseus addressed the council. "We have been beating our heads against the walls of Troy for too long. Perhaps it's time to try a different strategy. Tonight, I will sneak into Troy, wearing a disguise to avoid being recognized and attempt to steal the Palladium.

"Menelaus, you said something earlier that got me thinking. Paris gave you a hollow statuette disguised as a solid golden horse to get into your palace. Why don't we return the favor and do the same thing?"

Menelaus asked. "What do you mean?"

"The Trojans venerate horses. Why don't we use a hollow statue of a horse to get inside Troy?"

"But what good is a hollow statue?" Diomedes asked.

"We will build a huge wooden horse and hide men inside it."

Agamemnon asked, "But how do we get it inside Troy?"

"We don't. We let the Trojans do that for us." Everybody just looked at him for a moment. "We build the horse, and leave it on the beach with a plaque that says it's a gift to Athena for a safe passage home. To ensure that the Trojans don't burn it, we leave someone here to tell them it would make Troy invincible to attack by the Greeks if it was in their city, and that's why we built it so big, so they couldn't get it through their gates."

"What do you mean we leave someone here?" asked Agamemnon.

"We will pretend to sail home, but hide our ships behind the Tenedos Islands. When the Trojans take the horse inside the walls, we sail back, the men inside emerge from the horse, and open the gates for our army."

"And what if the Trojans burn it anyway?"

Odysseus paused for a moment. "The men inside die, and we lose the war."

Menelaus said, "I think it is a risk worth taking, and an incredible idea."

"Nothing else is working," said Diomedes.

"I agree, but tonight, Odysseus must sneak inside Troy. Tomorrow, we will skirmish with the Trojans. They don't seem too eager to come out from behind their walls. The plans for the horse will remain secret and are not to leave this room until after Odysseus returns with the Palladium. Let us see if that helps our cause first."

Agamemnon waited for an hour after the meeting before he summoned Odysseus to his hut. Menelaus stood up from his chair at the planning table when Odysseus entered.

"What have I done to deserve this invitation?" Odysseus asked sarcastically.

"Odysseus, come in and sit down." Agamemnon dismissed all his servants and slaves. When he was sure they were alone, he and Menelaus sat down across the table from Odysseus. Odysseus could see the seriousness of the situation on their faces. "We need you to swear that what we are about to tell you will not be repeated to anyone."

Odysseus looked puzzled and asked, "What's going on?"

"You must promise you will never reveal this secret, no matter what!" replied Agamemnon.

"All right, all right. I swear I will not repeat what you are about to tell me."

Agamemnon and Menelaus glanced at each other, and then Menelaus said, "Things are not always what they seem. You talked about deception today." Menelaus took a deep breath and asked, "What if I told you that Helen wasn't abducted?"

"You mean she really did fall in love with Paris?"

Menelaus said, "No, we're pretty sure that didn't happen either."

Agamemnon stood up and said, "We had good information that led us to believe that Priam was going to start a war with Greece, one kingdom at a time. He planned to start with Sparta." Agamemnon and Menelaus explained their plot to plant Helen inside the Trojan walls with the hopes of avoiding a war on Spartan soil.

Menelaus continued, "Helen was given all the information, and decided to seduce Paris and allow us to claim she was abducted so we could raise the Oath and go to war with Troy."

Odysseus remained silent for a long time. "I don't believe what I have just heard. Helen wasn't abducted, but came here solely for the purpose of invoking the Oath so you could go to war with Troy?"

"Yes. We had to choose to fight either there or here. War was inevitable," said Agamemnon.

Odysseus stood up and shouted, "But you gave *me* no choice! I could kill you! I would have chosen to stay home with my family!" He clenched his fists, and his face reddened.

"Then you would have died in Ithaca at the hands of the Trojans. We had to raise the Oath because if we tried to fight the Trojans one kingdom at a time, we would have all been killed."

"You don't know that!"

"Even now with our armies combined, the Trojans have almost driven us into the sea. What do you think would have happened had we been alone?"

Menelaus intervened. "That is all in the past. Many brave men have died, and we can't let their deaths be for nothing. Odysseus, you have sworn to keep this quiet. Now that you know the truth, will you keep your word?"

Odysseus sat down and shook his head in disbelief. "Yes, I will keep my word."

Menelaus said, "Good. You needed to know the truth because I want you to contact Helen when you are inside Troy. She will be able to help you steal the Palladium. I have thought about your horse idea, and she can help us there too." Menelaus put his hand on Odysseus' shoulder and said softly, "You love and miss your wife no more than I miss mine. You can imagine how concerned for her I am. I want you to tell her that I am proud of her bravery and fortitude."

Odysseus let out a deep breath and rose from his chair. "This has been an incredible meeting. I will give her your message. Is there any more I should know?"

Agamemnon replied, "No. Good luck."

That night Odysseus cut his hair unevenly and put grease in it. He smeared his face and body with dirt, tore his clothes, hunched over, and walked gingerly. He yellowed his teeth, blackened some out, and ate garlic to make his breath terrible. When Diomedes saw him, he said, "I almost didn't recognize you!"

"Excellent, that's exactly what I want!"

At midnight, Odysseus and Diomedes set out for Troy. The partial moonlight of a waning moon helped the two men reach the bank of the Scamander River, where Odysseus showed Diomedes the opening that had been over grown with shrubs and grasses. Diomedes said, "I will go with you."

"No, it would be too difficult for two to go unnoticed. Wait here." Odysseus took a torch and entered the tunnel. It was small and cramped, with just enough room for a man to fit through. The water was knee-deep in some areas, and the stench was overwhelming. Except for the occasional river rat, the tunnel was empty. Odysseus made quick headway. After traveling for what seemed like a mile, Odysseus saw a grate above him. He listened for a long time, and when he didn't hear anything, he gently lifted the lid and poked his head out. The street was clear. He quickly climbed out of the sewer, replaced the lid, then crawled over and sat in the shadows to wait for morning.

As the sun came up, Odysseus begged for food in the street. A Trojan citizen approached him and said, "I haven't seen you here before. What is your name?"

Odysseus thought quickly, looked at the ground, and replied, "My name is Rejenius. I came into the city last night from the Thracian peninsula. I fought mighty Ajax, but was severely wounded in the hip and knee. The Greeks burned my home and killed my family. I have no place to go."

The civilian said, "You need to bathe and get some food. A member of the royal family will be handing out food by the stables at noon. When we are sure the Greeks won't attack us, you can go down to the river for a bath."

"Thank you. You have been most kind." At noon, Odysseus limped over to the stable area and stood in line with the refugees. When he saw Helen, she looked as though she hadn't aged a day. She was still gorgeous. His mind wandered to the day she chose Menelaus as her husband, and the joy and celebration that took place. It seemed like only yesterday or maybe it was just a dream. As he got closer, Harleopi handed him a bowl, and he kept his head down. He stood in front of Helen, looked at the ground, and with shaking hands, he held out his bowl. Helen poured a ladle full of soup into it. Odysseus said weakly, "Thank you, my Queen."

Helen replied, "I was once so, but I am no longer a queen."

Under his breath, Odysseus said, "You will always be a queen to me."

Helen stared at the beggar in front of her. She heard something in his voice that was very familiar. As the man turned away, Helen grabbed his arm. "Who are you?"

"My name is Rejenius."

Helen turned him around and picked up his chin. "Where are you from?"

"I am from the Thracian peninsula."

Helen looked into his eyes. There was fire and life in them. These were not the eyes of a beaten down refugee, but of a king and a warrior. Helen's heart skipped a beat when she realized she was holding Odysseus by the chin. She thought quickly. "All right, Rejenius. Tell me what happened to you."

"Dear lady, don't allow me to bother you with my troubles. Let me go back to my doorstep and eat my soup on the other side of the stables."

Helen let go of Odysseus and watched as he limped, hunched over to a stoop a few yards away. She couldn't take her eyes off him to concentrate on what she was doing, she was afraid if she stayed there much longer, she would draw too much attention to him. She motioned to Aethra and Harleopi. "I am not feeling well. I should go back to my chambers." As Helen left, the two women looked over and watched the stranger sloppily drink the soup from his bowl.

Outside the Trojan walls, the Greeks attacked in small numbers. Agamemnon needed to create a distraction. He wanted to use the minimum amount of men to do it. They were caught off guard when the Trojans poured out of the Scaean Gate, led by Aeneas and Deiphobus. The Trojans drove the Greeks across the plain. It would have been a disaster if Menelaus and Nestor hadn't raised their reserve troops. The Trojans stormed the Greek battlements. They were thrown back when Menelaus attacked from the right and Nestor attacked from the left. The battle surged back and forth across the plains.

A Trojan soldier laughingly shouted to Menelaus, "Hey Menelaus, it seems as though Helen has a taste for Trojan men! "The comment stung, and Menelaus fought with a renewed ferocity.

Menelaus saw Deiphobus in the distance, and rode to confront him. Deiphobus shouted, "Don't worry, Menelaus. She is in good hands: mine!" He laughed aloud as he headed back into Troy. Menelaus was furious. He tried to fight his way through the forces between them, but it was too late. The Trojans had withdrawn into the city.

Inside Helen's chambers that evening, Helen said, "Harleopi, I want you to go to the rear of the stables, find the beggar named Rejenius that I spoke with this afternoon, and bring him here."

"Are you sure, Your Highness? He looked bad, and smelled worse."

"Just do as I say. Do not be seen bringing him here."

Harleopi nodded, and took a large blanket with her as she headed out into the night. Odysseus was crouched in a doorway behind the stables when Harleopi approached him. "Is your name Rejenius?"

"It is."

"I would like you to come with me."

Odysseus slowly tried to stand. "Where are we going?"

"Don't worry. Just come with me. My goodness, do you smell! Here, I want you to drape this blanket over your head and follow me."

Odysseus did as he was told, and the two of them stayed in the shadows as they made the slow trip back to Helen's chambers. While she waited, Helen instructed her servants to prepare her a bath. When Harleopi and Odysseus arrived, Helen removed the blanket and said, "Odysseus! How my heart has longed to see someone from home."

Odysseus straightened up and stood tall, and they hugged each other tightly. Harleopi ran to Odysseus. "My goodness, King Odysseus! I didn't recognize you."

The three of them exchanged hugs with broad smiles and joy in their eyes. Odysseus said, "You shouldn't have brought me here. It is too dangerous."

"We are safe. Deiphobus doesn't come here, and only summons me late at night. You must be hungry, and you certainly need a bath. Harleopi, go and get some food for our guest."

Odysseus started to say, "Menelaus and Agamemnon…"

Helen interrupted him. "Let's get you a bath, and then we can talk."

"I can't get too clean. I need some of the dirt for my disguise."

"You can roll in the dirt when you leave, but we must remove the smell." After the bath and some food, Helen dismissed Harleopi and turned to Odysseus. "Now tell me, why are you here?"

"Menelaus and Agamemnon have told me everything. Your husband misses you and is very proud of you."

Helen stood up and stared toward the window to the sea. "How I miss Menelaus and Sparta. I wish this were over and I could return home. It is like a never-ending nightmare."

"If you can help me, this war may be over soon. I am here to steal the Palladium."

Helen turned and said, "What do you need to know?"

"Where is the Palladium kept, how many guards surround it, and when would be the best time to steal it?"

"The Palladium is in the Temple of Athena, and there is only one guard protecting it at night. The best time to steal it would be late in the night when most everyone is asleep and the guard is the only one there. I have had many sleepless nights, and have gone there to pray for an end to this war."

"Can you tell me how to get to the Citadel?"

"I will take you there myself."

"My lady, you mustn't risk yourself like that."

"I have felt so helpless since I have been here. I am grateful for the opportunity to help in any way I can."

Odysseus put his hands on Helen's shoulders. "Menelaus has asked me to tell you that we are building a large wooden horse. Your task is to make sure the Trojans don't destroy it."

"What good is a wooden horse?"

"There will be men inside it, including Menelaus."

"But…"

"Listen to me, once the horse is inside the city, he wants you to wait until the people are asleep and wave a torch on the wall near the Scaean Gate, to signal the Greeks. Then you are to go back to your chambers, stay there and wait for him. I have to go now. I have already put you at risk long enough."

Helen said, "I will meet you where I first saw you, later tonight."

Odysseus stooped over and changed back into the beggar. Helen threw the blanket over his head, and he was led back out into the street where he disappeared into the shadows.

Helen felt more alive and excited than she had in a long time as she moved slowly through the streets. She wore a dark dress and a hood. When she passed a shadowy doorway, a hand reached out and pulled her in. Odysseus whispered, "This is what we will do: I want you to continue to walk down the street as you were. I will follow you in the shadows until we reach the Citadel. Then I want you to move into the shadows, and we will make a plan from there."

Helen nodded that she understood, and walked toward the Citadel. The silence of the city was eerie, and the dim moonlight cast long shadows. Helen heard the occasional catfight and dogs barking in the distance. She came around a corner, and the Citadel was there in front of her. She ducked into a shadow and waited for Odysseus to catch up.

Odysseus slid into the shadow so quietly that he startled her. "Is that it?"

Helen whispered, "Yes."

The Temple of Athena sat just inside the Citadel. It was dimly lit, and there were many shadows and dark areas around the perimeter. Odysseus saw the guard standing to the left of the entrance. Odysseus said, "I want you to lead the guard to the left side of the building, I will take care of him from there. Wait until I signal you that I am in position."

Like a shadow on the wind, Odysseus silently crept into position. He gave a slight whistle, and Helen started up the stairs toward the guard. The guard moved over to intercept her. "What is your reason for being here?"

"I merely want to pray to Athena for a swift victory over the Greeks." Helen removed her hood and revealed her identity.

"I'm sorry, Your Highness. I didn't know it was you."

Helen moved to the guard's side and said, "No harm done." She could see Odysseus moving rapidly from one shadow to the next as he approached the guard from behind. Helen felt her heart pound in her chest when she reached out and touched the guard's cheek with the back of her hand. "You must be lonely out here all by yourself."

The guard blushed slightly. "It can be a lonely place, at times."

"You can imagine how lonely I get, being the only Greek in all of Troy."

The guard swallowed hard and said in a small voice, "Yes, I suppose you would be."

Helen took him by the arm and led him toward the shadows. "Maybe we can help each other forget our loneliness." When they were deep in the shadows, Odysseus came from behind, held his hand over the guard's mouth, and swiftly cut his throat with a small knife. He let the body drop gently without making a sound. Helen said, "You must hurry, before his replacement arrives."

She watched Odysseus run into the Temple. He found the Palladium on a pedestal, picked it up with bloody hands, and returned to where Helen waited. The pair made their way to the back of the stables. Odysseus found his grate and dropped down into the sewer. Helen handed the blood-smeared Palladium down to him and replaced the grate. Odysseus looked up at her. "Thank you, and remember what I told you."

"I will." Odysseus disappeared into the darkness. Helen slowly walked away, but it was difficult not to scream with joy. She felt excited, alive, and needed. Maybe there was finally an end to her nightmare.

Odysseus slopped his way through the channel, and finally came to the end where Diomedes waited for him. "Well?"

"I got it."

"Let me hold it." Diomedes could see the statue in the light of the early morning dawn. "It's beautiful. Can I carry it back to camp?"

"You may, but remember who stole it and who it belongs to."

It was morning by the time Odysseus and Diomedes arrived in camp. They went directly to Agamemnon's hut, where Agamemnon and Menelaus waited. It had been another sleepless night for Menelaus, who paced anxiously, presumably to hear any word from Helen. When the returning heroes walked in, Agamemnon looked at the Palladium and said, "Fantastic!"

Diomedes replied, "It was Odysseus who took the risk. I merely waited for him."

Menelaus pulled Odysseus to the side. "Did you see her?"

"Yes, and she is as beautiful as the day you wed her. She is very homesick for Sparta and her family. She wants this war over as soon as possible."

"Is that all she said?"

"She didn't pour her heart out to me, but the look in her eyes said it all. She misses you very much and wishes she could see you again." Menelaus smiled.

Agamemnon placed the Palladium outside where all the men could see it. He shouted, "This is the Palladium, the statue that has protected Troy all this time. Thanks to the daring of Odysseus and Diomedes, we have it on our side. Without this, the walls of Troy are vulnerable and will soon fall!" A great roar and cheer rose from throngs of men. Disillusionment was replaced with a great optimism.

Inside Troy, the people found the murdered guard and saw that the Palladium had been stolen. Amid sadness and distress, Priam called an emergency council meeting. "I want the whole city searched! We must find out who stole the Palladium. The Trojan people are nervous and scared." The Trojans fanned out and searched the city, but couldn't find the statue. The people of Troy felt vulnerable;

someone had taken their most prized possession. They feared the worst—had a Greek snuck into their city and stolen it? If so, they no longer had spiritual protection. What would stop the Greeks from sneaking back in and destroying their city?

Helen watched from the corner with guarded breath. She had to lay low and couldn't let Priam detect that she was nervous. Surely if he found out she was involved, it would be her death. She looked out as the Trojans searched. Her king was outside the gates, somewhere waiting. Perhaps the gods were finally on her side again.

THE WOODEN HORSE

The Greek army moved steadily toward Troy and stopped just outside the range of the archers. In the center of the Greek line, Odysseus and the other Greek leaders rode proudly on their chariots. With a loud roar from the troops, a chariot rode out from behind the ranks and carried an object hidden under a blanket. When it was clearly in view of the Trojans on the walls, they removed the blanket to reveal the Palladium sitting on a pedestal. Odysseus raised the Palladium above his head and shouted, "I have been in your city, and I will be back!" Each leader raised the Palladium over their head to a thunderous cheer from the Greek soldiers. They placed the Palladium back on the pedestal, and rode the chariot back to the Greek camp. The Greeks pounded on their shields and created a deafening drumbeat as they tried to entice the Trojans to fiwght. The Trojans refused to come out from behind their walls, so the Greeks returned to their camp.

The Trojans felt insecure; the Greeks had violated their sacred space. Priam overheard a member of the crowd say, "That whore from Sparta probably had something to do with this! She is not Trojan; she is Greek. Odysseus was able to enter Troy unseen. If they did it once, the Greeks could do this again."

Priam quickly responded by calling another council meeting. "The people are in a panic. There is no telling what they will do. I want every possible entrance into this city shut down, barricaded, or guarded. If the Greeks came in unnoticed once, they will surely try again! I want sewer lids nailed down, extra guards posted at the gates, and no more refugees allowed in the city!"

Helen was weaving in her chambers when two guards arrived. "King Priam would like to speak with you in his chambers." Helen gave a worried look to her attendants as she walked out. Helen had heard the rumors that the Trojans felt someone had helped Odysseus steal the Palladium. She and her servants were the prime suspects. She could feel the anxiety growing in her stomach as she approached Priam's chambers. "What does he want? Did someone see me at the Temple? If so, it would mean death," she thought.

Helen entered Priam's chambers tentatively. Priam said, "Welcome, my dear. Come in and sit down."

Helen did as told. "Thank you, Your Highness."

"You have been here a long time, and have seen many things."

"Yes, I have, Your Highness."

Priam turned his back to her and said, "After all this time, it would be safe to say you are a citizen of Troy, would it not?"

"Yes, I am."

"I have considered you a citizen of Troy since the day you married my son, Paris." Priam turned back toward her and continued, "However, there are some who believe your loyalty lies elsewhere, that you haven't really adapted to being a Trojan."

Helen felt a bit anxious and adjusted herself in her seat. "Dear father-in-law, what are you trying to say?"

"I trust you know the Palladium has been stolen?"

"I have heard."

"I have been king for a long time, and have seen many things since this war began. I have never seen the people like this, not even when we suffered the death of Hector. They are very uneasy. They feel as though they have been violated, that they personally have been robbed, and they are looking for a scapegoat."

"Are you accusing me of something?"

"No, no, my dear, I'm not. Still, a few people have heard you talk longingly of Sparta. They feel you would be much happier if the war was over, and you were in Greece."

"It is true that I have had many sleepless nights feeling homesick. Isn't it a natural thing for someone to miss his or her home? I have watched many friends from my homeland die on the battlefield, just as I have watched many brave Trojans die. Yes, I wish this war was over, just like everyone else!" Helen paused for a moment, and then continued more softly. "I have been in Troy a long time. You have treated me well, even as a daughter. I consider Troy my home now."

"I just want you to be careful. No one knows what scared people will do, and since you are Greek, you are suspect to them."

"But not to you?"

"My dear, I believe you consider yourself Trojan. Besides, how could you have helped Odysseus? You were in the palace all night." With a hug, Priam said, "You may return to your room now. I just wanted to warn you about the sentiment among the people."

"Thank you. I will be sure to be careful." Helen couldn't relax. She wasn't sure if she believed Priam, and she worried that the Trojan people would turn against her. It was the same fear she'd held since coming to Troy; that someone would incite just enough of a mob and she'd be as good as dead. She sat quietly in her room, staring at the weaving wheel. How many more people would have to die before this stupid war would be over?

Inside the Greek camp, optimism mixed with skepticism. They possessed the Palladium, but still didn't know how to conquer Troy. Agamemnon met with his leaders. "We will try to knock down the Scaean Gate again. If we fail, we will try Odysseus' plan."

Nestor asked, "Why bother trying to knock down the gate? We have tried and failed, and will only lose more men. Why don't we just go directly to Odysseus' plan?"

"Troy no longer has the Palladium to protect it. We will attack again, while the city is vulnerable."

The following day, the Greeks assembled near the walls of Troy. They gathered around a huge battering ram with the head of a horse carved on it and rolled it toward the gate. The Greeks pushing the ram moved steadily forward while staying beneath wooden protective wings built on the ram. Arrows rained down on them like hail. The Trojans didn't come out to meet the attack, but waited for the Greeks to destroy themselves by pounding on the walls like waves against a cliff. Repeatedly, the ram smashed into the Scaean Gate. Again, it proved too strong to bash open. The Trojans threw spears, arrows, stones, and torches at the Greeks, who after sustaining heavy casualties, were forced to withdraw.

That night at the strategy meeting, Agamemnon said, "We have tried to knock down the gates and we have tried to scale the walls. Nothing has worked. We cannot continue this way. Odysseus, it is time to put your plan into action. What do you need?"

"First, we need enough lumber to build a massive horse. Mount Ida has been nearly stripped bare from all the funeral pyres and battlements."

Agamemnon replied, "There is a sacred cornel grove on the south side of Mount Ida. Assemble a company of men and get your lumber there, if you need more we can take it from the ships. I am sure you are all aware that we need to execute this project with the utmost secrecy. Tell the men we need the lumber to build an idol to appease Athena for stealing the Palladium. We will reveal the statue's true purpose only when we are ready to use it. We cannot risk a soldier leaking our secret to the enemy if he is captured."

When Odysseus returned with the lumber, Agamemnon sent the leaders out with a message for the men.

We have fought long and hard, and have lost many brothers and friends in this war. Now, we have stolen the Palladium from the Temple of Athena. To avoid Athena's wrath, we will build a statue of a horse to please her and win her favor.

Odysseus took his plans to Epeios, the master builder, and they assembled the best artists, architects, carpenters, and ship builders in camp. These men assembled at Agamemnon's hut and were sworn to secrecy. Agamemnon said, "Now that you have sworn an oath to keep this secret, you will not be allowed to leave camp for security reasons."

Everyone agreed, and they set to the daunting task of designing the horse. Odysseus said, "The horse needs to be big enough to hold at least thirty men and their armor."

A designer replied, "In case they need to get out of the horse fast, we will build the hatch under the horse's belly, to allow for a quick escape."

"Good, but we also need another hatch on the horse's back, in case the Trojans decide to burn it," said Odysseus.

Epoies said, "You will need fresh air to breathe, and yet not be seen or heard."

"We can bore hundreds of small holes all over the horse, at different angles, for cross-ventilation," suggested an artist.

Odysseus said, "The men may be inside the horse for at least two days. Since it needs to be large enough for them to be able to stretch, the body of the horse should be slightly elongated."

A designer asked, "What about human waste and the smell coming from inside the horse? Won't that give it away?"

Odysseus replied, "The men will eat their last meal twelve hours before they enter the horse to cut down on the waste. Beyond that, the smell of the fresh cut wood will disguise the odor for as long as needed. The men will be in the horse for no longer than two days. If they are not inside Troy by then, our plan has failed."

"Epoies, how long will it take to build the horse?" asked Agamemnon.

"Four, maybe five days."

"Good. There will be no moon in five days, so the Trojans will neither see the ships return in the night nor our army approach across the plain. I want the men to start breaking down camp. They need to be ready when the time comes."

Odysseus agreed, and the men set about the task of building the horse. The construction took place behind their fortifications, just below the crest of the plains and out of sight of the Trojans. Meanwhile, the army continued to march on Troy, to give the impression that the war was proceeding as usual.

The Greeks tried for two days to lure the Trojans to come out and fight, but they refused. Nervous after the loss of the Palladium, Priam called a meeting with his leaders. "We have lost too many men and too many leaders. Let our walls defend us."

Aeneas said, "King Priam, I understand your point of view, but Trojans don't hide behind walls like women! We want to fight. The enemy is here—let us face them."

Priam eventually agreed, and on the third day, the Trojans came out to fight. The battle was short, but fierce. The Trojans fought with a sense of desperation. Taken by surprise, the Trojans initially drove the Greeks back, but the Greeks regrouped and pushed the Trojans back behind their walls. The battle was over by noon.

That evening, Agamemnon said, "We have accomplished our goal. We kept the Trojans occupied and gave ourselves time to build the horse. It is time to tell the men the true nature of our plan and collect volunteers to go inside the horse. In case they have to fight the guards at the gate, we will need at least thirty men to stand a chance. I want it to be clear to the volunteers that this may be a suicide mission. If the Trojans uncover our plan, the men inside will no doubt be killed, or worse, burned alive!"

Odysseus replied, "This was my idea, so I definitely need to be in the horse. I can't ask my men to volunteer for something I wouldn't do."

Menelaus said, "We have been at war for a long time, and many men have come here on my behalf. I cannot ask any more of the men who remain. I understand the risk, but I also know that this will end the war, one way or the other. I must be in that horse!"

"I must be a part of this mission. I cannot sit and wait. I have fought too hard and too long. If the plan fails, I would rather be among those who were in the horse than those who waited for the signal," said Diomedes.

Nestor joined the pack. "I, too, want to be in the horse, to be one of the first to strike at the heart of the Trojans."

Agamemnon disagreed. "Nestor, my dear and honored friend, I must decline your request to join these men, not because you lack bravery, but because of your excellent leadership capabilities. I have too many leaders in the horse now. I will also need leaders outside Troy for this mission to succeed. Odysseus, as the leader of this mission, please choose a few men you trust to accompany you. I want the rest of you to go to your camps and announce our request for volunteers. Tell all the men who would like to volunteer to report to my hut in the morning."

The following morning, hundreds of men eager to join the mission swamped Agamemnon's camp. He climbed on top of a table and said, "Brave Greeks, I am inspired by your willingness to volunteer for this dangerous mission. You are all qualified and courageous, but there is only room for so many. To be fair, we will draw lots." By that evening, the Greeks had chosen the men, and among them were many of Helen's former suitors.

The men who were going into the horse met with Odysseus and Agamemnon that night. "I have called you here to explain what we can expect on this mission, and what is expected of you. We may be in the horse for at least two days. The bright sun will make it very hot inside, and the cramped quarters and body heat will make conditions even worse. While inside, we will have to wear minimal armor or none at all. Blankets will be on top of a dark tarp inside the belly of the horse for us to lie on. This will deaden any noise and prevent sweat from leaking out. The tarp will cover a hatch on the horse's belly. We can pull the tarp back and escape that way if needed, but the main hatch will be on the horse's back."

Diomedes asked, "How will we be identified when the battle begins?"

"The same way we are now; we will have our helmets, swords, and armor. We will have to put on our armor inside the horse and in the dark. Our gear will be wrapped in blankets until it's time to get out of the horse."

Diomedes interrupted, "Armor alone is not enough protection for battle. Perhaps our men can bring our shields to us after they open the gates."

Odysseus replied, "Good idea, we should do that. The men who want their shields brought to them will arrange with their soldiers. Also, because we don't know how long we will be in the horse, I want you each to bring goat skins filled with a light mixture of wine and water. There will be no food allowed in the horse, so the mixture will provide more nutrients than water alone."

Agamemnon asked, "Have we selected a man to stay behind and talk to the Trojans?"

"Yes, we had one volunteer." Odysseus motioned toward the crowd, and a small, wiry fellow with a slightly deformed left arm emerged from the back of the group. Odysseus said, "Introduce yourself."

The small man said, "My name is Sinon. I have volunteered because I want to do my part to help defeat the Trojans."

Agamemnon replied, "The fate of the whole mission may lie in your hands."

Sinon understood. "King Agamemnon, I swear to you that even if they torture me, I will not reveal the truth about the horse."

Agamemnon said, "Let's hope it doesn't come to that. Odysseus, you and Sinon must work on a story that is convincing and believable. The fleet will set sail on the morning the men climb inside the horse. We will sail to the other side of the Tenedos Islands, just a few miles off shore. We will wait there until night fall, and then sail back to our campsite. If the horse is inside Troy, we will silently approach the walls. Sinon will signal the men in the horse when it is safe to come out and open the gate. If he is dead or detained, it will be up to the men inside the horse to decide when to emerge. If he is able, Sinon will light a torch from the wall so that we can begin our assault. If he is not, someone from the horse will signal the ships. Are there any questions?"

"What if the Trojans leave the horse on the beach?" asked Nestor.

Agamemnon replied, "Then our plan has failed." There was a long moment of silence. "The horse will be finished tomorrow and we will put the plan in action the following morning. Let us coordinate our attack with the men inside the horse, so we can strike as quickly, strongly, and unexpectedly as possible."

Agamemnon pulled out the map of Troy that Menelaus and Odysseus created. Odysseus indicated a point on the map and said, "Here is the Citadel and palace. It is just behind the central town square, where the horse will no doubt be taken."

"Where are the soldier's barracks?"

"There are no barracks to speak of; most of the soldiers live in their own homes inside Troy," said Odysseus.

Menelaus said, "There is usually a small company of soldiers near the palace."

Odysseus continued, "As you can see, the palace is in the middle of the city. The streets break off and move around it on both sides. The armory is on the left, and the stables and chariots are on the right and rear of the palace."

Agamemnon said, "Nestor, when we come through the gate, I want you to take half of the men and split them into two groups: one group will go to the left and capture the armory, and the other will move on the stables. I will take the remaining men and advance on the palace. When those objectives are reached, the army can fan out through the city."

Menelaus said, "It was the Spartan Queen that was abducted. I would like to lead my men on the assault of the palace."

"I have no objections to that."

"One more thing, when Odysseus and I were in Troy as envoys, Priam wanted to kill us. The Trojan elder, Antenor, helped us escape, and now I want to repay him. Please see that Antenor, his family, and his house are spared."

Odysseus agreed. "Yes, we owe him that much." Pointing to the map, he said, "Antenor lives here. Pass the word so that no harm comes to him. Now, if there are no questions, our meeting is adjourned."

Odysseus rolled up the map and left the meeting. As he made his way back to his camp, Menelaus caught up with him. "Odysseus, wait a moment. Do you have some time? I would like to speak with you in my hut for a moment."

"I don't have much time. What do you need?"

"I would like you to show me where Helen's quarters are on your map."

"Follow me. We are closer to my camp." Once they entered Odysseus' hut, he unfurled the map. "When you go through the main entrance of the palace, you will see a reflecting pool and a corridor off to the right. Follow that corridor until you come to a courtyard. The only door on the right opens into Helen's quarters."

"I need to find her as soon as possible after we leave the horse. I fear a Trojan or a Greek soldier may blame her for the war and seek revenge once they realize we are inside their walls."

"I understand. I can't tell you how impressed I was with her help in stealing the Palladium."

"She has always been a courageous woman." Menelaus paused for a moment, and then it hit him hard, all of the fatigue he'd been feeling over the course of time that had passed—how much time had passed in this war Agamemnon thought would be quick and dirty? Finally he spoke. "I just hope that this is the end of the war and we can finally go home."

The day to get into the horse and put the wheels in motion was finally upon him; it was the final day of preparations before they would put their plan into motion. Menelaus and his men made last minute preparations for the fleet to sail. He stopped his work and walked over to admire the horse. It was a magnificent statue—part sculpture and part building, it stood thirty feet high and fifty feet long. Menelaus joined the other men as they practiced getting in and out of the horse quickly. He walked up to Odysseus and said, "I am surprised by how dark and roomy it is inside the horse."

Odysseus replied, "It only seems that way now. When we have our equipment in there with all of us, it will be much smaller."

"Let's see how it feels with thirty men inside."

Odysseus picked twenty-eight nearby men to enter the horse with him and Menelaus. As he climbed in, he said to Epoies, "I want you to tell me how much noise you can hear." When the men were all inside, Odysseus whispered to Menelaus. Then, he had everyone scream and move around. The men sat with their legs across from each other, like cogs in a gear. When they walked, they had to stoop over, as if they were walking in a small cave.

After they emerged, Epoies said, "I could hear the screaming, and the movement makes the horse shake, but I heard nothing more."

Odysseus replied, "Good we need to know what we can and can't do."

The guards on the Greek ramparts were being especially vigilant. If the Trojans attacked, they would catch the Greeks unprepared for battle. A large feast for the men going inside the horse was prepared. On the chance that the plan failed, Agamemnon wanted to provide them a proper last meal. Odysseus didn't want his crew to eat or drink after the banquet, in an attempt to eliminate or at least minimize the human waste during the mission.

The feast started early in the evening. The Greeks roasted wild boars and full steers, and the aroma drifted into Troy. The Greek morale was high; many men felt that, either way, this was the end of the war. The feast was not a time for celebration, as they had not won anything and had no reason to celebrate. The men focused on the task ahead; this was a time to honor the dead and those who might die in the coming battle.

After the meal, Agamemnon addressed the army. "Honorable men of Greece, it has been a great privilege for me to lead such courageous men in battle. I want to thank you for your service during this long and terrible war. With no end in sight, we have decided to try a new tactic. Now, our brothers have volunteered for a dangerous mission that will determine the outcome of this brutal war. Tonight, we honor them with this feast. May the gods bless their efforts!"

The soldiers stood and cheered for the volunteers.

Menelaus said, "Men, when I first sought your help, you were there. I ask you to be there for one last mission. Repeatedly, we asked the Trojans to return what is mine, and each time, we were rebuffed. The Trojans don't realize that this war is not about the honor of a single man, but the honor of a nation!" The men rose as one and cheered wildly. Menelaus continued, "I know there are many who feel Helen is the cause of this war, and may want to take revenge on her for the loss of a loved one. Let all men in this army know that I claim the right to exact the justice on her that I see fit. I now say that no man shall harm her. It is my right as her husband to give the punishment that is due."

Diomedes rose to speak. "Men of Greece, we have shared many experiences together, both good and bad. In the coming battle, I say give no quarter and expect none! Remember your friends and family who have died at the hands of the Trojans. Take no prisoners. The Trojans have been a worthy opponent, but it is time for us to wipe Troy off the face of the Earth and burn it to the ground so that it will never rise again!"

The army again cheered loudly. The men who volunteered to be in the horse left the feast to prepare for the mission in their own way, some listened to music, some slept, and some prayed.

Menelaus went back to his hut to rest; he had to climb into the horse before dawn. After tossing and turning for a few hours, he dressed and left his hut. He walked through the camp and up to the ramparts. He greeted the guards, but sought a place with some solitude, so he could be alone with his thoughts. The quiet of the night engulfed him. The night sky was especially clear, and the stars and planets appeared to be closer than usual, as if they were a million eyes waiting eagerly to see what was about to take place. Menelaus looked out across the plain to Troy. Its dark walls, dimly lit citadel, and palace rising from the middle looked ghostly. Menelaus thought, "I am so tired. I have fought long and hard, where will I find the strength to go on?" Then, as he was staring at the plains, he had visions of past battles. He saw Achilles killing dozens of Trojans, and could hear his voice calling for the Greeks to follow him. He saw Patroclus and Ajax fighting side by side. He heard Hector challenging the Greeks to fight. He closed his eyes and thought, "So many brave men have died on these grounds."

Menelaus took a deep breath and sat down. As he looked up at the heavens, he heard Helen's voice and laughter, and saw her running and playing with their little girl. He remembered her embrace, her tender kiss, and her soothing words. He thought of how her smile lit up a room. He felt the pain deep inside his heart; he missed her tremendously. He looked at Troy and as he thought of her being there, his anger and determination returned. "I swear by the gods on Mount Olympus, I will not let you be there another day longer. I will come to get you, even if I have to storm the walls of Troy myself." With renewed confidence, Menelaus returned to his camp and prepared to take his place inside the horse.

Sinon walked into Odysseus' camp and said, "I am ready."

Odysseus nodded and ordered his men to strip off Sinon's shirt and tie him to a pole. Odysseus took a cato'nine tails whip and lashed his exposed back. Sinon refused to cry out. After fifteen lashes, Odysseus put down the whip and untied Sinon. "Are you sure this is what you wanted?"

"Yes, it had to be done. We have worked too hard for this to fail now."

"We have grilled you with as many questions and scenarios we could imagine. Is there anything you would like to review?"

"No, I will go back to my camp and rest until morning."

An hour before dawn, the men met at the horse. Their spirits were high and there was excitement in the air. The Greeks broke camp at a furious pace to get the ships ready to sail. Menelaus, Odysseus, and Diomedes watched as their men climbed the rope and disappeared into the horse. Menelaus loaded the weapons wrapped in blankets into a basket, and lifted it inside to the men. Before Diomedes climbed in, he walked up to Agamemnon. They clasped each other's forearms in a form of handshake, and he said, "May the gods look favorably on our mission." Agamemnon nodded, and Diomedes climbed the rope.

Menelaus gave his brother a hug. "This is it, the moment we have been waiting for. We are as ready as we can be!"

Agamemnon said, "I will see you inside Troy."

Menelaus nodded, took the rope in his hands, and climbed to the back of the Horse, but before he dropped down into the horse's back, he looked out over the water. He saw the pink horizon as dawn was approaching. With a slight smile and nod, he joined his countrymen inside the horse.

The last to climb inside was Odysseus. His eyes met Agamemnon's. They both knew how dangerous the coming day would be. They nodded to each other with respect, and Odysseus took the rope in his hand and vanished into the wooden horse. Agamemnon took a ladder and placed a plaque on the front of the statue, then said a silent prayer for the men inside.

The horse was roomier than Menelaus imagined it would be. The men fit inside and had ample room. However, when Odysseus closed and locked the hatch, it appeared to grow smaller, darker, and more cramped. The air holes provided the only light and served as a way to see and hear what was happening outside the horse. The men jostled loudly for a more comfortable position among the blanket-wrapped weapons and supplies. Odysseus said, "Settle down, men. We can't make this much noise or have this amount of movement when the Trojans arrive. Most likely, we won't see or hear the Trojans until they are right under us. From this point on, we will communicate by hand signals or whispers. Messages will get from one end to the other by passing it from man to man. We all know the importance of remaining silent and unfound." Lookouts stationed in the front and rear of the horse looked through the air holes for anyone approaching.

On the beach, Agamemnon called Sinon forward and asked, "Are you ready for this?"

His clothes were ripped and filthy, and he was covered in dried blood from his beating. "Yes, Your Highness, I have been taught and briefed on many possible scenarios. We have developed a story that is sure to be believed."

"The success or failure of this mission lies in your hands. The Trojans may be more forceful and hostile than we can predict."

"Your Majesty, I am ready to give my life for our cause and for my country. No matter what the Trojans do, they will not get me to talk."

"Good man. Now, turn around." Sinon turned around, and Agamemnon tied his hands behind his back. Then Sinon walked toward the far end of the ramparts and disappeared over the barricade. Agamemnon turned his attention to the men loading the ships. "Let's move! We need to get out of here. Burn anything we can't load on the ships; we don't want to leave anything for the Trojans." The men stacked everything that wasn't going with them in a huge pile. For the first time in ages, they were confident and upbeat. This plan offered something different from the constant slaughter they had experienced, and it may have been the solution to all the fighting. Before the ships set sail, the soldiers set the huge pile of debris on fire.

The sentries on the Trojan walls noticed the huge plume of smoke rising in the distance. It was unusual to see so much smoke so early in the morning, and it was too large to be a campfire. Funeral pyres usually occurred late in the evening, and this seemed to be right in the middle of the Greek camp. The guards watched in awe as the Greek fleet came into view; once again, it seemed to fill the entire sea. They sounded the alarm. The Trojan people and the army woke and hurried to the walls. Helen heard the alarm, looked out her window, and saw the people running toward the walls joyfully shouting, "It's over! They're leaving!"

She rushed to see why everyone was shouting. Helen stopped a passerby and asked, "Why is everyone so excited?"

"The Greeks are sailing away! They are leaving! The war is over!"

Helen looked at Harleopi in disbelief as they ran to the walls and watched the Greek fleet sail off into the distance. As more and more people arrived, the shouting and cheering grew louder. Helen remembered what Odysseus had told her, but she didn't realize the ships would be leaving. She turned to Harleopi and whispered, "I don't believe it. This can't be happening."

"They will be back, won't they?" asked Harleopi.

"I don't know, I'm not sure what is happening."

Helen looked at the jubilation on the Trojan faces, and then stared at the ships as they got smaller and smaller. She felt anxiety and emptiness building in her stomach, but she smiled, waved, and cheered with those around her. After a few minutes, Helen whispered to Harleopi, "We must get back to my quarters. I cannot bear to celebrate the Greek fleet leaving."

When they got back to her quarters, Aethra met them and said, "I have heard the commotion. What is happening?"

Harleopi replied, "The Greeks have sailed away."

"What will happen to us?"

Helen said, "We will think of something, but for now, I want you to act as though you are happy the war is over."

"They are coming back, aren't they?" wondered Aethra aloud. "We don't know."

Helen thought, "Perhaps this is the beginning of Odysseus' plan." She tried to reassure her attendants. "I remember that Odysseus said there may be more to this than meets the eye, so let's just wait and see what develops. For now, we must act as Trojans."

When Priam arrived on the walls, he felt the energy of his people. They still celebrated and shouted, "They're leaving! They're leaving! We won! We won!" Priam was about to ask for an explanation when he saw the fleet sailing away. Unable to believe his eyes, he watched for a moment. As if he were talking to Agamemnon, he said, "Why? Why are you leaving now? We did not win a decisive victory, so why are you leaving? What has happened?" He watched as the people sang, danced, and shouted. Horns blew, and the entire Trojan population crowded onto the walls with tears of joy running down their faces. Troy exploded into a frenzy of activity.

Priam had his doubts. "Aeneas, I want you to send a company of men to see what is happening with that fire." Aeneas sent two sets of charioteers to investigate the Greek campsite. The charioteers approached the abandoned barricades of the Greek camp slowly. They could see the ships fading in the distance as they cautiously passed through the ramparts and entered the camp. They saw the huge bonfire burning the left over trash from the Greek camp, and as they moved past the fire and down the beach, the massive wooden horse came into view.

The Trojans gazed at the wooden horse in disbelief. Suddenly the camp felt eerily quiet. They were scared and uncomfortable, and hurried back through the ramparts and rode back to Troy as fast as their horses would run. The people celebrating on the walls saw the chariots coming across the plain, as lines of dust billowed up behind them. The Scaean Gates opened wide, and the men reported breathlessly to Priam. "Your Highness, the fire is only garbage, and the camp is empty." The soldier stopped to catch his breath. "There is one more thing. There is an enormous wooden horse in the camp!"

Priam was confused. "A what?"

"An enormous wooden horse!"

Priam thought for a moment then ordered, "Assemble a few companies of men. I must see this for myself, but I will not leave the city defenseless if this is some kind of trap!" The Trojans assembled a large force of men, and Priam accompanied by many in his council marched out of Troy.

The Greek fleet sailed slowly out to sea, and the men stared back at Troy. They had been there for such a long time, and now they could see it in a different light. Agamemnon listened to the men on his ship speak of how the memories of friends and relatives who had given their lives flooded back into many of their minds. A feeling of melancholy for things that could have been cast over everyone, even Agamemnon. They all looked at the huge fire burning on the shore, and spoke quietly about the men in the colossal wooden horse. Many of those men were kings and friends of the men in the ships. The soldiers on the ships knew how brave the men in the horse were, and hoped the mission didn't end in disaster. Finally, Agamemnon could no longer see the beaches of Troy. The fleet pulled around the other side of the Tenedos Islands, and all nervously awaited nightfall.

After the Trojan charioteers rode away, the men in the horse were concerned. "Did they hear us? What's happening out there?" they whispered. The anxiety of uncertainty built up inside the men. They were getting restless; some men twitched their feet, and others drummed their fingers on their legs. As the sun heated up the atmosphere, the temperature inside the horse rose. Odysseus passed the word, "Be quiet and still. There may be someone outside."

Menelaus' mind raced. "How long will we be here? The minutes seem like hours. Maybe this won't work. Maybe the Trojans aren't coming."

One of the lookouts turned and whispered, "Shhh, listen!" The men stopped, they heard the sound of approaching horses. The lookout said, "There must be a thousand Trojans just outside the ramparts!"

The men in the horse were still and silent, and listened intently. They knew that anchored on the other side of the Tenedos Islands, the Greek fleet could only wait. The next move belonged to the Trojans.

Priam rode in the front of the ranks and ordered, "Spread out and search the whole area." He looked out over the sea and saw that the fleet had disappeared, but was worried about its sudden return. He moved slowly toward an opening in the ramparts and looked at the hulking wooden horse that stood in front of him, letting his eyes skim over its construction. Priam studied the horse for a long time and took in the whole scene: the empty Greek camp, the huge debris fire, and the enormous wooden horse standing on the beach.

CHAPTER TEN

THE FALL OF TROY

Priam moved closer to the wooden horse; he had never seen anything like it. The royal guard followed him as he walked around and touched the massive statue. Compared to the noise of war, the empty beach was strangely quiet, broken only by the sound of crashing waves. Priam turned to his High Priest, Laocoön. "What do you think this is?"

Laocoön said, "I don't know what to make of it, but I don't trust the Greeks, even those bearing gifts."

"Do you think this statue is for us?"

"I think it is a trap, a ruse. This is not what it seems. I don't know what it is, but we should be careful."

Priam wasn't as skeptical as Laocoön. "I don't know about that. Look at this plaque hanging from its neck:

> *The Greeks dedicate this offering to Athena as thanks for their safe return home.*

"I don't care what that says. I still think this is a dangerous trick. We should burn it," said Laocoön.

Priam replied, "I don't want to offend Athena, especially since we already lost the Palladium."

Laocoön said, "Listen." He picked up his spear to throw it. Priam ran over and tried to stop him, but he was too late. Laocoön threw his spear at the side of the horse, but it bounced off the wood because of the angle he threw it and only made a dull thumping sound. "It's hollow like a drum."

Priam replied, "I wish you hadn't done that. I expect it to be hollow; it's huge."

"We shouldn't take anything from the Greeks. Burn it and get it over with."

As they discussed the fate of the horse, they heard a commotion coming from farther down the beach. The soldiers brought a captive to Priam and threw the man on the ground at the King's feet. "Look what we found hiding in the bushes by the marsh."

Priam looked down at the small, dirty man on the ground before him. His clothes were in tatters; he had his hands tied behind him; and his back showed fresh wounds from a recent whipping. "What's your name?"

The man remained silent and stared at the ground. A Trojan soldier kicked him in the ribs and shouted, "The King asked you a question!"

In a small voice, the man replied, "Sinon."

Priam asked, "Why didn't you sail away with the Greeks?"

Sinon said nothing. Two Trojan soldiers grabbed him and pulled him to his feet. One of the soldiers held him by the head while the other placed a knife between his skull and his ear. He said, "Maybe he's hard of hearing. This will help!" and sliced his ear off. Sinon screamed, and rolled on the ground with blood running down his neck. The soldier asked, "Now can you hear me?" Sinon groaned and nodded. "Good, now answer the question."

Sinon sobbed, "I will tell you my tale. Please, don't hurt me anymore."

The soldier said, "We make no promises. Talk!"

Sinon struggled to his knees and kneeled before Priam and his entourage. He spoke slowly and timidly. "It is true I am a Greek. I came here as a squire to my master, Palamedes. I enjoyed all the benefits of that position because Palamedes was an honorable and respected warrior." He stopped talking and looking at the men's goatskin water sacks. "Please, I haven't had any water in two days."

Priam said, "Tell us more, then maybe you can have some water."

Sinon continued, "Odysseus held a grudge against Palamedes. Odysseus framed him, falsely accused him of being a traitor, and had him stoned to death. I swore I would get revenge for my mentor. When Odysseus heard of my threat, he began to terrorize me and to devise ways to destroy me." Sinon began to sob and bowed his head. "There is no point in telling you anymore. If you think all Greeks are the same, then you can kill me now. Odysseus would be pleased, and Agamemnon would pay a good price."

"Continue, or we will kill you."

Sinon looked up at Priam. "The Greeks wanted to leave for some time because they thought the war unwinnable, but the winds were never favorable, so they consulted the seer Calchas. He told them they needed a human sacrifice, just as they did to get favorable winds to sail here. Odysseus chose me as a sacrifice and none opposed him. They beat me and whipped me, but I managed to escape because I have a friend or two left in the Greek camp. I ran away, hid in the swamp, and watched as they sacrificed a poor slave girl in my place. I'm sure they will take out their anger on my family when they get back to Greece." Sinon placed his face against Priam's feet. "Please, great King. Allow me to live, to return to Greece to help my family."

Priam's heart softened to the pitiful man. "Untie him, and give him some water."

The guards untied Sinon, who threw his arms around Priam's legs. "Thank you, Your Highness!" Sinon received water, which he drank in great gulps.

Priam said, "Now that I have spared your life, tell me what this great horse is for. Is it some religious object, or some type of weapon?"

"Please don't ask me that. Although they tried to sacrifice me, I cannot betray my countrymen."

Priam motioned to the soldiers. Three men grabbed Sinon; two of them held him while the third placed a knife between his remaining ear and his head. Priam asked again, "What is the meaning of this horse?"

Sinon remained silent, so Priam nodded, and the man sliced off his other ear. Sinon fell to the ground crying. The blood ran through his fingers as he held his head where his ear used to be.

Priam commanded, "Pick him up." Two soldiers picked up Sinon and held him firmly by the arms and shoulders. Sternly, Priam said, "Now, tell me what I want to know."

Sinon remained defiant. "I am not a traitor!"

Priam signaled again. The soldier grabbed a handful of Sinon's hair, jerked his head back, and placed a sword against his throat. Priam said, "I have removed your ears, now I will remove your head." Sinon felt the blade cutting his skin, and as the warm blood started to flow down his neck, he cried, "Please! I will tell you true."

The soldier removed the sword from Sinon's throat. Poor Sinon fell to his knees, put his hand to his throat, took a deep breath, and said, "The horse was built to please Athena. They believed they may have incurred her wrath because they had stolen the Palladium from her temple."

Priam said, "That's what it says on the plaque. Tell me more."

"The horse was meant to win favor for the Greeks when they return home. But, if it were placed in the Temple of Athena, it would make the Trojans impervious to future Greek attacks. To destroy it would mean the ruin of Troy."

Laocoön walked to the edge of the surf and shouted, "I tell you, it is a trick! Burn it!" As he shouted, a large serpent emerged from the sea and wrapped itself around him. His two sons rushed to help their father, but serpents also attacked them, and all three drowned in the surf.

The Trojans were stunned and frightened. Someone shouted, "He threw a spear at the horse, and look what happened to him!"

Priam looked at Sinon. "We will take the horse inside the city."

"You can't. To prevent you from doing that, the Greeks purposely built it too big to fit through your gates."

"The Greeks aren't as smart as they think they are. If I want the horse inside Troy, it will be inside Troy." Priam turned to his soldiers. "I want the engineers to transport this to Troy as quickly as possible."

Trojan engineers removed the large wooden wheels and axles from two oxcarts strong enough to support the horse. Once the Trojan townspeople heard that the Greeks had indeed left and it was safe, they hurried down to the abandoned Greek camp to see where their enemy had lived for so long. They watched as the engineers dug a small channel under the front of the horse, and then used a large lever to lift the front and place wooden support blocks under it. Next, they attached the axle and wheels to the front of the horse's platform. They repeated the same procedure at the back of the horse, and soon, the horse had four wheels and was ready to be pulled into Troy. The Trojans harnessed three teams of horses by rope to a freshly installed hook on the front of the platform, and the horse started its slow, steady journey. Sinon was tethered to the hind legs of the horse bloodied and beaten he was forced to walk behind it as it made its way across the plain. The people saw the horse as a symbol of their victory over the Greeks. Some threw flowers on the horse's platform, musicians and dancers led the parade, and everyone cheered as their trophy rolled toward the city.

There was no road to speak of leading into Troy, so the horse bumped and swayed as it made its way across the plain. Inside the horse, the heat continued to build as the midday sun beat down on the wood. Fresh air was at a minimum. The men in the horse were sweating profusely. Some tried to lie down and conserve energy, others closed their eyes and meditated, and some felt sick from the lack of fresh air and the erratic movement.

When the horse reached the Scaean Gate, the parade stopped. It was indeed too tall to fit through the gate. Priam watched from his balcony on the wall. When the horse stopped, he said to Aeneas, "Watch, the Greeks think they are clever, but we have a few tricks up our sleeves as well." The Trojans let down two large, thick ropes from the top of the walls. They attached these ropes to the back of the platform and pulled. The rear of the horse gradually left the ground, and when the head was at a thirty-degree angle, it was low enough to fit through the gate, the horses started to pull it into Troy.

When the horse tilted forward, the men inside were taken completely by surprise. Odysseus made a gesture to remind them to be quiet. As the horse tilted, they slid toward the front. They scrambled to grab their clothed weapons and armor so they wouldn't clang. The men ended up in a large heap at the front of the horse. As the head passed to the other side of the wall, the end was let down slowly, and the wooden horse was inside Troy without damaging the horse, the walls, or the gate. The men inside the horse slowly untangled and crawled back to their places. They could hear the people of Troy cheering and knew the party was underway.

A Greek lookout passed the word to Menelaus that he could see her walking along the wall and stopping to stare at the horse. Menelaus wanted to move to an air hole where he could see her, but feared his movement would be detected and jeopardize the entire mission. He sat still and closed his eyes, waiting for nightfall.

Helen had watched from her window as the Trojans pulled the horse into the city, and she remembered what Odysseus had said to her. She now walked along the top of the walls and looked at the horse from many different angles. The Trojans were celebrating loudly below her. When they first saw the Greek ships sailing away, they were overjoyed, but soon grew skeptical that it was but a Greek trick. Once they felt the Greeks were really gone, the city erupted in a huge, impromptu celebration. They slaughtered dozens of hogs and steers for roasting, and the palace opened up its stores of wine. The people danced in the street, sang, and hugged strangers. They hung banners from rooftops, and shop owners gave away free samples of food to the townspeople. Hundreds of Trojans circled around the horse to get a better look at it, but were afraid to touch it out of fear of incurring Athena's wrath. The tensions of all the years of war were lifted, and they felt a euphoria they hadn't felt before. Free from the yoke of Greek attack, they even left the Scaean Gate open.

Helen made her way back to her chambers where Deiphobus was waiting. Laughing and gloating, he said, "We won! The Greeks have left, the war is over, and we have won!"

Helen turned away and looked out her window at the wooden horse. "Is that why you came here? To gloat?"

"Well, it looks like old Menelaus has finally given up. I knew he wouldn't last."

Filled with hatred for her newest husband, Helen faced him and hissed, "The Greeks may have left, but you'll never be the man that Menelaus is!"

Deiphobus stood uncomfortably close to Helen's face. "Be careful, my sweet. You need me now. The war is over and the Greeks have left, so your value has just fallen. Without me, you will be considered nothing more than a cheap adulteress." Helen slapped him hard across the face. Deiphobus raised his hand to strike her, but thought better of it. "No, I will take care of you later. Now is a time for celebration, and I won't let a whore ruin it for me." Helen watched Deiphobus walk out, and she clenched her teeth and fists.

That night, the city of Troy was raucous with celebration. Music and singing filled the air, and everywhere, people danced in the street with friends and strangers. Priam and his council stood at the top of the palace steps and looked down on the horse standing in the middle of the market square. Still tethered to the horse, Sinon sat on the platform near the back legs. He looked like a broken man as people came by to shout, "You dog, you Greek pig! My husband died in the war!" They spit at him or threw stones. A guard was stationed nearby to prevent the people from killing him. The towns folk cheered when they saw Priam at the top of the stairs, he and the council waved back to the joyous masses.

Cassandra stood with her father and faced the adoring crowd. She possessed the gift of prophecy, and ominously said, "That horse will be the destruction of Troy."

"What do you mean?" Priam asked.

"There are soldiers inside the horse."

Unfortunately for Cassandra, she also had the curse of not having anyone believe her prophecies. "That is nonsense," Priam responded, "They would have suffocated by now if there were men in there."

Aeneas said, "It is certainly big enough to have soldiers inside."

Deiphobus asked, "Why don't we just tear a few boards from the top of it and look inside? We can end all this speculation."

Priam refused to touch the statue. "I don't want to damage it. We may invite the wrath of the gods. Laocoön merely threw a spear at it, and look what happened to him!"

"If we can't prove for certain that there are not warriors inside the horse, then we will place guards around it for the rest of the night," suggested Aeneas.

Helen was standing with the royal family and heard Aeneas' recommendation. She knew that it would be a disaster for the Greek plan. Determined to put their minds at ease, she said, "I know a way to prove that there are no men inside the horse."

"How?" asked Priam.

"The Greeks have been away from their families for a long time."

"So? What does that have to do with the horse?"

Helen seductively responded, "The men have also been away from their wives for a very long time. When I was a little girl in Sparta, I earned a nickname because I possess a very special gift. They called me Echo."

In unison, all the people at the top of the stairs said, "Echo?"

"Yes. I have the gift of impersonation. I can impersonate anyone's voice."

Deiphobus said, "I don't believe you. I have never heard this before."

"I don't believe you. I have never heard this before," replied Helen, with a perfect imitation of his voice.

Hecuba said, "That is incredible!"

"That is incredible!" echoed Helen, in Hecuba's voice.

"Impressive, but how will that prove no one is in the horse?" asked Priam.

"I can go to the horse and mimic the voices of the men's wives. The Greeks have been here so long, they must be very homesick and miss their wives greatly, they will mistakenly think their wives are here, and if they are in the horse, they will come out."

Aeneas was skeptical. "How do you know which wives to imitate? Do you know something we don't?"

Helen stroked Aeneas' chest and cheek. "Don't be so suspicious, Aeneas. If there were soldiers inside the horse, they would most likely be the leaders or the bravest of the Greeks. I have met the wives of many of these men. If there are men in the horse, I assure you they will not be able to resist the temptation to see their loved ones."

Priam said, "I'd like to see this. Let's give her a chance. Clear an area around the horse!" The soldiers moved the people back, a large circle was cleared around the base of the horse, and Priam's entourage gathered around. Priam raised his hands over his head. "I want silence!" The people all quieted down and the music stopped. Priam looked at Helen, and gestured toward the horse.

As Helen walked forward, the lookouts inside whispered, "Helen is outside the horse." It was dark and miserably hot, and the thin, dim rays of light that came through the air holes provided little illumination. Many of the men looked like silhouettes. They were weak from heat exhaustion and lack of fresh air, and a few were starting to get delirious. The water and wine mixture provided them with some nutrition, but not enough to combat the brutal conditions.

Helen approached the horse, and in a perfect impersonation of Odysseus' wife, Penelope, called out, "Odysseus, where are you? It has been so long since I've held you. Please come to me. Don't you miss my warm embrace, my loving kisses, and the sweet smell of my perfume? My arms ache to hold you again, to be together in our bed, and make sweet passionate love once more. Come to me, Odysseus. Come to me now." Odysseus wiped his forehead, took a deep breath, and licked his lips. Menelaus put his index finger to his lips and whispered, "Echo."

Helen went from one wife to another. Some of the men whose wives she imitated were in the horse, and some were not. When Helen imitated Anticlus' wife, he attempted to cry out, but Menelaus clasped his hand over his mouth. Anticlus suffered from heat exhaustion and was delirious. Menelaus could feel the cold sweat on his body as he tried to keep him from calling out. The other men sitting nearby moved quietly to help Menelaus; some held his arms and others held his legs. Desperate to be released, Anticlus thrashed and struggled. Menelaus didn't know whether he was suffocating or trying to escape, but he couldn't take the risk. Finally, the fighting and twisting stopped, and Anticlus lay dead, accidently suffocated.

All the Greeks froze. Did the Trojans hear them? Did the horse shake? The men listened carefully, and finally heard Helen say, "King Priam, I have done my best to expose whoever may be in the horse."

"You are very believable. I don't think I would have been able to resist your temptations had I been in the horse." Priam raised his arms and addressed the crowd. "Tomorrow, we will place the horse in the Temple of Athena, but tonight, we celebrate our victory over the Greeks!"

The people all cheered, the musicians played again, and the dancing and singing picked up where it left off. A spontaneous parade formed, and the euphoric Trojans danced through the streets, picking up more people along the way. Odysseus whispered to Menelaus, "The noise from the party will drown out any little noise we may make." Odysseus then passed the word to his men, "Start putting on your armor." The men unwrapped their armor and helped each other put it on.

Helen returned to her quarters and called for Aethra and Harleopi. "I want you to secretly prepare our things for a trip."

Aethra asked, "Where are we going?"

Noticeably anxious, Helen snapped, "Don't ask questions; just do as I told you!"

"My lady, does this have anything to do with the party outside?" asked Harleopi.

"I want you to stay close by. Do not leave your rooms tonight. It could be very dangerous for us out there; the Trojans are very drunk, and we must remember that we are Greek. I'm sure there are those in the city who haven't forgotten that." Helen hugged both of her attendants and said, "I love you both. Please understand that this is for your own safety. Now go and do what I asked."

The servants left, and Helen went across the hall to the rooms she shared with Deiphobus. She knew he was at the celebration, and would be gone for hours. Helen found his armor, spear, shield, sword, and helmet, and hid them—some in his quarters, and some in hers. Helen sequestered herself in her room, watching and listening to the party going on outside her window. Every Trojan celebrated their victory. The Scaean Gate had been closed, and even the guards celebrated. Who could blame them? It was the end of a long, hard war, and they thought they had won!

The party finally wound down. Many Trojans were very drunk, and everyone was exhausted from the celebration. Soon, there was no one on the streets or the walls. Helen snuck out of the palace, and walked quickly toward the walls facing the sea. Along the way, she grabbed a torch and moved quickly up the steps to the top of the wall. She spotted Sinon further along the wall waving his torch, and she imitated his movements. She'd temporarily pause to see whether anyone had spotted her. When she caught up with him, Sinon explained that the men guarding him drank heavily and left with some women, and did not notice that Sinon had untied his ropes and freed himself.

The Greek fleet waited a mile off the coast. When they received the signal they hoped for, they moved rapidly to shore, like silent ghosts floating across the sea. Helen and Sinon waved their torches for a few more minutes, and then hurried back down the steps. Helen returned to her chambers, while Sinon knocked on the side of the horse three times with a spear.

"That's it! Let's go!" whispered Odysseus. He threw open the hatch, and let two ropes down to the ground. The rush of fresh cool air was invigorating. The men quickly slid down the ropes and fanned out to their appointed positions. Menelaus and some men went directly to help open the Scaean Gate by pulling across the huge wooden latch that held it closed, others sought out the unconscious guards and slit their throats. The Greeks on the walls watched as their army approached like a flood of shadows across the plain. The Greek army poured through the Scaean Gate, lit their torches, and fanned out through the city. Some of the men from the horse waited to get their shields and lead their men, but Menelaus did not. As he ran toward the palace, he knew that his Spartan soldiers would follow him. The screams of the Trojans started out slowly, but intensified as the army flooded into the city.

The screams were heard inside the palace and a general alarm was sounded, calling the soldiers to grab their armor and defend the city. Deiphobus drunkenly stumbled to his room to retrieve his armor and weapons. He tore his room apart, but couldn't find them anywhere. Then it dawned on him. "That Greek whore!" He grabbed a large knife and hurried to Helen's quarters. Helen was in her night robe when Deiphobus burst in, waving the knife. "Where are they? Where did you put them?"

Helen stepped back, out of range of his knife. "What are you talking about?"

"Don't lie to me; you know what I'm looking for. I may die tonight, but I will get the satisfaction of doing what every Trojan has wanted since you came here, you little whore!" Deiphobus stepped toward her and Helen backed up to the wall.

From behind, Deiphobus heard a shout. "Deiphobus!" Menelaus had fought his way to her chambers, killing those in his way, and running past those he could. Now, he stood in Helen's room, breathing heavily from his sprint. When Deiphobus turned to face Menelaus, Helen grabbed a dagger lying on a small table next to her bed and drove the knife deep between his shoulder blades. Deiphobus groaned and turned halfway around to look at her, but Menelaus jumped on him and drove his sword deep into his stomach, then ripped it up toward his chest. Deiphobus moaned loudly and fell off the sword onto the floor. Helen watched as the pain, frustration, and anger that had built up inside Menelaus exploded in a fit of rage. He hacked at Deiphobus' arms and legs with his sword. Menelaus dismembered him as he screamed like a beast in the jungle. He knelt next to Deiphobus' destroyed body and shouted, "You've seen too much of Helen. Now, you will never see again," as he gouged out his eyes with his sword.

Menelaus stood and turned toward Helen. His body was splattered with gore, and Deiphobus' blood dripped from his sword. Helen was scared. She had never seen Menelaus like this before. Terrified, she thought, "Is he going to kill me too? Did he believe the rumors and slander about me? He surely must have heard them." Helen was ready to accept her fate. She said to herself, "What will be, will be." She cautiously moved toward Menelaus, held her head high, dropped her robe, and stood naked before him.

Menelaus had prayed for this moment for a long time: Helen was finally before him. The emotion welled up inside him. He dropped his sword, and they leapt into each other's arms. Tears of joy fell freely from their eyes, as they hugged and rained kisses all over each other's faces. Between kisses, Menelaus whispered, "My darling, I have missed you so much. I can't believe I am holding you again."

"My dear Menelaus, my dear Menelaus, you are finally here. I have missed you too!"

"We must leave here immediately. They are going to burn the city."

They heard the cries of battle taking place outside the window. Helen put on her robe and said, "Wait, I must get my servants."

"Leave them, there is no time."

"No! They are my friends!"

"Hurry!" Menelaus knew there would be no arguing with Helen when it came to Aethra and Harleopi.

Helen stepped around the pool of blood and Deiphobus' lifeless body, and ran to a back door. "Harleopi, Aethra, grab our things! It's time to go!" The two women scurried out, each carrying a large bundle. They gasped at the body on the floor and stared at Menelaus.

Menelaus said, "I remember both of you! Come now, it's time to go. Stay close to me."

The three women followed Menelaus to the reflecting pool in the middle of the palace. They passed soldiers engaged in hand-to-hand combat and dismembered bodies sprawled throughout the palace, and were careful not to slip on the blood-covered marble floors. Greeks ransacked everything in sight. Some used their swords to pry the gold rings from around the marble pillars.

Menelaus called to three nearby soldiers, "You three come here! I want you to help me escort these women to the front gate!" Menelaus turned to Helen and her attendants. "Cover your heads with a shawl; you may have many enemies out there!"

As they made their way to the front of the palace, Menelaus saw Priam and his family fighting Achilles' son, Neoptolemus, in front of the Temple of Zeus. Helen peered out from under her shawl and caught Priam's eye. She could see by the heartbreak on his face that he realized the horse was a trick, and Helen was in on it. She felt sad for Priam; he had always treated her well. She watched in horror as Neoptolemus dragged Priam by his hair through the blood of his freshly slain son and drove a sword deep into his ribs. She caught her breath and froze until the soldier pushed her on.

As they ran down the palace steps, Helen saw that parts of Troy were already on fire. Bodies littered the streets and the Trojan people screamed and ran around aimlessly. When they passed the Temple of Athena, Helen saw Cassandra and heard her screams as she was raped at the foot of the statue of Athena. Once again, guilt sunk its gnarly claws into her heart. This was all because of her.

The sights and sounds were overwhelming, and the carnage was brutal. The fountain in the middle of the square ran red with blood. They had to step over the bodies of the soldiers, men, women, and children that lay slaughtered in the streets. Menelaus knew how dangerous it was for them to be in the midst of the battle. The three Spartans helped herd the women through the streets, and slay any non-Greek who stepped into their path.

The small party finally made it to the Scaean Gate. Greeks guarded the gate so that no one would escape the bloodbath. Menelaus said to his soldiers, "We will be all right from here!"

The soldiers bowed and ran back into the chaos behind them. Menelaus found a wagon and helped the women into it. As they rode away, Helen and her servants looked back at Troy, the place that had been their home for the duration of the war. She saw the Trojans fighting gallantly. Some fought from rooftops and others tried to organize a defense, but the sheer number of Greeks overwhelmed them. Menelaus said, "Troy is finished. We will finally be going home."

The wagon moved quickly across the plain, illuminated by the burning city behind them. When they reached the ships at the beach, Menelaus approached the man he trusted most with Helen's life, a Spartan palace guard named Lurineus. "Guard these women

and make them comfortable. I will return when the battle is over."
He helped the women down from the wagon and gave Helen a hug.

Helen asked, "You're not going back, are you?"

"I can't ask my men to fight for me when I am not willing to join them!"

"Be careful, and come back to me." Menelaus and Helen embraced and enjoyed a long kiss. He climbed in the wagon and rode back toward Troy. Helen and her attendants boarded the ship, and Lurineus led them to Menelaus' stateroom.

The screams of battle grew louder as Menelaus approached the gates. The fighting was still intense. He found his men fighting their way through the palace. The resistance was strong, but disorganized; the Greeks had caught the Trojans completely by surprise. The Trojans didn't have time to form a strong cohesive fighting unit, and any small bands that developed were promptly overrun. The palace was swarming with Greeks, and the treasury was looted quickly and completely. The Greeks pillaged everything of value, including gold, jewels, and women. They killed everything else.

Menelaus watched the great wooden horse, surrounded by the growing inferno start to burn as well, set ablaze by the radiant heat from the burning city. He thought, "The horse can serve as a funeral pyre for Anticlus, the same way Troy will serve as a funeral pyre for many Trojans."

The slaughter lasted all night and into the morning. Finally, the noises of battle died out, and the only sounds left were the sobs of the weeping survivors as they were led away into slavery. Agamemnon left a company of men behind for the day to scour the city for treasure, finish off wounded Trojans, and capture hidden survivors in the smoldering city. The majority of the Greeks returned to the ships to celebrate their victory. Behind them followed a parade of women and wagons loaded with treasure to divide among the victors.

Menelaus returned to his ship early that morning. He was exhausted from his time in the horse and the battle for Troy. He wanted to spend time with Helen, but first, he bathed in the warm waters of the Aegean and feasted on wine and meat. He took Helen to his private quarters aboard his ship, closed the door behind them, and said, "The moment is finally here."

"Dear Menelaus, my heart has ached to hold you again." She took him by the hand and led him to the bed, stroked his cheek and kissed him softly on the lips. They removed their robes slowly and embraced as they lowered themselves onto the bed. They caressed each other and kissed deeply. Their long nightmare was finally over. After the two were finished with their lovemaking and before he fell asleep, Menelaus said, "I just want to rest a little; there is much work to be done. Wake me in a few hours! "Menelaus held Helen as he slept, content and relaxed.

Helen woke Menelaus with a kiss. They dressed and stood arm in arm on the bow of the ship to watch what was happening on the shore. Menelaus could not be prouder of his men and his wife than he was at that moment. He took in the scene with a huge smile on his face. The soldiers cheered for them, and as word spread that Helen stood on the ship, many men ran to see the great beauty they had fought so hard to bring back to Greece. A crowd of soldiers gathered around and applauded. "Hail Menelaus! Long live Greece!"

Menelaus raised his arms above his head and shouted, "Men, for all of you who have never met her, this is my wife, Helen!"

"Helen!" They all shouted.

"Since the day she was abducted by the Trojans, you have stood with me through many hardships and sorrows. I tell you now that I am forever grateful to all of you!"

The crowd cheered as the reunited lovers shared a kiss. They climbed down from the ship, and Menelaus escorted her to Agamemnon's camp. Everyman they met along the way offered congratulations and compliments. Agamemnon had his hut restored, and when Menelaus and Helen entered, Agamemnon said, "Well, here they are! Come in, come in." Agamemnon went directly to Helen and gave her a hug. "My dear, you are as beautiful as you are brave."

"I don't feel brave. I feel tired and relieved that it is finally over."

"There are few women who could have endured what you have!"

Menelaus interrupted. "It has been a long war. Now it is time to prepare to leave for home."

Agamemnon said, "Yes, but first we must have a victory celebration, and later this evening, we will divide up the treasure we have won!"

Helen said, "Menelaus, is it possible to return to Troy to recover some of my valuables? I hid them before the fall of the city, and I may have overlooked them in my haste."

"There is no need for you to go back there. The city is completely destroyed, and there are sights you don't need to see. If you tell me where you hid your treasures, I will retrieve them."

"If you think that is best. I saved some treasure from Paris and Priam by hiding it with my gowns and robes when we first arrived in Troy because I wasn't sure what would happen when we got here."

Agamemnon said, "Menelaus, you can take a few men with you. What you bring back is yours and won't be divided among the rest of the men."

"All right, I will leave immediately. I want to be back in time for the celebration." Helen and Menelaus returned to his ship, and Helen told him where she hid her valuables as he prepared to return to the city. As Menelaus prepared to go back to Troy, Helen noticed a large holding area farther down the beach. As she neared the large pen, she saw Queen Hecuba, Cassandra, and Hector's wife, Andromache, among the prisoners. They were held as slaves to be handed out as part of the treasure later that evening. The three women were dirty and tired; Helen looked in their eyes and felt pity for them. Once, they were powerful women married to the leaders of Troy, and now they were nothing more than the spoils of war to be divided amongst the victors. As Helen stood by the fence, some of the women recognized her and shouted, "There she is! There's the whore who brought us to this!" Other women ran to the fence and spit at her. "May the gods curse you, you dog!"

Helen walked away and reminded herself, "That could have been Hermoine and me, had the Trojans attacked Sparta."

Menelaus gathered a small group of men and set out for Troy. As he approached the city, the rancid smell of burnt flesh grew stronger. He passed through the front gate and saw the remains of the wooden horse in the center of town. Three wheels were mostly burned away, and part of one of the charred front legs was all that stood. Hot spots burned throughout the city. Bloated corpses were scattered everywhere, and the stench was overpowering. Dogs carried off pieces of the dismembered bodies, and Greek soldiers stripped the dead Trojans of their armor and piled dead Greeks onto wagons to prepare for the funeral pyre. They would leave the Trojan corpses where they lay. In the distance, Menelaus saw Antenor rummaging through the remains of his house. The Greeks had spared his life, but the fire didn't spare his home. He made eye contact with Menelaus, and then continued to gather what he could salvage from the ruins. Many Greek soldiers were already tearing down the walls of Troy. Some didn't want Troy to rise again, and others wanted to take a block of stone home as a trophy. Menelaus made his way through the palace and found the servant's chambers. Under Harleopi's bed, Menelaus pried up two large, marble tiles and found a large quantity of gold and jewels that Helen had hidden there. He loaded the treasure on a wagon and returned to the ships.

At his campsite, Menelaus received a visitor. The man said, "My name is Acamas of Athens. I have fought long and hard in this war, and now I have come to ask for the return of my grandmother, Aethra."

Menelaus replied, "Acamas, I want to thank you for your service and your help in my quest to restore my honor and that of all of Greece. That decision falls to my wife." Menelaus called for Helen. "I would like you to meet Aethra's grandson."

"It is a pleasure to meet you."

"He wants to take Aethra back to Athens with him."

Helen summoned Aethra, who appeared from a back room. Aethra said, "Yes, Your Highness?"

Helen said, "I want you to meet your grandson."

Aethra looked at the man standing before her. He bore such a strong resemblance to his father, Theseus. "Acamas! You have grown so much."Aethra was overcome with joy, ran to him, kissed his cheek and hugged him tightly.

Helen was excited for her. "Aethra, you have served me well, and became more than a servant. I consider you a member of my family. I give you your freedom to return to Athens with your grandson, if you so wish."

Aethra wiped the tears from her eyes. "My lady, you were always dear to my heart, but it is time for me to go home."The two women embraced lovingly, and Aethra went to gather her belongings.

When Aethra finished, Helen summoned Harleopi to say goodbye to Aethra. "You have been like a mother to me." Helen, Aethra, and Harleopi embraced, and then Aethra turned and walked away with her grandson.

As Aethra walked away, Odysseus appeared at the campsite with a thin, worn out little man with no ears at his side. Menelaus said "Odysseus my friend, welcome." Odysseus and Menelaus embraced.

Helen exclaimed "Odysseus I am so pleased to see you." Helen hugged Odysseus tightly.

Odysseus replied. I am pleased to see you both. I have with me the man who convinced the Trojans to take the Horse into the city at the cost of his ears. He may be small but he is as brave as any warrior in the Greek army. His only request was to meet the woman he has admired for so many years. Helen I would like you to meet Sinon."

Helen approached Sinon and said "Yes I remember you being tied to the horse inside Troy and the people abusing you." Sinon replied, "Yes my Queen, that was me. Many years ago I went to Sparta when your hand was being offered in marriage. I had no property and nothing much to offer, but I had hoped for a chance to see you, but it wasn't to be. When I heard you had been abducted I had to be in the army to bring you home."

"I am sorry that you have lost your ears in this war."

"My Queen, the loss of my ears is a small price I would gladly pay again to stand in your presence." Helen moved forward and hugged Sinon tightly and gently kissed where his ears used to be. "I am so very impressed with your sacrifice along with the sacrifices of all these men on my behalf, I would like you to join us as we prepare to eat."

Menelaus said. "Yes, Sinon, please join us and you as well Odysseus."

"Thank you my friend, but I must decline, I have much to do with my preparations to return home.

"I am most honored to dine with you, thank you so very much." Sinon said as he smiled broadly."

That evening, the Greeks prepared the funeral pyres on the plains for all those who lost their lives in the sacking of Troy. Agamemnon delivered the eulogy. "These brave men gave their lives fighting for the noble cause of restoring our country's honor. We will remember them always!" The bodies were stacked on the huge woodpiles and lit on fire. The army returned to the beach and started the victory celebration. Huge barrels of wine were placed throughout the campsite, and multiple fire pits roasted wild boars and steers.

The Greeks piled all the treasure taken from Troy into huge mounds in front of Agamemnon's hut. Agamemnon called his leaders forward, one by one, and allowed them to take their share of the plunder back to their men. There was so much wealth to divide that no one complained about his share. After doling out the treasures, the captive women were given to the leaders as concubines. Odysseus took Hecuba, Agamemnon kept Cassandra, and Andromache was given to Achilles' son, Neoptolemus. The remaining women chosen and taken by the soldiers.

The soldiers drank and ate heavily; there were musicians, dancers, games, and races to entertain the battle-weary men. The relief from the stress of the war was as great for them as it had been for the Trojans. The leaders sat at a massive table, and Agamemnon raised his sword to the sky and shouted, "Men of Greece, victors and conquerors of Troy, I salute you! The men raised their swords and cheered. "Let it be known from this day forth that Greece is an honorable country and will defend its people."

"Long live Greece!" roared the crowd.

Menelaus raised Helen's hand and shouted, "With your help, your sacrifice, and your courage, the honor of my family and the honor of our country have been restored!"

"Hail Greece!"

Menelaus and Helen went back to the ship early, but the rest of the Greeks partied well into the night.

It took a full day for the Greek fleet to prepare for the voyage home. Menelaus and Helen met with each leader, and thanked him for his courage and honor for fulfilling his oath to protect their marriage. Helen was overjoyed that it was finally time to leave Troy and put the horrors of the past behind her. Menelaus loaded his ships with gold, jewels, and women, and left a few hours earlier than the rest of the fleet. The Trojan War was over. Helen let out a sigh of relief. Finally, she was heading home!

CHAPTER ELEVEN

HELEN GOES HOME

Helen stood on the stern of the ship with Menelaus and looked back at the city of Troy. The famous walls were scorched black in places and demolished in others. The Citadel no longer shimmered in the sun—it was now a charred heap. Great flocks of vultures circled above the city and feasted on the remains of the victims below. Helen thought, "At last, it is finally over. What a waste, such a beautiful place destroyed by revenge and pride."

Menelaus watched Troy fade into the distance and thought, "I will never forget the men who died there, friends and foes." He placed his arm around Helen as they watched Troy disappear over the horizon. Due to the casualties of war, he set sail from Troy with thirty ships, down from the fifty ships he arrived with so long ago. He sold some to Allies whose cities had seaports, including the Athenians, the Cretans, and the army from Cyprus.

Menelaus was at sea for two days when the signs of a major storm developed on the horizon. He saw the storm clouds blocking his path home, and decided to go southeast, around the storm. Sailing farther behind Menelaus, the rest of the Greek ships, tried to go directly through the storm. Was this the hand of Fate? Menelaus already had doubts about going directly home to Sparta. He heard the whispers and rumors. Some thought that Greece shouldn't have gone to war over a woman, let alone an adulteress. They blamed Helen for the death of their loved ones. Menelaus used the huge storm as an excuse to sail southeast to Egypt.

When Menelaus arrived in the Egyptian capitol of Memphis, Egypt was enjoying a time of peace, but they were plagued by sea-raiders from the north. They looked upon the incoming Greek fleet with suspicion. The Greeks were tired of war and had plenty of treasure to spend. Menelaus, Helen, and the commanders of his ships were taken to the great palace. They met with Ramses III, and placed a chest filled with gold and jewels at his feet.Menelaus said, "Great Pharaoh, we are on a journey home and were blown off course by a massive storm. We are not on a mission of conquest and do not pose a threat to your country.We merely wish to rest and repair our ships for the journey home!"

Ramses replied, "I have heard of a great war in Troy to the northwest. My emissaries tell me it was fought over an incredible beauty. I see before me such a woman. You are welcome to enjoy the hospitality of the Egyptian people while you prepare to return home."

Helen stepped forward and bowed. "Great Pharaoh, you are very gracious and generous.Thank you for your kind words and hospitality."

Ramses took Helen's hand and led them toward the entrance of the palace. He was proud of his city, and as they stood at the top of the steps and looked out over the land, he said, "Memphis has many wonders and beautiful temples, but none can compare to the beauty I see in you. Menelaus, you and your men must join us this evening to celebrate your great victory over the Trojans, and the continued peace between our countries."

The small group walked down the steps of the huge palace and through the large throng of people who gathered to see the woman who caused the fall of Troy. When they returned to their ships, Menelaus said, "I think we will stay here a while. I don't think it is wise to go home to Sparta so soon after the war. I have heard rumors of people blaming you for the war. It may not be safe for you there. Let's give the people some time to cool down."

Helen replied, "I want to go home as much as anyone, to see Hermione and Sparta, but I am happy to be with you, wherever we are."

That evening, the Egyptians presented the Greeks with a large feast and celebration. The Greeks ate meat and food they had never seen before. The exotic sights and smells of Egypt and the great Temples of Memphis, kept the men occupied for a week or so, but their desire to go home was overwhelming. The leaders called for a meeting with Menelaus. Captain Karulius said, "King Menelaus, we have followed you wherever you have led us, and we have not complained. It has been a very long time since we have seen the mountains of Sparta and breathed in her air. You are reunited with the one you love, and we too long for the arms of our families."

Menelaus replied, "Forgive me for my blindness and selfishness. I let rumors and hearsay about my wife's safety cloud my thinking. That is a cowardly way to live. We will sail for Sparta as soon as we can ready the ships." The Greeks set sail for Sparta the next day.

The fleet sailed north until it reached the shores of Asia Minor, and continued west until it moved into the familiar waters of the Aegean Sea. They crossed the Aegean and entered the warm waters of the Laconian gulf.

When they spotted the coast of Greece, the other ships sent a message to Menelaus indicating they wanted to stop on the shore. Menelaus agreed and beached the ships. The excitement among the soldiers was contagious. Some jumped out of the ships into the surf before they ran ashore, and others joyfully shouted, "We are home!" and fell to their knees in the sand. Helen smiled broadly and ran barefoot along the beach. She opened her arms and spun around, as if absorbing the air itself, and playfully kicked the water in the bay. Menelaus sent emissaries ahead to Sparta to let them know they would sail up the Eurotas River and arrive in Sparta at noon the next day. When the emissaries arrived in Sparta, the news flashed through the community like a lightning bolt. The Spartan people scrambled to get the message to those whose husbands, sons, and brothers had gone to Troy.

The next day at noon, thirty ships carrying the Spartan contingent who fought in the Trojan War sailed up the Eurotas River. When the fleet came into view of the people lining the banks of the river, horns started blowing, musicians started playing, and the crowd cheered. There wasn't enough space for all the ships to land at the small Spartan docks, so some beached on the banks. The people came from all across Sparta to welcome the returning army. Men ran to greet their families, and tears of joy were shed all along the banks of the river. Harleopi's parents arrived to welcome their daughter home.

Hermione came down from the palace and ran to Helen. "Mother!" she shouted as she jumped into Helen's arms. In the years since Helen left Sparta, Hermione had grown into a young woman.

Helen said, "Look at you!

Menelaus said, "You have grown into a beautiful young woman." Hermione hugged her father. Menelaus climbed on top of a table and shouted, "Friends, I want to thank you all for your patience and support." Gesturing for Helen to join him on the table, he continued, "Our mission took a while, but in the end, we were victorious!" Helen waved and the crowd went wild. Helen and Menelaus kissed and waved, and Hermione joined them on the table to more thunderous applause. Menelaus waited until the crowd quieted down and shouted, "I am grateful to all of you. To show my gratitude, I invite the whole country to be my guest for a celebration to take place in three days on the palace grounds and the streets of Sparta!"

The crowd roared its approval, and the royal family started the long walk through the crowd to the palace. The palace servants lined the hallways to greet Menelaus and Helen as soon as they walked through the front door. Helen greeted every one of them with a hug, and Menelaus gave a slight hug to the women and a handshake to the men. They were anxious to tour the whole palace, survey their home, and settle into their chambers,.

Menelaus met with his head of security. "Loiceteus, thank you for keeping the palace and my daughter safe."

"Your Highness, we have been friends for a long time. You know I would do anything for your family. I am only sorry I was too old to go to Troy."

"You have always been there when I needed a friend, and I am forever grateful for that."

The two men walked toward the large banquet room, and Loiceteus said, "Your Highness, if you wouldn't mind, I would like to spend my remaining years with my family on our farm."

"I understand. Thank you for your service." The men shook hands and Loiceteus continued down the hallway and out the front door of the palace.

The palace and the town were buzzing with activity because the day for the welcome home ceremony had arrived. The leaders of the army slept in the palace, some soldiers stayed with their Spartan families, and others stayed with generous townspeople who opened their homes. There were fire pits and large barrels of wine spread throughout Sparta and the palace grounds. The Spartans roasted wild boars, half steers, and goats a day in advance to prepare for the huge crowd. The parade began on the banks of the river, led by the palace guards and General Loiceteus. Musicians, dancers, and acrobats followed the guards, and women throwing flower petals in the air trailed behind. Next in line was the army. The men wore their full armor and marched in formation. When the army got to town, the people cheered and shouted from rooftops. Banners hung from every window that read, "Welcome Home" or "Helen, we love you!" Menelaus and Helen stood in a decorated wagon at the end of the parade line. The crowd cheered them wildly and fell in step behind them as the parade snaked into the arena. Menelaus had arranged a day of games and competitions for his party guests in the stadium. He competed in the horse races, foot races and javelin throw, though he didn't win any of them.

After the games, Menelaus stood in the royal viewing box and faced the crowd. "It is with great respect that I address you today. It has been my honor to lead these courageous and honorable men in such a terrible war. I am forever grateful for your sacrifice and patience. My family was torn apart, and you came together to help restore my honor and dignity." Menelaus stopped speaking for a moment and scanned the crowd. "As a gesture of my gratitude, to the families of the men who gave their lives in this struggle, I will grant an equal share of the treasure from my share."

The crowd gasped, and then stood and applauded. Menelaus raised his glass of wine and the crowd followed suit. "I salute each and every one of you: those living, and those who gave their lives for this noble cause!"

They all drank together and cheered loudly. The crowd chanted, "Helen, Helen!"

Overcome with gratitude and emotion, Helen composed herself and addressed the crowd. "I thought I may never see Sparta again until our fleet landed on the shores of Troy. I knew then that I was going to be coming home. I have always been proud to be Spartan, but never as much as I am right now! I stand before you eternally grateful for the sacrifices you have made to bring me home to the greatest place on earth!"

The crowd cheered jubilantly, and someone called out, "We love you, Helen!" The celebration lasted for three days until all were satisfied.

Menelaus received emissaries from other kingdoms who told the tragic stories of other members of the army. Some members of the returning Greek fleet drowned during the storm in the Aegean, and others were exiled from their own kingdoms by their wives and started new towns in other countries.

When Menelaus heard that Clytemnestra murdered Agamemnon along with his concubine, Cassandra, he was devastated. Agamemnon had been his protector and mentor. He was sad that he was not there to help his brother and perhaps prevent this tragedy. Helen was also saddened by the news. She loved Agamemnon, but she loved her sister as well. She knew Agamemnon simply pushed Clytemnestra too far, first with

Iphigenia's sacrifice, and then by bringing Cassandra into their home. Helen and Menelaus didn't discuss the situation, but both recognized the hurt in their hearts.

Hermione grew into a beautiful woman and planned to marry Neoptolemus, the son of Achilles. During the war, Menelaus had promised his daughter Hermione to Neoptolemus. Neoptolemus arrived to marry her and planned to take her back to his city. Their wedding drew officials from all over Sparta. As wedding preparations were being made, a young man came to Sparta. He entered the great hall, and when Helen saw him, she knew immediately that he was Odysseus' son. Helen said to Menelaus, "Look at this young man. He looks just like Odysseus when he was young."

Telemachus approached Menelaus and Helen. Menelaus said, "Young man, your resemblance to my old friend is uncanny. Are you the son of Odysseus?"

"Yes, my name is Telemachus. I have come seeking information about my father. He has not returned from Troy."

Menelaus was concerned. He turned to Helen and said, "They can continue the preparations without me. Excuse us for a moment while I talk to Telemachus."

Helen replied, "I will tell them to continue without both of us. Odysseus was my friend, too. I will join you."

Telemachus followed Helen and Menelaus to the garden behind the palace. Telemachus said, "There has been no word about my father's whereabouts since he left Troy. I thought you might have information about him."

"I was with your father in the wooden horse he conceived to help end the Trojan War. He was a brave and honorable man, and a very close friend of mine."

Helen added, "I remember when your father came into Troy, disguised as a beggar to steal the Palladium. I was so homesick, and it felt wonderful to see the face of an old friend."

Menelaus felt sorrowful that he didn't have better news to share with Telemachus. "Your father did many brave and courageous things during the war. We could speak of his valor all night. I will tell you what I know. During our journey home, I heard that Odysseus was lost in the same storm that destroyed so many of the Greek ships. His ship survived the storm, but was shipwrecked on the island of Calypso, where he is being held against his will."

"Then he is alive!"

"He was alive when I was told this tale."

"Yes, you have given me hope. I was too young to remember much about my father, but now there are many men in my home. They seek my mother Penelope's hand, and are destroying our home."

Menelaus was appalled. "That isn't right. Your father would handle them in a very appropriate way if he were there."

The tales of Odysseus continued and caused many smiles as well as tears as Menelaus and Helen remembered his courageous deeds and the influence he had on their lives. Finally, Helen said, "I have something that will ease the pain." She produced an elixir she acquired while in Egypt. "This will help you forget your sorrow and remember the good things of your past." The three of them then joined the celebration in the palace.

The next day, Telemachus prepared to leave early. Before he left, Menelaus gave him many gifts, and Helen presented him with a tapestry of weavings she made. Telemachus thanked them for their hospitality, and rode away in his chariot.

The following day, as Helen was weaving, a young girl shyly came into the room. Glancing occasionally over her shoulder toward the door, the girl sidled up to Helen. She was dressed in a clean white dress and wore a small tiara of flowers on her head. Helen asked, "May I help you?"

The little girl blushed brightly and produced a small bouquet of flowers from behind her back. In a small voice, she said, "These are for you."

Helen smiled broadly. "What beautiful flowers! Thank you very much. What is your name?"

The little girl looked down at her feet, "Katinus."

"What a beautiful name."

A voice from the doorway said, "She has been dying to meet you for the longest time."

Helen looked up to see Harleopi standing there. She ran to her old friend and wrapped her in her arms. "Harleopi! I haven't seen you in years. How are you? You look wonderful."

"As do you, my Queen. This is my daughter, Katinus."

"She is adorable," said Helen as she hugged the little girl.

"She has heard so much about you and just had to meet you."

Helen laughed. "How wonderful! I can tell you stories about your mother, as well."

Harleopi said, "She wants to come and work for you."

"When she is old enough, she can come here with me."

The little girl smiled and ran to hug her mother. Harleopi said, "You always treated me more as a friend than a servant."

"That's because you are my friend." The three of them walked to the garden and continued reminiscing.

One night after Menelaus returned from one of his many trips around Greece he approached Helen and said, "I am weary of hearing all the slurs and insults that are whispered behind my back about you and the Trojan War. It pains me to hear them call you whore, adultress and worse. I feel we should come forward and explain to the people the situation we were in at the start of that war and the reasons for our decisions."

Helen replied, "My dear Menelaus, it hurts me to hear the insults as well. But I think it is too late to change what people think, many are already set in their beliefs and nothing will change that."

Menelaus continued, "Agamemnon and Priam are dead and it would not hurt them to tell the people what they conspired to do and it would restore your reputation."

Helen walked over to Menelaus gave him a hug and said, "Menelaus, I love that you care so much about what people think of me, but to place blame on Agamemnon and Priam after they are dead would make us look petty and shallow. Please do not speak to anyone of this, I don't want to relive that horrible war and the decisions made because of it. As far as I'm concerned we can let the Trojan War stay in the past where it belongs. People will believe what they believe about me, it is enough for me that you know what happened and why."

Menelaus kissed Helen and said, "If that is what you wish, then that is how it will be."

In the thirty years since the Trojan War, Helen aged gracefully. She had a few streaks of grey in her hair, but retained her figure. She was still the high cheek boned, classic beauty, but she developed tiny wrinkles on the edges of her eyes and mouth. Menelaus outlived almost all of the soldiers who fought with him in Troy, and he aged charmingly as well. With a full head of white hair, and a well trimmed white beard, he had the appearance of a wise old teacher.

Soon, however, he grew frail. The end was near. As was expected for a man of his stature and power, Menelaus had many concubines. Men were allowed to keep other women outside of their marriages, and Menelaus was no exception. He fathered numerous children outside of his marriage to Helen, and as he reached the end of his life, the eldest of these sons, Megapenthes, came to Sparta. Like a vulture circling a dying animal, he came to ensure he received what he thought he deserved. Megapenthes was a strong, slender, muscular young man with yellow hair and the familiar features of Menelaus. He had been to Sparta years before, and Helen knew who he was. Previously, he was courteous and polite, but now his ambition began to show through. He met with Menelaus and Helen in their chambers; Menelaus was bed-ridden and was very weak. Megapenthes said, "Dear father, it pains me to see you so weak and frail like this."

"Do not pity me. I have lived a good life and been fortunate enough to have been loved by a good woman. Now, the gods are calling me home."

"I will try to make you proud of me."

"Son, I am proud of you, as I am proud of all my children." He reached out for Helen's hand, and said, "I have had many reasons in my life to be proud, but having you as my wife has made me the proudest of all."

Helen replied softly, "Yes, my dear. I have been blessed by the gods, who made you my husband. Now rest and save your strength."

Menelaus nodded and closed his eyes. Megapenthes and Helen left the chambers and walked silently together to the garden. Helen said, "I fear he doesn't have long to live."

"Yes, he looked very weak." They sat by the pond and quietly looked into the reflections on the surface. Megapenthes asked, "What are you going to do when the time comes and Menelaus has passed on?"

Helen pondered his question for a moment. "I never really thought about it. I don't want another man, but I think as the Queen of Sparta, the people will expect me to take a husband."

"That is why I am here. I have come to claim my inheritance to the throne of Sparta."

Helen was flabbergasted. "What? I am still the queen."

Megapenthes stood up and declared, "It is my birthright!"

Helen stood also and said, "It was my birthright from my father, and it is mine now!"

Megapenthes replied, "It is time for a change. The people should know that you plan to empty the treasury and go to Egypt."

"That's not true! How dare you insult me in this manner? You can't spread lies about me."

"Many people believe that's what you did when you went to Troy. If you did it once, why wouldn't you do it again? When Menelaus dies, I will spread the word that I have discovered your plan to steal the treasury and sail to Egypt. Lies can be very powerful, and I will use them against you. If you stay in Sparta, I will start a civil war and you will die, which is fine with me, but I cannot let you stay here and undermine my rule. I brought a large company of men with me, and we will fight for what is mine!"

Helen watched as Megapenthes turned and walked away. Stunned, she sat down and thought, "What would Menelaus think of Megapenthes? Surely, he wouldn't condone his son's actions.

Menelaus would be so disappointed. He is so weak; I don't want to excite or alarm him. When he recovers, I will tell him about this snake."

Menelaus lived for another day, and passed away in his sleep. Helen was devastated by the loss of her husband, protector, and best friend. She couldn't eat or sleep and wept openly and constantly. The Spartans built a large funeral pyre on the outskirts of town, near the river. Dignitaries from all over Greece came to pay their respects to Menelaus. The King's body was placed on top of the funeral pyre, and after a few officials had spoken, Helen climbed the platform beside the pyre and said, "We have come here today to honor a great man, a compassionate, courageous, and honorable leader. A man the Spartan people were proud to call King, and I was fortunate enough to call my husband. Menelaus loved Sparta with all his heart, as I loved him with all of mine. Today we grieve because we lost a great leader, but we should also rejoice in knowing that he brought Sparta respect and honor throughout the world. Now I say goodbye to the only man who has filled my life with love, joy, honor, and respect, until the gods ordain we meet again!" Helen picked up a torch and lit the funeral pyre. Tears rolled down her cheek as she watched the flames consume the love of her life. The next day, the glowing embers were doused with wine, and Menelaus' remains weregathered and put in a large urn. The Spartans placed the urn in a monument built for Menelaus on the other side of the Eurotas River.

Some of the dignitaries who paid their respects to Menelaus also had other motives. One of the men from the far western corner of Sparta approached Helen inside the palace. "A beautiful woman such as yourself should not be without a man. I want you to know that I am here for you, if you so choose."

"Thank you, I will consider your offer."

"There is no need to go Egypt."

Helen was surprised. "What are you talking about?"

"I have heard from many people that with Menelaus gone, you can finally take what you want and go to Egypt!"

"Dear sir, I can assure you that I have no plans to go to Egypt. Now if you'll please excuse me."

Helen returned to her quarters and spoke with Katinus. "I am not interested in taking another man as my husband, but I feel I must if I want to continue to live in Sparta. Megapenthes has started to spread lies, and there are not many loyal soldiers left. Many will believe him."

Katinus, who started working for Helen about 15 years earlier and like her mother before her, she became Helen's trusted confidant and friend. Katinus replied, "My Queen, I don't understand what you mean, but I have heard the story as well. I want you to know that I don't believe them, and I will follow you wherever you go."

"Katinus, you are a faithful friend, but it would be best if you didn't know the full extent of the unfolding events. Tonight, we will go to the royal treasury."

The next day, Helen sent emissaries out to all the surrounding kingdoms and stated that she sought a husband. Megapenthes heard of Helen's plan and was furious. "She was warned, but now she plans on taking a husband and denying me my birthright!" Megapenthes paced back and forth in his tent. "Tonight, we will take what is mine. I want her dead!"

Helen entertained some of the dignitaries that stayed after the funeral and wanted to be considered among the suitors for her hand. The ambassador from Thebes said to another, "She is a remarkably beautiful woman who seems to have defied aging."

The ambassador from Corinth replied, "There are only a few suitors now, but there will be dozens of men here shortly. Now is the time to make a good impression before the word spreads."

"Who wouldn't want to try and tame the woman who destroyed Troy?"

Helen left the party early and called Katinus to her quarters as she prepared for bed. Katinus was combing Helen's hair when they heard shouts and the clashing of swords. Helen heard this same noise in Troy and knew what was happening. She turned to Katinus and said, "Hurry! I must get dressed." Helen quickly dressed and ran with Katinus to the secret passageway behind her mirror. Menelaus installed the escape route for just such an emergency. It led to a small room on the far side of the palace where they could hide until they had more information.

Helen said, "I want you to go and find out what you can, and then come back here as quickly as possible."

Katinus nodded and ran back through the passageway. She emerged from Helen's quarters and found a battle raging in the palace. Megapenthes' forces had stormed the palace, overwhelmed the palace guard, and taken the ambassadors hostage. Katinus overheard Megapenthes say to the ambassadors, "My fight isn't with you, but you will serve my purpose until I find Helen."

Katinus picked up a serving tray and walked calmly through the palace until she reached the door to Helen's chambers. She looked around to be sure that she wasn't followed, and then quickly went back through the secret door behind the mirror. When she reached Helen, she didn't recognize her. Helen wore make-up to make herself look like an old woman. She even blackened two teeth, yellowed the rest, and completed the transformation with an old wig. She stood stooped over and used a gnarled walking stick. Her hands shook and she spoke in a raspy voice. Katinus told her about Megapenthes' plan, and Helen said, "We must make our way to the stables. I have hidden four chests of treasure there. We will take a wagon to the river."

Helen and Katinus walked quickly through the passageway. Once Katinus saw that the room was empty, they entered Helen's chambers and then the main hallway. Katinus helped Helen, who walked slowly and unsteadily, as they made their way to the stables. Soldiers ran through the main hallways searching for Helen. When they saw the two women, one of the soldiers stopped them, looked them over, and asked, "Who are you and what are you doing in the palace?"

"My name is Katinus. I am a servant of the Queen, and this is my grandmother who came to visit me. I am taking her home."

The soldier walked slowly around Helen and checked her over. "You are a servant of the Queen? Where is she?"

"I just left her in the main dining hall."

The soldier believed the ruse. "You can leave."

Once they reached the stables, the stable master recognized Katinus. "Young lady, what do you want here at this hour? It is a very dangerous night to be moving about."

"Dear sir, if you would be so kind as to help me. I am taking my grandmother home to my mother's house. The Queen told me that she prepared a wagon for me in the back of the stable."

"Yes, I know the one. The Queen was here just this afternoon."

They went to the back of the stables and uncovered the four large chests that Helen had hidden under large piles of hay. Helen started to help Katinus load the wagon, ut the stable master said, "Old woman, don't do that. You'll hurt yourself."

In her normal voice, Helen replied, "It is I, Helen, your Queen. Help us load this wagon."

The stable master just stared at her. "Your Highness?"

"Yes, it is me! Now help us!"

They loaded the chests on the wagon and covered them with hay. As they started to ride away, Helen said to the stable master, "You didn't see me." The stable master nodded, and Katinus drove the wagon toward town.

The wagon rolled steadily down the small hill toward town, but two soldiers stopped them before they reached Sparta. "Who are you, and where are you going?"

"I am Katinus and this is my grandmother. We are on our way home. Why have you stopped us?"

"We are looking for Queen Helen. We have reason to believe she has committed crimes against the state."

In a raspy voice, Helen said, "My husband died in Troy." Helen slowly stood, and she raised her voice and shook her walking stick at the soldier. "I hope you find her. She caused that war, and *that* was a crime against the state. What do you think of a woman like that?"

The soldier backed away. "You may go. Sorry to bother you."

The women rode through the town to the docks on the riverbank. Katinus found a ship captain and asked, "How much to hire your ship to sail to Rhodes?"

The captain said, "The cost is ten gold talents, but it is the middle of the night!"

Katinus opened one of the chests and removed the gold. "I'll give you twenty gold talents to sail now and ten more when we get there."

Impressed with their offer, the captain helped the women load the chests on the ship and they set sail. The full moon shone brightly on the water and the surrounding landscape. Helen and Katinus stood on the bow of the ship and looked at the palace on the small hill in the distance. A tear rolled down Helen's cheek. She realized it might be the last time she would ever see her beloved Sparta. Katinus asked, "Why are we going to Rhodes?"

"I have an old friend there named Polyxo who may be kind enough to let us stay for a while." The women stood silently on the bow for a long time.

The next morning, Helen emerged from her cabin without the old woman disguise, but as Helen, the Queen of Sparta. The captain saw her and recognized her immediately. "Your Highness, I am honored that you have chosen my ship for your voyage."

"Thank you. How long will it take to reach Rhodes?"

"My Queen, is that the first stop on your trip?"

"What do you mean?"

"The word in Sparta is that you are bound for Egypt."

"That is a lie spread by Megapenthes to steal my throne. I am going to Rhodes to form a plan to recapture what has been taken from me—my home and my country."

"You can count on me to help anyway I can. With a favorable wind, we will be in Rhodes in a week."

The ship sailed to Rhodes without incident. Meanwhile, Megapenthes declared that Helen was sent into exile as an enemy of the state for her plot to steal the treasury.

The ship sailed gently to the coast of Rhodes. Helen looked out at the rolling mountains and green forest, and said to Katinus, "What a beautiful country. I hope Polyxo allows us to stay for a while."

When the ship docked, Helen was escorted to the small palace on the hill overlooking the sea, and was greeted by Polyxo. Polyxo was a small, olive-skinned woman with streaks of grey in her dark hair. Her face was weathered and lightly wrinkled, with big dark brown eyes that were lively and clear. Although she was old, she was still svelte and strong. Polyxo said, "Helen, the destroyer of Troy, I hope you haven't come to destroy Rhodes as well!"

Helen was surprised. "Polyxo, please! Why would you say such a thing?"

Polyxo smiled slyly. "I am teasing you, my old friend. It is good to see you again; it has been so long!"

Polyxo hugged her, but Helen had an uneasy feeling. "Polyxo, I am happy to see you again as well. You look wonderful."

"Come, let's get something to eat, and then we can talk. You must be exhausted from your trip."

"Yes, it was quite a long trip. Your country is beautiful."

After lunch, Helen was shown to the guest quarters and she settled in. Four chests were brought in, and she opened them to confirm their contents. Two trunks held gold and jewels, and the others contained dresses, gowns, tiaras, and other necessities.

Helen and Polyxo walked in the garden behind her palace. The beautiful garden was full of many different types of flowers, trees, and spas where Polyxo and her guests could bath or swim. Polyxo asked, "Why have you come here? Are things going well in Sparta?"

"I suppose you heard that Menelaus passed away a few weeks ago?"

"No I hadn't heard. I am so sorry for your loss. Was it unexpected?"

"He had been ill for some time and went gently in his sleep. I miss him tremendously."

Helen and Polyxo sat quietly in the shade of a large oak tree. "I know what you mean. I lost my dear husband many years ago. Do you remember Tlepolemus? He was once one of your suitors."

"Yes, I remember him. He was a very tall, handsome young man with long curly black hair."

"Yes. He was killed in the Trojan War."

"I'm sorry to hear that. Many brave men died in that horrible war."

"I miss him still. I think of him every day. I never remarried." After a brief pause, Polyxo said, "So, what brings you to Rhodes?"

"One of Menelaus' sons claimed the throne and spread false rumors about me stealing the Spartan treasury and sailing to Egypt. He and his men attacked the palace and overpowered the guards. I was taken completely by surprise, and I had to leave or die. I'm hoping you will let me stay in your beautiful country while I try to figure out how to reclaim my throne. I can pay for my lodging."

"Don't be ridiculous. You are welcome to stay here as long as you need."

"Thank you. You are a good friend. Many of the men and women who were my friends have died. I may be here for a while."

Polyxo said, "Take your time. You are safe here."

A few days later, Polyxo hosted a great feast and invited dignitaries from all over the island. Many of them were anxious to meet the women they had heard so much about. Helen sat at the head table with Polyxo, and watched the wrestlers, dancers, and jugglers as they celebrated her presence on the island. The celebration brought back many fond memories for Helen. She remembered the many celebrations they had in Sparta. That time seemed so long ago. Now she was a widow, had been thrown out of her country, and her name was slandered once more. A feeling of melancholy swept over her, but she tried to smile through her sadness.

After the feast, a dignitary approached Helen in the garden. "My lady, you are absolutely stunning and effervescent. I can see why men fought a war over you."

Helen coldly replied, "That war was not fought over me."

"Pardon me. I am mistaken."

"That war was fought because of revenge and greed."

Helen was the center of attention for the rest of the evening, and fielded questions about the Trojan War. "Was Achilles truly a great warrior? How big was the wooden horse?"

Polyxo became annoyed and couldn't keep her animosity for Helen in check any longer. "What about Tlepolemus? How did he die? Do you even know? How many men died because of your adultery?"

The entire party fell silent. Helen was surprised and hurt by her attack. "I beg your pardon. There are many rumors about that war, most of them are untrue, and that is one of them. Now if you will excuse me!"

The party guests stood in shocked silence as Helen walked out and went back to her chambers. Helen said to Katinus, "We have to leave here as soon as we can. Polyxo is not the friend I thought she was. She is bitter and dangerous."

"Yes, but where will we go?"

"We are going home to Sparta. I was wrong to leave in the first place. It is my home, my throne, and my country. If Megapenthes wants a fight, he will get one."

When the sun rose, Helen and Katinus found a ship that agreed to take them home to Sparta, but it couldn't leave until late that evening. Polyxo heard of Helen's plans to leave, and called a meeting with her servants and attendants. "That whore has caused me and thousands of people so much pain. I will make her pay for her sins. She will not leave Rhodes." Polyxo opened three huge trunks and chose three faithful servants. "I want you to put on these costumes after lunch. When Helen takes a bath, I want you to seize her."

Helen went to lunch with Polyxo as usual. The two women said nothing to each other for a long time. Finally, Polyxo broke the silence. "I understand you have made plans to leave."

Helen replied, "You are very well informed. Yes, I think it would be best if I left and returned to Sparta."

Polyxo said flatly, "I want to apologize for my outburst last night. It was out of character. Perhaps I had too much wine. I don't want you to feel as though you are unwelcome."

"Thank you. I still think it would be best if I returned to Sparta. I will be leaving this evening."

"If you think that is best." The two women finished eating in silence.

Helen and Katinus finished packing their chests for the trip home. Helen said, "I think we are ready. All we have to do now is wait until it's time to leave."

Katinus replied, "I am anxious to get home."

"I am, too. I miss Sparta. It's so hot here; I think I will go to the garden to take a refreshing bath—my last treat before we get on that ship."

"I will prepare the water."

Helen bathed in the garden and tried to relax. Katinus walked past Polyxo with a bucket to fetch more water when the guards and servants rushed in. Two guards grabbed Katinus and she watched as three servants dressed as the Furies, old hags with bat wings, sent by the gods to punish wrongdoers, attacked Helen. Helen heard Katinus scream and saw the Furies coming after her. She jumped out of the bath and started to fight her attackers. The Furies screamed in high-pitched voices and tore at her flesh with eagle talons sewn into gloves. She punched, kicked, and clawed at them, but they tackled her to the ground. Although Helen fought with all her strength, they overwhelmed her, punching and kicking, clawing and scratching her and tying her hands behind her back.

Katinus was powerless and could only scream, "No, No!" She struggled in vain to be released. Helen felt a loop of rope drop over her head and around her throat. She struggled with a renewed desperation as the rope was pulled tight. Polyxo shouted, "Did you think you were never going to pay for your sins? This is for the thousands you killed, and for my beloved Tlepolemus!"

The attackers dragged Helen, bloody and naked, across the ground by the rope around her neck. Her breath was taken away as the rope tightened around her throat. The attackers threw the rope over a branch and lifted Helen into the air. Her legs kicked and thrashed violently as she struggled to breathe, she saw Katinus sobbing helplessly. The attackers watched as Helen swung in the air and Polyxo looked on with a satisfied smirk. Helen struggled for air, her mind screamed for help, but she couldn't talk. Helen felt her breath leave her body; her strength was gone, her body went limp, and her mind went blank. The Furies watched as the final twitches in Helen's body ceased, and then walked silently away as Polyxo stood and stared. The guards released Katinus, who ran to Helen, untied the rope, and gently let her body down. Katinus wept uncontrollably as she held Helen's lifeless body.

Katinus cried, "My Queen should at least have a funeral. Does your hatred for her go so deep that you would deny her that?"

Polyxo replied, "I am satisfied with her death. I am not so angry as to deny her a proper funeral. You may make the arrangements."

"Thank you, would you be so kind as to allow me to take her remains home to her beloved Sparta?"

"Yes, you may do so."

Katinus arranged for a large funeral pyre to be built on top of a hill overlooking the sea. A huge crowd gathered once word got out that Helen had died in Polyxo's palace. However, there was no one in attendance to give the eulogy. Polyxo refused, and would not even attend the funeral, but she allowed Katinus to say a few words. "It is a sad day for all of us who knew Helen, the Queen of Sparta. There were many rumors about her, but to me, she was more than my Queen. She was a confidant and a close friend. She will be missed terribly by all who loved her."

Katinus walked to the edge of the funeral pyre and lit the fire. The flames grew larger and larger, and as they consumed Helen's body, the blaze was seen for miles out to sea and all over the island. The next day, Katinus doused the last embers of the pyre with wine, gathered Helen's remains into a large urn, and set a course for Sparta.

Word reached Sparta about Helen's death long before her remains arrived. When Katinus docked, a large crowd was waiting for her. Harleopi met her daughter, Katinus, at the dock. Megapenthes arranged for Helen to be placed next to Menelaus in his shrine across the river. They placed the urn on the flower-covered wagon, provided by Megapenthes, and started the slow ride through town. The streets were lined with people. Many wore black, and loud moaning and weeping filled the air. The people filed in behind the wagon and followed it to Menelaus' monument.

Megapenthes met the funeral column at the shrine. "Today, the heart of Sparta is filled with sorrow. We have lost our beloved Queen. She had been vilified and demeaned, yet she stood tall. To all who knew her, she was an honorable, loving, and courageous leader. No one loved Sparta more than Helen, and no one loved Helen more than Sparta!" The tomb was opened and Helen's urn was placed inside next to the love of her life, Menelaus.

In the coming months, many people came by to pay their respects to Menelaus and Helen. One day, as Harleopi and Katinus placed small tiaras made of flowers on Helen's monument, a group of people came to honor her memory. One of the men said, "Here is where Helen is buried. Her beauty caused the Trojan War."

Harleopi approached the group and said, "Sir, if I may, what you have just said is not entirely true. While it is true that she was incredibly beautiful and men would do anything to possess her, she was much more than that. I was with Helen in Troy during the Trojan War. To the people who know what truly happened, Helen was indeed more than the beautiful Queen of Sparta. She was a friend, a brave and compassionate leader and in many eyes a Greek hero!"